# A Wicked Device

by

Jack Thompson

Bloomington, IN
authorHOUSE™
Milton Keynes, UK

*AuthorHouse™*
*1663 Liberty Drive, Suite 200*
*Bloomington, IN 47403*
*www.authorhouse.com*
*Phone: 1-800-839-8640*

*AuthorHouse™ UK Ltd.*
*500 Avebury Boulevard*
*Central Milton Keynes, MK9 2BE*
*www.authorhouse.co.uk*
*Phone: 08001974150*



*First published by AuthorHouse 7/3/2006*

*ISBN: 1-4259-4583-X (e)*
*ISBN: 1-4259-3642-3 (sc)*

*Printed in the United States of America*
*Bloomington, Indiana*

*This book is printed on acid-free paper.*

# ACKNOWLEDGEMENTS

This story is a figment of my imagination. Those who know the Deutsche Welle TV building in the Berlin suburb of Wedding will recognise some similarity with the headquarters of my *Deutsche Fernsehkanal.* But there is no-one at Deutsche Welle remotely like Kai Struck, Maguire or even Charlie Barrow. Almost all the other characters are entirely fictional and bear no resemblance to anyone, alive or dead. The only 'real' people in this book are Kyriakos and Dmitri, owner and head waiter at the 'Dionysos' restaurant on Potsdammerstrasse where I have eaten some hearty meals and spent many happy hours. I owe much to the unending patience of my wife, Kathryn, and to the hospitality of good friends in Berlin. I should like to thank The National Archives and the documents department of the Imperial War Museum, Duxford, for permission to quote from official transcripts of interrogations conducted at the time of the Nuremberg Trials in 1945 (the quotations were taken respectively from documents PRO, WO 309/1423 and IWM, FO 645, Box 157) Any mistakes of description or attribution are my own, for which I apologise to those who may be affected.

Jack Thompson
London, May 2006

# PART 1

# Chapter 1

The car rattles down the darkest street in Berlin. But the din can't hide the shot. Maguire brakes hard, spins the wheel and hares back to the crossroads.

"What the hell are you doing?" I bawl.

"Didn't you hear it?"

"Of course I bloody well heard it. So what?"

"Someone in trouble."

"Mac, please. If there's a maniac loose with a gun, I do not want to meet him. Not here. Not anywhere."

I prattle on. I'm young - well, relatively young. I want to go on living.

He takes no notice of course. He parks the car at an awkward angle and staggers out into the night.

"Stay there." he says.

"You're kidding. If you're going to get yourself killed….."

"Listen," he says. And we listen. To the clear air and the rumble of traffic in well lit streets just a few blocks away.

Someone moans. Maguire shuffles his big flat feet as fast as his bulk allows - into the gloom near to where the Wall used to run.

He kneels.

"Chap's in a mess," he says.

"Mac, all I wanted was my bed."

Another shot pings off the building behind us. I flatten myself to the flagstones. Another moan.

Someone's running.

"Bugger's scarpered. We can take a proper look now."

Maguire rolls the man on to his back and lifts his head. He's in his early forties, short and slim. His rimless glasses hang from one ear. The front of his denim shirt is soaked in blood.

I grope for my mobile.

"Hell, what's the number for the ambulance?"

Maguire holds up a hand and the man slumps into the cradle of his arm. I bend lower.

"I know him, Mac. I fucking know him."

And if I hadn't known him, I wouldn't be sitting on this balcony looking at the ocean and the setting sun.

# Chapter 2

Axel cruises the airport bars. His favourite haunt is The Pavilion. It's all self-service and decked out with copies of old German film posters bearing the faces of stars long gone. Axel sidles up to unsuspecting travellers. They're smoking, sipping coffee, slurping beers or chewing rolls, stuff they don't want but it helps to pass the time.

"Your photo?" Axel pretends to press the button on his digital. A smile and a nod.

The wife giggles. "Hey, Bernd, what about it then?"

And Bernd, dewy-eyed with alcohol, grunts his approval.

"Let's try another one, shall we?" Axel presses again. "Five euros, please. Won't be a moment." He retreats to his printer, parked on a nearby table.

The regulars have seen it all before. And sometimes he pushes his luck.

"Shove off."

He never takes offence. He doesn't care.

Today is Monday. I am flying to London. I watch him pack his cases. Everything in its place. No straps dangling. A fashionable little mobile, what the Germans call a *Handy*, pokes from his shirt pocket. He catches my eye and takes off his specs.

"No." I say. "No pictures."

"You're a real regular," he replies. "You were very rude to me once."

"For which I apologise. And, yes, I am what the airlines call a frequent flyer. It's very boring."

His *Handy* trills. The smile fades. He excuses himself but stays within earshot.

"I have pix of the people you asked me to watch out for," he tells his caller. "I will see you tonight."

He stiffens and frowns. It's the first time I've seen him angry. And he's trying to master a stammer.

He stuffs the phone back in his pocket. His eyes water with a deep melancholy. My flight is called and I bid him good-bye.

A week later, I land back at Tegel. And he's there on the concourse. I wave. He's smiling again. I head for the taxis. There's a queue but I know it'll clear soon enough. I feel a tap on my shoulder. It's Axel offering me a lift into town.

Why I accept, I don't know. And it doesn't occur to me to ask how he knew I'd be on a certain flight. We wander out to the car-park.

"I don't know your name. I'm Charlie Barrow by the way."

We're hurrying because it's drizzling.

"Axel. Axel Dreissig. Get in, please."

I dump my bag on the back seat of his little red Polo. Not new, but clean and spruce. We shake hands at last.

Taking a left a kilometre from the airport, he follows the narrow road along the Saatwinkler Damm and Seestrasse and on into the depths of Wedding. He's a careful driver. And courteous, even when others cut him up or blare their horns.

He wants to talk and he wants me to listen.

"Do you smoke?" he asks.

I tell him I gave up years ago although the craving sometimes returns.

"Me too," he says. "I used to get through forty a day. But I stopped. It was an act of defiance." He glances at my puckered brow.

"You've seen them," he snorts. "Those people in The Pavilion. Addicted. Addicted to almost everything - cigarettes, drink, junk food, TV game shows and *Bild*. Weak." Another snort. "Germans are weak." And for once he hits the horn and scowls at a passing cab.

I'm not sure how I'm supposed to react. "You're not weak," I say. "And you're German." But he's not in the mood for poor jokes.

"Look at them all." he cries with a sweep of the hand. "The uneducated mass. Kept in their place by corrupt politicians. Dumb them down. Feed them the lowest common denominator. They won't protest. Not even the five million out of work."

I get more of this as we dive into Wedding. It's dark now. The rain turns the road surface into a light-show, a million reflections from shops, pubs and apartments.

"We've had two world wars, we've been laid to waste and we've been cowed into submission by dictators. And we still do as we're told," he rants.

I don't want him driving me all the way into central Berlin. But before I can ask him to drop me at a convenient rank, we're turning into Ruegenerstrasse and pull up outside a soulless modern block.

"Have you time for a drink?" Axel asks. I accept and again wonder why.

We climb the stairs to the first floor.

"Remember that phone call you took at the airport," I say. "The first time we spoke?" I'm hoping to catch him off guard but he says nothing until we're inside and he's handing me a glass of white wine.

"My one indulgence," he says. "A nice, clean Kreuznacher from the Nahe valley. I wish I could retire to somewhere like that." He raises his glass and sips.

I look round. Axel has hung blown up stills from Riefenstahl's film of the '36 Olympics, sunny shots of Aryan maidens and a sepia replica of Furtwaengler conducting the Berlin Phil in front of the Nazi hierarchy. But no swastikas. And no pictures of a manic *Fuehrer*.

He ignores my curiosity.

"The call came from my minder," he explains. "I have to see him again tonight. With some more photographs. He's a fool. He talks about 'meets' and 'drops'. He's picked it up from trashy novels."

I push my luck a little further. "And your stammer?"

"I have a hard time controlling it," he sighs. "It comes on when I get angry. Having to take orders from that bastard. Look, I've got an arts degree. And what am I? A bloody photographer making half a living snapping the idiots at Tegel and the other half spying for fools in The Movement."

I prick up my ears and he notices.

"Don't get excited," he says. "All I have to do is stay alert, keep an eye open for certain people."

"But The Movement? Funny sort of outfit to be working for." I'm trying to be disingenuous but he doesn't respond. He goes into his kitchen.

I examine his bookshelves. There are copies of 'The Storm of Steel' by Ernst Juenger and Goebbels's very own 'Michael, the Diary of a German's Destiny'. In the corner sit piles of newspapers and magazines, CD's and a laptop.

He brings in a light meal, a salad he's prepared earlier in the day.

"All salads these days." he says.

He sets it down on the low table in front of me. "No meat. No fish. No eggs. No dairy products. Herr Lenz has decreed it."

The healthy German is evidently a vegetarian or, better still, a vegan.

"Herr Lenz?"

"Heinrich Lenz. Our Leader." He suddenly stands up straight, back stiff as a pencil.

I get the full works. Lenz is telling them that Germany will be great again, fit to dominate the rest of Europe. Not through wasteful conquest - that was Hitler's mistake. But by example, intelligence, discipline and organisation. This will be the antithesis to the communists' nanny state and their indulgence in espionage and supervision. These won't be necessary in a society where people are as busy as bees, caring for the environment and enjoying the arts and sport.

"Who are these people you take photos of?" I ask.

"Now you're getting nosy, Mr Barrow." He sticks a fork into a piece of tomato, dips it in vinaigrette sauce and pops it into his mouth. He wipes his lips with a paper napkin. "But then you're a journalist. Aren't you?"

"How do you know that?"

"I've seen you on the *Kanal.* You're easily recognisable with that bushy hair and the lived in face. You read the news in English. I found you one day when I was flipping the remote. Then I got on to the website."

"Am I in your picture collection?"

He doesn't trip up. "Yes. Though why, I don't know. They never tell me why."

He wears that look of melancholy again, puts his head in his hands and sniffs.

"I'm a coward. I know it. I hate violence."

"But you have to do what they ask?"

"I'm in too deep. My minder takes the piss out of me. I accept it and slink away with an envelope full of cash and instructions for next time."

"Why are you telling me all this?" He doesn't stop to think about a reply.

"Because you're safe."

"I wouldn't bank on that."

"Meaning....?"

"Meaning that I don't just work as a newsreader for the *Kanal.* And I'm not your father confessor. You're giving me material I could use in a piece for a British newspaper. Could I quote you? And if I did, what would your minder have to say about it?"

"I don't know that I care any more," he says.

"Simple question, Axel. Why?" It's the first time I've used his name. He throws up his head and looks beyond me to the street outside.

And he has mastered the art of the oblique reply. "I've never given a moment's thought to the people I'm asked to photograph, until the other day. Then it hit me. I ought to be building up a catalogue, an archive, something The Movement can put to better use. Something that will further The Struggle. Heinrich Lenz is always talking about The Coming Struggle." He looks at me as if expecting some sort of penetrating comment.

"But The Struggle *never* comes, does it, Axel?".

"No. Never," he mutters sullenly. "We're always being told to be patient. We fight elections. We put up posters. We push leaflets into people's hands. We hold meetings on street corners in Marzahn and Lichtenberg."

"And the skins are out there brandishing their flags?"

He pauses. "Oh they love it. Bawling and shouting like the fools they are. Have you ever been to Marzahn and Lichtenberg?" He spits. "Shit-holes. Nothing but tower blocks for the workers."

I wait for him to sort out his thoughts.

"And we always fuck up at elections. The old parties win hands down. Even the communists." He laughs. "At first they called themselves the Party of Democratic Socialism. Now it's the Left-Alliance. What a farce."

I want to get back to the pictures and the people he's been asked to photograph. Are they always the same?

"The last lot were terrifying," he says. "Stocky and dark. Jeans and black leather jackets. Moustaches and broad shoulders. They could have been Arabs or Kurds, or Chechens."

I am more than keen to know why a neo-fascist organisation in Germany is interested in travellers from the Middle East and the Caucasus. But Axel doesn't go down that road.

"He's always right - my minder, you know. Always accurate. Down to the smallest detail. Never misses a trick. It makes the job easy. Except with those two. I had to make sure they didn't spot me."

It's time for me to go. We shake hands. He asks if we can meet again. I say, of course. We exchange *Handy* numbers and agree to talk in the morning.

But he doesn't call and my efforts to get through are thwarted by an infuriating voicemail message. *"Vielen Dank fuer Ihren Anruf. Bitte, hinterlassen Sie eine Nachricht nach dem Ton!"* I let it drop. When we see each other again, Axel is at death's door.

# Chapter 3

Axel lies in a hospital bed, in a room lit only by a table lamp. His life-support machine flickers and beeps as he strains to explain why he was out and about at two in the morning.

"My minder called - said there'd been a delay. I was to wait until one thirty before handing over the photos." He coughs and blood oozes from his mouth. "I did lose my temper that time. Told him it was bloody inconvenient."

His face wears his usual look of melancholy. He makes a supreme effort to stay conscious. Maguire and I stand stock still and watch. There's nothing we can do.

"It wasn't far," he croaks. "Across Brunnenstrasse. Down Voltastrasse. Past that old AEG building. You work there, don't you?" He fights for breath. "Max Urich Strasse. Always black as pitch. A dump for stolen cars."

He coughs again. But there's no blood this time.

"I never knew his name, you see. It was always the same one. He had blond hair and wore a black car coat, and loafers. I remember the loafers. He never let me see his face. I said I'd brought the pix and handed over two folders. Usually he'd pull out a torch and look at them. Not this time.

Just stuffed them inside his jacket." He tries to moisten his lips but the tongue is dry and shrivelled.

"I asked for my money. He laughed at me. He said 'Not this time, Axel.' I don't know how I managed it. I screamed at him. Called him scum and a cheat." He screws up his face at the memory.

"He kicked me hard. In the balls. My head hit the pavement. Then he bent over with a knee in my guts."

Axel subsides into the pillows.

His voice is a whisper. I stoop to listen. "He said he'd reported me. I was too bolshie. He had new orders - something like that." His eyes roll.

"I remember - he spat at me. Then the shot." He lifts a hand and tries to point.

"I heard feet. And felt an arm."

The machine beeps insistently. The note has risen a notch or two.

Axel looks at Maguire. But doesn't see him any more.

# Chapter 4

The police station on Jaegerstrasse is not where I want to be at five thirty in the morning. The colours are pastel. Walls, doors, window frames and carpets. I suppose they're intended to chime in with the image the authorities want to project. Consumer friendly and environmentally sound. But they clash with the yellow and khaki worn by Berlin's sullen law enforcers. The room's too warm. I feel the weight of my eyelids.

She introduces herself as Inspector Renate Seelig of the grandly named *Kriminalpolizeiliche Sofortbearbeitung.*

"It's a section formed to react swiftly to emergencies," she tells us. At least, that's the official version. She's lean, of medium height, has cropped fair hair and a well chiselled face. She wears her uniform as if it's tailor-made.

And she provides decent coffee, thank God.

Maguire takes it all in his stride. "I am a public-spirited soul," he says. "Which is why I stopped when I heard the shot."

She puts more routine questions and he answers concisely. Then wants to put some of his own.

"Surely, this was nothing more than a straightforward fracas between two members of the underworld, Inspector?

The victim intruded on his killer's territory. A felony like a thousand others in Berlin?"

Seelig gives him a long, hard look. I know what she's thinking. "Is this Englishman - who speaks better German than his friend - is he trying it on?" She slides the laptop closer to her and delicately taps the keys. "Shall we go through it again, Herr Maguire?"

"Yes, officer. Let's do that," he answers. "May I ask - again - who was this man?"

"I suppose I'll have to tell you, especially if you end up in court explaining your presence in Max Urich Strasse at that time of night." She turns to me and raises an eyebrow.

"We were on our way home," I say. "We came off shift at the *Kanal* at two fifteen and we were heading for our beds, when Philip Marlowe here decides to meddle in things that didn't concern him."

Maguire grins. But aware that I am well nigh comatose, he injects a little pace into proceedings. "Well, officer?"

"His name was Axel Dreissig. He was in his early 40's, lived at an address in Wedding and worked as a photographer."

We nod.

"And.....?" Maguire probes, exuding patience.

"And what?" replies Seelig. She sits back in her chair and folds her arms.

"And he was a little more than your average nobody, wasn't he?" Now he's telling her - no more bullshit. "In fact, he was a member of The Movement, a signed-up supporter of a neo-Nazi organisation on which the *BKA* and the *BND* have had their eye for some time. Recently, they have been paying even more attention to it, because the government is worried that this bunch of nutters will win more votes at the next election." He pauses for breath. "Ask Mr Barrow."

I'm trying hard not to look as if butter won't melt. Again I know she's asking herself, how does this man have access to stuff which is hidden in my files? She has the air of a predator about to spring at its prey.

"Will you please tell me how you arrive at that astonishing conclusion?" she asks.

"This fell out of Dreissig's clothing." Maguire produces a sheet of paper from his jacket pocket and dangles it in front of her.

"And what is that?" She wears an expression half way between disapproval and shock.

"This is a leaflet," explains Maguire, warming to his task. "It was published, if I can grace it with such an epithet, by The Movement. It calls on all true Germans to rally at the Brandenburg Gate on November the 9th. That, I might remind you, is the anniversary of *Kristallnacht* and the Munich *Putsch*. They propose marching past the Reichstag to the government quarter where they will demand the expulsion of all foreigners. And this." He holds up a piece of plastic bearing Axel's photograph. "This is clear proof that our friend was an *active* member of The Movement."

Maguire tries hard not to look smug. Seelig is rattled but still in control. "You are withholding evidence," she says, softly.

"On the contrary, Inspector. I am about to pass these items to you in front of a witness. But before I do, let me say that, when Mr Barrow and I try to save a man's life after he's been brutally attacked, when he practically dies in my arms, and when we co-operate fully with the police, we expect a little give-and-take."

"You have been very helpful, Herr Maguire. I acknowledge that. But you are beginning to try my patience." She is moving round from behind her desk. Maguire tenses and I blink in an effort to stay awake. "You are also being obtuse and rather silly. Herr Barrow looks as if he should be tucked up in bed. Now, why don't you do him a favour and come to the point?"

It's my turn. "I may be dog tired," I snap. "But I am still *compos mentis*."

Seelig looks up, startled by my sudden burst of energy.

"I knew Dreissig. I'd met him before. He told me what he was. And more besides. Just before he died."

"Withholding evidence again. You two really are something."

Before Maguire can jump in, I decide to unruffle her feathers.

"Inspector, Maguire and I have walked right into the middle of a good story. And there's nothing you can do to stop us reporting what's happened and our part in it." I'm not sure I'm on firm legal ground here but it's worth a try.

"And you want my help?" She's calmed down, goes behind her desk again and looks at the laptop. Then sighs.

"Not at this time of night, gentlemen," she says. "You are exhausted, Mr Barrow. Herr Maguire also needs a break from the excitement. And since I was dragged from my bed to deal with this emergency, I too would like to put my head down for a while."

She flashes a smile. Maguire can't take his eyes off her. Mine are closed.

"Come back at midday and we shall see what we can do for one another. Note my words. I use language very precisely." And not a little stiffly, I think.

"But this will be out in the open by lunchtime," wails Maguire.

"As part of our bargain, I'll make sure it isn't," she replies. "I am very adept at keeping material under wraps. In any case, it's too late for the papers. As you know, the Berlin press is slow on the uptake. The people you have to worry about are your rivals in TV and radio."

"In which case," pleads Maguire, "make it eleven o' clock"

# Chapter 5

I get back to the hotel at seven. Everybody else is up and about. Margit on the desk looks at me as if I've risen from the dead.

"Talk to you later," I call out as I head for the lift.

I undress and shower and throw myself into bed.

I drift into sleep but I'm still in the car with Maguire. We'd spent ten hours churning out English-language newscasts at *Deutscher Fernsehkanal.* It's an international network, paid for by the German government and housed in a renovated factory.

"Too many bloody egos in that place," says Maguire. It's time for a little character assassination.

"Yours and mine?" I turn and smile as he slides the Peugeot out of the car park. "Management believes it makes for creative tension, as long as no-one actually hits anybody."

"I came damn close to it tonight," shouts Maguire over the noise of a whining gearbox. He'd had a spat with the German duty editor. A mother of a row over an item on Iraq. Lots of dead bodies in gruesome detail.

"You can't run it," said the German.

"Bollocks," replied Maguire. "We show war like it is." He broadcast the footage and the German threatened a formal complaint to higher authority.

Maguire is a strange mixture. A shambling figure afflicted by asthma and myopia and a staunch defender of animal rights - he shares his apartment with two dogs and seven cats. He can be blunt, rude and immovable. But he knows his job.

I let all this swirl around in the subconscious and finally fall asleep.

Inspector Seelig invades my dreams. She sits at her desk and smiles. Then she's spinning, falling apart and coming together again, flying round the room at Jaegerstrasse like a wraith. She speaks but I don't hear the words. She starts to strip. She never gets very far before the sequence fades and repeats itself.

My head shoots off the pillow. A pale light comes through a gap between the curtains. My cheap alarm says it's ten o'clock. I have an hour.

"Why do you put up at the Felsen?" Maguire once asked me.

"It's clean, it's comfortable and it doesn't cost the *Kanal* overmuch. It's my one concession to their requests for economy."

And it's damn convenient, I thought, close to a Greek restaurant on the corner of Schoeneberger Ufer and Potsdammerstrasse, from which I often find it hard to tear myself away after a good meal and a *viertel* or two of cheap red wine. And it's far enough away from the studios in Wedding to give me a sense of having a home in Berlin.

I'm not going to Jaegerstrasse. Not yet. I'm taking unilateral action. I can think of nothing else as I shower again, hurriedly shave and dress. I call a cab and stalk up and down the lobby inwardly cursing the time it takes to arrive. Margit decides the best course is to pretend I'm not there.

"Max Urich Strasse? Where the hell's Max Urich Strasse?"

"Wedding. You know Wedding, don't you?"

"Of course I know Wedding but….."

"Then just go. I'll show you when we get nearer. And don't mess me about. I don't want a tour of the sights. Head for Invalidenstrasse and Gartenstrasse."

He curls his lip and shoves the gearshift into drive.

Berlin taxi drivers are never so happy but outwardly morose as when they're given instructions. They hate losing face and missing a chance to make a little extra on the fare. But they're only too willing to pass up all responsibility if the passenger knows best. This one curses the rain and mutters about traffic jams, one way streets and cyclists. But he does as he's told.

He drops me at the spot where we stumbled across the wounded Axel Dreissig. The area still bears the scars of the Cold War. I'm a couple of blocks from Bernauerstrasse where desperate Berliners were filmed jumping from second floor windows to freedom in the West. Wander around and you'll find bits of the Wall, in pockets of land once planted with mines but invaded now by couch grass, nettles and ground elder. It's a home for Turks, Kurds and the destitute overspill from Erich Honecker's collapsed communist paradise.

I'm squatting on a wet pavement trying not to ruin a decent pair of trousers. The rain's seeped into my shirt collar. What am I looking for? Spent cartridges? Blood? The police tapes have gone and the rain has washed the sidewalk clean.

I whirl round. I'm being watched. I can feel it. And I spot him, maybe fifty metres away, across the street, hiding behind a tree. He's tall, flaxen-haired, wearing a black car coat. He stands, feet apart, arms folded. He's imbibing my personal data like a CCTV camera in an airport lounge.

He runs. The slap of his footwear is the sound Maguire heard in the early hours.

I swallow hard. My overcoat is sodden. I must get to Jaegerstrasse. But cabs are few and far between in this part of town.

I brace myself to walk down the hill to Gartenstrasse.

Is he waiting for me? Will he attack? I jog the kilometre to the S-bahn at Humboldthain. The train takes an age.

*** *** *** ***

"I rarely swear, Charlie Barrow, but where the hell have you been?" Maguire has jumped in before Renate Seelig can issue an official reprimand. "The Inspector has a mind to charge you with wasting police time. I have a mind to support her. And we've got to get a beat on this story."

"I've seen him." I'm hoping this might swing the moral advantage my way. But they look at me as if I've gone mad. "And he's seen me."

"What are you talking about, Herr Barrow?" Seelig sits prim and proper at her desk. I recollect my dream and try chasing it away with a rapid shake of the head.

"Are you all right?" she asks.

"I'm fine," I say but I don't feel it. I plunge into an explanation of my excursion to Wedding. She's showing interest but Maguire has different ideas.

"Frau Seelig. You'll excuse us, please. We have work to do." He heads for the door.

"Not so fast," she says. He stops in his tracks, turns and stands to attention.

Seelig lets time pass and Maguire's shoulders relax. "I'm not going to be bounced into giving two television journalists *carte blanche*." She motions to Maguire to sit down again. "I respect your freedom to report without official interference. But I have a favour to ask."

"A favour?" Maguire and I exchange worried glances.

"I want to see the finished product before you put it out."

Maguire whistles. "You didn't say that last night. You didn't even hint at it."

"You don't understand, Herr Maguire."

"I understand only too well if you mean you insist we chuck out the bits you don't like."

"That's not what I'm asking for."

"What are you asking for?"

"When you've collected your material, I want to watch the editing process. I want to see how you put it together into a finished product."

It's a laughable idea. And I sense that Maguire thinks it's impossible. But this woman is angling for a bargain. And we don't know what it is.

He tries again to deflect her. "Let me explain, Inspector. First we have to persuade our editor that we can handle this. That'll be difficult because he's an awkward sod. Either he won't be interested, or he'll want to hand it over to the German team. They'll mess it up because they're not directly involved in the story. And in any case, they'll look on it as the brainchild of the English, who are all crazy and stupid and, by definition, that makes it a total waste of time. And if the police officer investigating the case insists on hanging around, the editor will laugh in our faces and that'll be the end of that."

Seelig is unfazed.

"Then I'll have to apply a little pressure, won't I?" She peels round into the centre of the room. Somewhere along the way we've been seriously wrong-footed.

She shakes our hands. "Don't worry, gentlemen. I shall be discreet. And please do keep in touch."

# Chapter 6

It's four o'clock in the afternoon. Berlin's at its worst. Low, mottled, cloud and another heavy downpour. Maguire drives us to the *Kanal.* I'm not looking forward to this shift.

"You're not due on till five," he says.

"If I don't get in early, there won't be time to repair the damage. Crimes committed against the English language, Mac. Abominations of grammar and syntax, perpetrated by the lively young people we call translators. They've got degrees in German, Russian, Czech and God knows what else. But when it comes to English, they're half educated."

Bullets of rain defy the best efforts of the wipers. But Maguire pushes on, smiling as he listens again to my perennial gripe.

"There's always a pile of work before the first.....show." I sniff the dampness against which the heater fights a losing battle. "I hate that expression. It says the sole purpose of what we do is to entertain."

"Heads and brick walls, Charlie. Our bosses care about ratings and moving pictures. They're not interested in words. You and I wage that war every day of our lives."

I nod reluctantly. "I wouldn't mind so much if I didn't have to work with those American neo-cons. They think television exists to spread their views on everything from gung-ho politics to supply-side economics."

"Of course they do, Charlie. That's why they were put into this world. Anything that doesn't fit the Republican canon is heresy. All foreigners are subversives, even the Germans who pay their wages. Arabs are not to be trusted. Russians are stupid. Their heating systems fail in winter and their aircraft keep falling out of the sky. They made a mess of Afghanistan and they're making an even bigger one of Chechnya."

He turns off Unter den Linden into Neustaedtischer Kirchstrasse.

"The French are bloody arrogant and even the Brits are suspect notwithstanding Tony Blair and suicide bombers in London. It won't change Charlie."

We're passing the U.S. embassy, an unprepossessing fortress bristling security.

"I wonder why they took up residence down here?" I ask. "It's not like them to hide their light under a bushel."

"It's so they don't have to answer questions," muses Maguire. "Say the words *sputnik* or Vietnam, Enron or Abu-Ghraib, and they clam up. Try it in the newsroom with your neo-cons. It works."

We're on Friedrichstrasse now, heading north and I'm gloomier by the minute. I glimpse pedestrians pushing against rain, sheltering in shop doorways or diving into the U-bahn. The city wears delusion and disappointment like threadbare gabardine.

"What do you make of our friend then?" I glance at Maguire who's concentrating on a tram he's trying to overtake. He says nothing until we squeeze past and cross its tracks a little too smartly for the motorman's liking. We hear the repeated clang of his bell. Maguire does a quick spurt, cutting up a delivery van. This time we get the full force of a farting horn and flashing headlights.

"Same as you, I guess," he says, unperturbed by the effects of his driving. "What does she want? This deal she's trying to strike. Smells a mile off. But I suspect that if we want to do the Dreissig Story, we'll have to play along - somehow."

I listen to the swish of traffic and the rumble of tyres on sets.

"I'm thinking of getting out, Mac."

"Out of the deal with Seelig or out of the *Kanal*?"

"You know what I mean."

"Surprise me, Charlie." Then he makes me feel guilty. "I can't quit," he says. "Too many bills to pay. In any case, German labour law says they can't sack me. So I stick it out."

And I ask myself again - what else can Charlie Barrow do at the age of 49? Maguire second-guesses me.

"You've got a decent CV. You've worked in British military intelligence. You're fluent in five languages. You've gone through the mill in Ulster knocking the shit out of villains on both sides. And you've come out relatively unscathed. You've made a bob or two out of freelancing. You won't starve."

"I sometimes wonder why the *Kanal* took me on." I'm fishing for compliments to get out of my depression.

"Kai Struck wanted a *Mensch*, Charlie. A somewhat wizened on-screen presence, a shock of grey hair, a face that'd been knocked about a bit, lending authority to the output. At least that's what he told me."

We park at the back of the building in what used to be a rail yard with the old tracks embedded in concrete. It's stopped raining but I don't feel any happier.

We show our passes and are told the *Chefredakteur* wants to see us.

# Chapter 7

"Absolutely, no way." Kai Struck is in his late thirties, athletic, short fair hair, fresh faced, wears jeans and a pink shirt open at the neck. His blue linen jacket is draped across the back of his executive's chair.

"I cannot release you from your normal duties to chase a story that, frankly, is of no interest to this network. A murder in a Berlin suburb? The victim a non-entity, a member of an insignificant right wing party, and no one arrested? Do me a favour, Maguire. Tell me what the international dimension is and I might look on more favourably. But there isn't one, is there? And you, Charlie Barrow, should know better than to ask."

The room hums quietly with air-conditioning and computers. I glimpse the outside world through a row of slanting windows, a landscape of sodden rooftops and the glow of street lighting as the winter afternoon closes in.

"You know what's wrong with this organisation, Kai?" Struck is about to cut me off but I push on. "It's reactive. It never originates anything. It follows where others have led….."

"Why do you always pour shit over everything we do, Barrow?" The use of my surname means he's losing his temper. He hits the desk top with the point of a biro.

"I don't pour shit." I say. "I spend most of my time wiping this network's arse. I work hard to improve the output. I try to make sure it reaches the highest standards and competes, God damn it. Only you won't see it, will you? When you get a chance to steal a march, you don't take it."

Maguire thinks it's time to get Struck back on side. "Herr Struck, you know how passionate Charlie is about these things….."

"Oh, I know how passionate he is. And how stupid." He looks daggers at me. "Let me spell it out to you. This is a government financed television station broadcasting to the wider world in two languages, covering international stories and reflecting life in Germany….."

"Precisely," I interject. "Which is why you should do this story. Hell's teeth, two of your own people are involved in a case in which a member of a neo-Nazi organisation is murdered in Berlin. This at a time when the government is gunning for the bastards. I might remind you, that that same government has gone to the courts to get The Movement declared illegal. If that's not life in contemporary Germany, then what is? And if it's not a chance to show others, including critics inside the government - and don't tell me you don't know who they are - if it's not an opportunity to show them how this network can do some real journalism, what do I have to say to shake you out of your complacency, Herr Struck?"

Struck shifts in his chair. "This is not for us," he says. "It's a job for the domestic stations." He turns his face away from us and stares petulantly out of the window. Then puts his feet on the desk. He's wearing loafers.

"Is that all you've got to say?" I ask.

"It is all I have to say, Herr Barrow." He gestures as if he's lining me up in the sights of a gun.

"Then fuck you, I resign." I jump out of my chair and summon all the venom that's been accumulating for weeks. "You can find another bloody presenter for your English 'shows'." I head for the door.

Maguire is blocking my way. "Don't be fool, Charlie."

"I wouldn't stop him if I were you," calls Struck. "Presenters are ten a penny. I can pick them up off the Ku'damm any time I like."

Maguire stands, his mouth wide open.

"Get out." Struck has turned to face us. "And don't come crawling back to this organisation, Barrow. You're through."

"You bet I am," I yell, making sure Struck's two secretaries in the outer office are witnessing the whole scene. I beckon Maguire to go past me. Then take enormous pleasure in slamming Struck's door.

We're in front of the elevator door.

"I still have a programme to produce, Charlie." Maguire speaks quietly, almost meekly. "I can't walk out."

"I'm sorry, Mac."

"So am I. We are now as far away from getting this thing to air as we are likely to be and Inspector Seelig might not forgive us."

"I couldn't take any more from that arsehole." I'm still shaking. Please, God, don't let me have a heart attack. Not in here.

Mac displays his usual quiet smile. "What will you do now?" he asks.

"I need a meal and a stiff drink. And I know where to go."

Mercifully the lift arrives. We stay silent in the presence of our fellow passengers who look at us as if we're untouchables. We reach the lobby.

Maguire throws up his hands and bursts out laughing. "Ah well. I shall now attempt to retrieve something from the decay of this colossal wreck." He waves his arms about like an uncontrollable windmill, a mime show that takes in the whole building.

"You will never repair the legless trunks of this Ozymandias, Mac. It's too far gone for that."

"I compliment you on recognising a quotation from Percy Bysshe Shelley. Would that I had time to read more of him." He steps back into the lift, ascending to a production room I shall never enter again. There'll be the buzz of rumour and comment from those glad to see the back of me. And that will be that. Charlie Barrow. Forgotten and not much missed.

As I move through the swing door out on to Voltastrasse, Struck emerges from the other elevator. There's something familiar about his gait. And if a look of total scorn can kill, I'm dead already.

# Chapter 8

Dizzy with my new found freedom but dimly aware that I have walked out of a good job and probably behaved with a reprehensible lack of professionalism, I look across the table at Renate Seelig. She is no longer in uniform. She wears denim, jeans, shirt and jacket and a multicoloured necklace of fluospar. Her blue eyes shine with the reflected light of a candle.

She rang my *Handy,* telling me to meet her at a North African bistro in Kurfuerstenstrasse, not the brightly lit Damm in the West but a quieter street north of Schoeneberg. It's the secluded haunt of whores and dealers but, for all that, highly convenient and a short walk from the hotel. The rain has stopped. There are even stars in a clear sky glowing with the heat and light of the city. But the pavements smell fresh again and there's a faint hint of resin from trees almost leafless as autumn moves into winter. I am vaguely conscious of being followed but too adrift from reality to worry about it. The bistro isn't busy and stays mercifully free of muzak. The food is a mixture of French and Moroccan, dominated by a couscous of lamb, beef and chicken with onions, chick peas, tomatoes and courgettes mingling in acceptable proportions.

I stare into a half empty glass of wine. "Why do you still want to see me? Especially after what I did this afternoon."

"Yes," she says. "I gather that was quite a spectacle, Charlie Barrow. Decisive, Irreversible. Struck is not a man to forgive and forget, I'm told."

"Who told you?"

"Don't be so touchy. Maguire of course. He called me after you left Voltastrasse."

"Struck can go to hell."

The dizziness returns. I am free and light-headed. But with no income other than a modest armed forces pension and a few savings, I might be about to find life a little difficult. Mild panic bores into the back of my skull. I swig my wine. "I asked you a question, Inspector."

"And I shall answer." She in turn sips her wine. "You are a marked man."

I try to interrupt but she brushes me aside.

"In two senses of the word. The case, the story, the murder of Axel Dreissig, has marked you out, not least because you are thoroughly familiar with the background. I can tell, Charlie. You are obsessed with The Movement. You keep asking yourself, what is it? You want answers. You are a journalist and I know you are going to pursue this until you have found the truth and someone to listen to those answers."

She pauses, practises her beguiling smile but again holds up her hand. "And you have been marked by the villains. The man you believe killed Dreissig has seen you. Therefore you are in danger. And as the investigating officer, I am responsible for your safety."

I laugh softly. "Why do you slip into this formal language, Inspector? It's almost pompous and I don't think you are a pompous person."

She frowns, concentrating on the food in front of her. “What is wrong with good, formal, German? Too many Germans abuse their language. Formality means precision and accuracy. I need those in my line of work.”

I put my hands together and bow my head. “I did not mean to offend. It’s just that I find it strange, like a gear change at the wrong speed.”

She is still frowning. “If I am calling you Charlie, you must respond in kind. My name is Renate.”

“Renate,” I say, self-consciously. “Nothing pompous about that.”

The studious face of a senior police officer melts into that of a handsome woman, out for a relaxing evening with a friend. It seems the right time to pause and we begin to eat. But I am too inquisitive.

“I know it’s none of my business but you do seem young for your rank. And there can’t be many women of your seniority in the Berlin force.” Before she can break in, I add, “I do know something about police procedure.”

“Yes, Charlie. I know you do. I looked you up on our files.” Now she is toying with me and enjoying it. “I know about your time in Northern Ireland - and more. I know you questioned terrorists.” She leans towards me. “And I know you bent the rules.”

I am not shocked. My record is an open book for every security force in Europe. But I have triggered Renate Seelig into reminding me of a past I prefer to forget, of work I was forced into after my years in military intelligence analysing the weaponry of the Warsaw Pact. They decided to cash in on my skills as an interrogator of defectors and insisted I was needed in Belfast and Crossmaglen. I spent too many hours in unwholesome interview rooms and dank cells coaxing or beating information out of hardened criminals and committed rebels.

"Oh, I bent the rules, all right." I drink to wash away the memories. "Do you bend the rules, Renate? Does the *BND* or the *BKA* bend the rules?"

"Charlie Barrow, you are forgetting your English gentleman's good manners. I should like another drink, please."

I call for a second bottle. The art of conversation has deserted me and I hold my tongue.

"Charlie." She speaks quickly now, as if wanting to get this part over and done with. I concentrate on my food.

"I am 43. Divorced. No children. A career police officer. I specialise in quick response to reported crime and, for reasons at which you have guessed, I have a more immediate interest in neo-Nazi skulduggery and its links to terror outside this country. And I am good at my job."

"I am sure you are." I can't think of anything else to say.

She leans across the table again and takes my hand. By now the management has yielded to the temptation to play music. It is rather enchanting. Sinuous and Levantine. And not too loud.

"You don't need the *Kanal* to do this investigation," she tells me. "Your file says you still freelance for other outlets. British newspapers, an Australian magazine - even an academic journal in Budapest. Do you speak Hungarian?"

"Yes I do. But I don't write it well. They translate what I send them. The trouble is none of them pays too generously." I am doing some quick thinking. I can sell a story about The Movement to contacts in London and Melbourne. It will be hard graft. But it will be real journalism, the sort I haven't done for months. We are still holding hands.

Temerity returns. "Am I to assume that you will help," I ask, "that you will give me leads I can follow, fruitful, profitable leads, Renate? Freelances can't afford to waste time on dead ends."

"Neither can police officers." She releases me. "Come to the office tomorrow and we shall talk about it."

I should be required to show caution. I should distance myself from a tempting offer.

I once made friends with a senior police officer in Budapest. But that had been strictly business. This is a deeper commitment.

"What about Maguire?" I have an obligation and I intend to fulfil it.

"He's tied to the *Kanal.* But I think you can trust him if you want him along."

Now I should ask Maguire's question. What's the bargain? What is she getting out of all this? She must have scores of agents in the field. The police don't use journalists to conduct investigations by proxy. Journalists get in the way.

The candle splutters and the second bottle arrives.

"All I really want," I say, "is to fly back to London. And the first thing I shall do when I get there is sit down at my old piano and play some jazz."

"I don't believe you, Charlie Barrow." I sigh and she laughs lightly. "Don't say you want me to become formal and pompous again."

"You aren't pompous, Inspector Seelig. Just - correct."

"Not that correct, Mr Barrow."

# Chapter 9

Renate Seelig lives in a brand new four-storey block in Kreuzberg SO36, a sobriquet derived from a postal code used in the days before the Wall came down. It was once an outpost of alternative cultures, a source of protest against efforts by the government of West Berlin to destroy the squats of the radicals and gentrify the property that survived the Allied air raids. The radicals lost the battle and the old has been replaced by modern apartments offered at rents lower than those payable in the modish areas of Schoeneberg and Wilmersdorf. Renate has made a smart move.

Over coffee in her sitting room, its walls lined with paperbacks and a motley array of prints and photographs, I give my own version of my life story.

"I sometimes think I have died," I conclude, "that I'm peering like a ghost at a crystal ball in which it's all happening in another world."

"You spend too much time in cafes and restaurants, Charlie, looking on at others. It isn't healthy." She holds my gaze and gives me her artful smile.

"You have been married?" she asks.

I'm locked into silence again. She gets up and returns from her kitchen with two glasses of malt.

"I was abandoned for someone younger and more exciting." I swallow hard. She doesn't interrupt. "I've had my share of affairs and relationships. But when I made love I could never get rid of the memories of her. She was very beautiful."

The outside world is blocked off. No traffic. No wind or rain. She leans over and kisses me on the forehead.

"I think we should seal our bargain," she says.

*** *** *** ***

I creep away from Renate Seelig's apartment at about six. I leave her sleeping, with a note of my *Handy* number and a reminder that I will call her in mid-morning.

As I step out of the pristine lobby, I get a reminder of the past. A street light throws its beam on to a plaque set in the pavement. It tells me this was where the Wall ran until Kreuzbergers, east and west, ripped it down with their bare hands in November 1989.

I walk south to Oranienstrasse hoping to catch an early 129 bus heading west. I pass a piece of spare land, concrete and weeds, another remnant of the no-man's land that divided East and West Berlin. It serves now as a used car lot. But I see it as a convenient short cut and haul myself over a line of railings. A stiff wind blows the insistent drizzle into my face. I let myself indulge in visions of Renate, warm under the duvet. Our lovemaking was a signature on a contract. I can only move forward from this point.

I don't see the rats until it's too late. They are feeding off some carrion, hard by the wheel of a second hand Golf. I walk straight into them and freeze when one scuttles over my shoe and races away squealing into the shadows. I peer at the shoe and see what has preoccupied them. It lies on the concrete, bloody and decomposing. A human hand, half wrapped in a blue plastic bag. There's no-one around. A taxi ambles along Oranienstrasse and I hear the faint sound of a siren. A step further and I know more or less what it will be. Another plastic bag and a protruding foot, as unsightly as the hand.

I retch, turn, stagger back over the railings and keep running. With my chest heaving like an old bellows, I press the buzzer. No answer. I try again. And again.

At last her voice crackles over the intercom. I attempt some sort of breathless explanation.

"Charlie. Not again. Not tonight."

I protest. I don't want sex. I want reassurance. I want to tell her what I've seen, with a cup of coffee warming my hands.

"You look awful," she says, as she opens the door. She wears a green track suit and a pair of flip-flops.

"I feel awful. Because....."

"Because?"

I tell her. Renate holds me, turns me round and slips off my overcoat.

"Sit there." She moves into her kitchen. I hear a tap running. She returns with a glass of water. I gulp it down. She gives me another and a Kleenex. She spends the next ten minutes coaxing something like a coherent story out of me. I am ordered to stay where I am until coffee has been made. It comes black and strong and I stare into the mug as if my whole being were contained in a liquid circle of reflected light.

When she next stands before me, she's in uniform, smart and efficient.

"Show me."

We walk out to the car lot, her hand on my shoulder. Early risers peer at us. If anyone has thought of offering a clever remark, they are dissuaded by her scowl. Back-up are already there, blue lights flashing and yellow, phosphorescent jackets in abundance. She hasn't seen the evidence yet but my story has convinced her to make the calls I never heard her make.

"Show me." she says again. I point to the ground by the Golf's wheel. Rat droppings and blood. The body parts are still there but covered with blue sheeting.

A sergeant tells her what they've found.

"A dismembered body, Inspector. Male. Youngish. Some of the parts were dumped in green waste sacks. Haven't found the head. But there are some banknotes and a plastic card."

"A card?" I ask. Renate shoots me a glance which says, "Keep quiet."

The officer hands it over. She pulls me to one side and takes out a pocket-torch.

"Well, well, well, Charlie Barrow! You can't get away from them, can you?"

We look for the name. Jens Koard. It means nothing except that The Movement seems to have embarked on an internal and very violent purge. Dreissig was shot. A clean death in a way. This one has been butchered.

The forensic team arrive. Renate tells me to be patient, to hang around while she consults them. I walk away and stare at nothing in particular. Twenty four hours ago, I was tossing and turning in my bed after this woman had interrogated me. Later I'm in the back streets of Berlin, observed by a man who might be a killer and reminds me of someone I know. I walk out of my job and dine with the officer who questioned me. And I spent the night with her.

She turns from her chat with the medics and, ignoring their reaction, interrupts my thoughts by placing her hand on my shoulder again. She leads me quietly back to the main road.

"Go to your hotel. There's a taxi-stand on the corner. Take a scalding hot shower. Shave and eat some breakfast. Meet me in my office at eleven."

I mumble my thanks and bend to give her a peck on the cheek.

"Not now, Charlie. Not here. Talk to you later."

I don't want to be on my own. But I do as I'm told.

# Chapter 10

I drink more of Renate's coffee. Maguire and I sit in her office again. He has a faraway look in his eyes as if he's weighing up a wealth of information on the impact of my walkout from the *Kanal.* It will be fascinating to hear his news but not yet. I am trying to exorcise bad memories, of rats and severed limbs, and the ride from Oranienstrasse to the hotel.

I chanced upon a garrulous driver, a surly Berliner, *Ossi* to the core, who reckoned I was a suitable sounding board for his views on Turks, Arabs, Jews, scrounging asylum seekers and rich Russians buying property in fashionable suburbs. There was no escape, as the rain lashed the streets of a city covered in thickening layers of grey storm cloud.

In the end I told him to shut up.

Then came the rant. "You English. *Immer Scheiss machen.* Why didn't you accept Hitler's peace overtures in 1939? It would have saved us all a lot of trouble." He threatened to dump me somewhere near Alexanderplatz.

"Do you want the fucking fare, or don't you?" I'd had enough of this rodomontade. But we were already in the lower reaches of Potsdammerstrasse and it wasn't worth discarding him.

"OK, OK," he countered and muttered something inaudible into his steering wheel.

There were few surprises at the hotel. The first message I picked up came from Struck's office. It ordered me to quit my room or pay the bill myself as from yesterday. The second was more promising. Would I ring Fred on my old paper in London? Fred is a foreign news editor, with eyes over which not a strand of wool can be pulled.

"I'd heard," he said.

"Heard what?" I played along in the hope of coming out of this poker game with a promise of filthy lucre.

"Heard you'd walked out of the Krauts' TV show." There was no need to ask how he learned of my bust-up with Struck. There are others at the *Kanal* who file surreptitious copy to London and Fred knows them well.

"So you're looking for work?"

"I'm already on to something." I marshalled my arguments for selling the Dreissig murder to him. I told him that if he gave me time, I would file a whole lot more after a preliminary piece on the events of the last twenty-four hours. I pitched in with stuff on The Movement, its likely impact on forthcoming elections, its appeal to disaffected German youth, and its apparent willingness to do a brutal clean out of its Augean stables.

"Sounds good. But you know what I always say."

"Yes, Fred. Facts and no waffle. Rest assured."

And with that we had a deal which brought me some relief.

Renate sits down at her desk, re-arranges three pencils and pulls the laptop towards her. We are like three members of a dumb-show just after the curtain's gone up. She bursts out laughing.

"What a pair. I suppose you want me to open proceedings simply because I am the one in authority."

"Of course," I say sheepishly. "We await orders."

The smile changes to a frown. I have goofed.

"Don't push the anti-German satire too far, Mr Barrow."

The frown becomes the scowl that cowed passers-by in Kreuzberg in the early hours.

"I'm sorry," I reply. "I have no such prejudices, as you well know, Inspector."

Maguire's face tells me he's baffled. He can't decide whether we are serious or playing a game he doesn't understand.

Renate coughs importantly and taps her keyboard. A printer in the corner churns out a single sheet of paper. She leans back to retrieve it and passes it over to me. "Your first contact," she says. "Memorise the name and address. It's not his real name. When you've finished, it goes in the shredder."

"Last night...." I have blundered again. Maguire's face lights up. I blunder on. "You talked of links to outside terror. Would you like to expand on that or is the world going to be full of surprises when I embark on this investigation?"

"I can't you give you details, Charlie, because I haven't got them - at least none that you don't have already. We know Lenz has Middle East and North African connections. Even though he hates foreigners, some are more equal than others, to quote a phrase. They're necessary allies in the struggle against the degenerate German state. It may have firebombed asylum seekers' hostels and killed a few aliens but The Movement has a peculiar habit of trying to avoid Arab targets. Every now and then though, it screws up. Not so long ago, two Algerians were beaten senseless in Rostock. Which was a very bad case of mistaken identity on the part of Lenz's people because Algeria is where most of his Arab contacts come from."

Renate hits a key on the laptop. "Lenz also hates Americans."

She points a finger at the screen."He's on record as saying they deserved Nine Eleven. After Madrid, Beslan and London he's added the Spanish, the Russians and the British to his list."

She opens the desk drawer and pushes an envelope towards me. "We found these in Axel Dreissig's apartment." Maguire and I glance at the photographs. Two men of what the police usually call Middle Eastern appearance are sitting at a table covered with coffee cups.

"That's the bar at Tegel," I say. "And these are some of Lenz's Arab friends." I look more closely. "Or are they people he wants rubbed out?"

"That's what we'd like to know," she says.

"My guess is they'd done deals with The Movement and Axel's minder was under orders to keep tabs on them. It's no more exciting than that."

"A guess isn't good enough."

"Which means you've got your own people scouring the walkways at Tegel?" I ask.

"Something like that, yes."

I hand back the piece of paper. The shredder whirrs and it's gone for good.

The plan is for me to meet her man at eight that evening and for Maguire to act as go-between while I am out in Indian Country. I note that Maguire seems to have tacitly accepted the bargain we've struck.

"I don't want you phoning Jaegerstrasse from dodgy locations," says Renate. "Restrict your calls to Mac's *Handy*. They can all be traced of course and this bunch have some clever people who know all about hacking into networks. But it's the safer bet. There must be no calls to his home number or to the *Kanal*."

"How often do I phone?"

"Twice a day at most. And shuffle the times around - unless of course you're in trouble."

"You expect trouble?"

"We're dealing with thugs, Charlie."

I have enough training in me to avoid most tight corners but up to now the idea that I might be killed hasn't occurred to me. Her face tells me she knows what I'm thinking and is saying nothing.

"Struck is watching me like a hawk," says Maguire. "Or rather he's having me watched."

"I'll bet he is," snaps Renate. "Which is why I say - no calls to the *Kanal*. And, by the way, I'm running checks on him."

"Why so?" asks Maguire.

"Just a feeling," she replies. "His reaction to your proposal. The way he dealt with Charlie." She nods towards me. "As if he was just waiting for an excuse to get rid of you."

"I can keep tabs on him," says Maguire.

"Do that. But quietly."

He hands me a sheaf of print-outs, copy from news agencies, background on The Movement and the German far right. Then he tells me he's spoken to a contact at another network who's interested in the story.

"How much have you told him?"

Renate shows her worry lines.

"Just a straightforward tale about The Movement - the leading figures, where it gets its main support from. Nothing about the two murders - or your interest in them."

Maguire raises his hands in half-hearted protest.

"Don't take it any further," she orders. "Not until Charlie gets back to Berlin."

He rises. " 'Hope may vanish, but can die not'. I take my leave."

"More Shelley?" I ask.

Maguire gives me a cherubic smile, shambles to the door, waves and is gone.

Renate places her hands on my shoulders.

"I won't be far behind, Charlie."

I don't know why. But I'm not reassured.

# PART 2

# Chapter 1

It is six o'clock, already dark, and the rain has returned, persistent, cold, sweeping the streets like a monstrous power shower. I use an internet café on Potsdammerstrasse to file some copy for Fred. It's stuff on the murders, based on formal statements from the police that both victims had, incidentally, been members of The Movement but there was no suggestion that the killings were politically motivated. I leave it at that for the time being.

I take S-bahn Line 7 from Hackescher Markt, a district transformed inside a decade from a row of blackened archways into a fashionable collection of bars, restaurants and shops selling tourist tat. The train, maroon and cream like its old-fashioned predecessors, whisks me eastwards through the smartly functional station at Alexanderplatz, across Jannowitzbruecke, its stark girders still reminiscent of the Cold War divide, and into the grim suburbs that once made up the workers' Elysium.

Even German trains can be delayed. This one is held in a cutting lined with hedgerows of hawthorn and remnants of summer weeds, lit up by the fluorescent lights of the carriage, a thin ribbon of territory neglected and untouched by the planners.

I drum my fingers on the covers of a notebook and become aware of suspicious looks from fellow passengers. A bald, beady-eyed man in his forties sporting a Bismarck moustache, a brown leather jacket and jeans, stands before me. He asks for my ticket and I suddenly remember that I failed to cancel it in the machine back at Hackescher Markt.

"This is not valid," he says with the air of a teacher catching a schoolboy smoking behind the toilets.

"It is perfectly valid," I reply in an effort to bluff my way out of the inevitable crisis.

"I bought it at Hackescher Markt. I paid six euros for it. But I forgot to cancel it. I apologise for my forgetfulness." I try to smile.

"That means it is not valid," he says, po-faced and motionless.

"Look, I'm sorry. It was a genuine mistake….."

"I am fining you forty euros."

"You are doing what?" I huff. The eyes of all in the compartment bore into me.

"I am fining you forty euros." He is tapping something into the small screen of an electronic device dangling from his shoulders.

"You must be joking. If you think….."

"If you do not pay now, we shall notify you of the fine. If you do not pay on notification, we shall prosecute. You will give me your address."

I snatch at my notebook, rip out a page, scribble my details and thrust it at him.

"I shall give you this in return," he says, his face as firmly set as before. "It is a record of this interview and a demand for payment. You must not lose it."

He marches off. Those around me summon up a collective sneer. *Ossis* do not like strangers. And I was definitely a stranger in a strange land. I glower back. At least I haven't paid up. They don't flinch. I turn abruptly to stare through the window at the detritus of old rolling stock parked in the huge marshalling yards of Lichtenberg.

The name reminds me that we're close to the old home of the *Stasi* with its offices at Normannenstrasse 22. It's an address those of us who once had an interest in these things know well. Thousands of agents worked in an enormous office complex, spying on their fellow citizens and on each other, watching and waiting for the slightest sign of dissent, and for the opportunity to blackmail.

Lichtenberg. Damn. The fracas with the ticket inspector and my musings on the *Stasi* have distracted me. I've gone past the station where I was supposed to get off. I nip out at Friedrichsfelde Ost, cross over and wait forlornly for a train to take me back towards town. Ten minutes later I am where I was meant to be. I stand on the platform at Noeldnerplatz and hesitate. I'll call the whole thing off. It's a sham, a wild-goose chase. And I'm not up to it.

The rain has stopped. I need a drink. I wander out of the station into a street that glories in the name of Archibaldweg. I find it so comic that I laugh hysterically and draw startled glances from passers-by. I see the lights of a bar. *Dicke Heinrich*. Fat Harry's. It's empty except for one old soul cooped up in a corner behind a newspaper. He ignores me. Mine host, as gross as the name of his pub implies, isn't over courteous but at least serves me a very large Warsteiner which I carry to a table as far away as possible from my fellow tippler. I drink, wipe my mouth with the back of my hand, take a deep breath and contemplate the future.

There are more papers folded into a rack near the door. I haven't caught up with the news for the best part of twenty-four hours. They have both stories by now - Axel Dreissig and Jens Koard - but nothing on the front pages. There's no mention of their membership of The Movement, just idle speculation about links to an underworld of drugs and male prostitution. Renate has laid her false trails.

My contact lives round the corner in Kolonie Paradies. A Berlin *Kolonie* is a collection of garishly painted huts, with allotments wrested from spare land. This is where *Ossis* used to hide from the prying eyes of Normannenstrasse and tilled their private plots to supplement the diet offered by the state-run food stores.

Even now, city dwellers try to live a quiet life, tending vegetables and flower beds. But I can hear the city beyond these little picket fences. It crashes and hoots, roars and rumbles, and threatens, like the Big Bad Wolf, to blow these houses down.

I go over the basic information in my head, making sure I've recalled the details. Fechner at Number 35. Common sense tells me to slow down. So I sit and aim to spend time with my beer. Fat Harry puts on a CD. Appalling German pop in keeping with the bar's kitschy décor. I drain my glass and step outside.

Kolonie Paradies is a short walk away but I need my street atlas and torch to work out how to get there. Its wooden sheds and plots of sodden, well tilled earth, reeking of dead leaves and manure, nestle against another S-bahn line.

I push open a flimsy gate which scrapes the footpath and sets my teeth on edge. I knock on a door barely illuminated by a 40-watt bulb sheathed in dust and cobwebs. I wait a full minute before the lock is drawn and a man in his late thirties wearing spectacles with thick lenses, a grey sweater and brown corduroy trousers scrutinises me through the gloom.

"You are Mr Barrow?"

I acknowledge my identity and show him my passport. He beckons me inside.

"I can offer you tea, coffee or schnapps. Or all three. Please, sit down. The room is untidy. But only with books and papers. Actually I clean it thoroughly every week. Very Prussian. For that is what we are. Prussians. Whether communists, Nazis, neo-Nazis, democrats, shopkeepers, bureaucrats or footballers. It's the Prussian in us that counts. Order, cleanliness and utter boorishness. And we feel so sorry for ourselves."

I'm thrown by this. "I quite like Berlin," I say lamely.

"Do you really? You are very kind. I wish I could say the same. Pleasant enough in summer but depressing in winter." He smiles. "Your drink? You didn't specify."

I ask for schnapps. He moves to a corner of the room where he busies himself with a bottle and glass and hands me a generous measure. Before I can thank him, he says, "So, you want to meet the movers and shakers in The Movement?"

"I'm told you can arrange it, Herr.....Fechner."

"Yes, I can arrange it."

There is an awkward pause in which I sip my drink. He laughs softly. But it is almost a threat. "You are not too sure of me, are you? Am I one of 'them' or a mere go-between?" He sits back and gazes through his pebble lenses. I try to stare him out but am the first to blink. He laughs again.

I've had enough of this shit. "Herr Fechner, I am a journalist who wants to do a story on The Movement. I want to find out why, after all that's been said and done in this country.....why a new species of fascism is finding followers and, apparently, blooming. Is it just unemployment? They tell me it's as high as twenty per cent in parts of the East. It creates disaffected youth with time on its hands and a propensity for violence. Or is it a response to what the *Ossis* see as the colonial mentality of the West, now that capitalism has triumphed but failed to bring fat pay packets and holidays in Spain?"

I think I've wrested the initiative but he takes time to reply.

" 'We will take your rubbish at scrap value and even pay a little extra on top.' That was Guenter Grass, arguing against Reunification."

"I remember that little book. He was furious at the way Bonn swept in and took over. The East colonised by the West."

Fechner is not impressed by this. He looks round the room as if expecting a pile of paper to provide inspiration. A smart laptop has taken up residence among the debris on an old wooden table. But Fechner ignores it seemingly repelled by the intrusion of modern technology into more traditional methods of storing information.

"They didn't even bother to consult the Christian Democrats who'd survived in the East, never mind the rest of the population," he says bitterly. "You have however been doing your homework, Mr Barrow. And you have drawn the usual conclusions. I read them so often in the press. The formula is simple. No jobs equals skinheads and neo-Nazis. As easy as that." And he clicks his fingers.

"It must have something to do with it," I venture.

"It does have *something* to do with it," he retorts. "But it is far from the whole picture. Tell me, what kind of people are you expecting to meet if I choose to help you?"

I don't answer immediately. This time he removes his spectacles and rubs his eyes.

"I should like to meet unrepentant SS officers if there are any still alive," I say. "But I expect I'll end up with youths with shaven heads and polluted minds. There might be the odd young firebrand who rants and raves at election rallies about criminal foreigners taking German jobs. He will probably call for a Germany that is both nationalist and socialist. And he'll appeal not so much to the jobless as to the unskilled who still have jobs, to the self-employed, and to adults who say they support violence against people with black skins or dark complexions, but haven't got the guts to do the dirty work themselves. That's best left to the youngsters."

Fechner spreads his hands over the ribbing of his corduroys. Then says, "Well, that's better than most of the stuff I read."

"Don't patronise me, Herr Fechner. Either you are the contact the police regard as genuine or you're a sham and you're wasting my time."

"Calm down, Mr Barrow. It would not be wise for you to lose your temper with me. I might just send you packing." He shifts in his chair and studies a piece of paper he's retrieved from the pile at his feet. During the pause I try to pick out the titles of some of his books. They might give me a clue to his real identity. But the room is too dark.

"Your rather emotional survey of the types who have either joined The Movement or tacitly support it at the ballot box is not too wide of the mark. But these people are much more complicated than you suppose." I am about to interrupt with some remark about 'once a thug, always a thug' but he holds up his hand.

"I am now going to tell you what to do next." Again he examines the paper in his hand. I listen to the muffled sounds of the city beyond Kolonie Paradies and wait. I am sure I hear noises a little closer to hand, a quiet footfall and the rustle of clothing. Fechner speaks without looking up.

"You will go to Dresden," he says. "There you will meet, among others, a young woman called Marion. She is Jewish and a neo-Nazi. Does that surprise you, Mr Barrow?" I don't react. "She has many things to tell you that will."

"I'm sure I shall be astounded." I now know that we're not alone. "Tell me, how do I get there? And do I go on my own?"

The curtain at the back of the room is pushed aside. Two burly figures step forward, one male, one female. Everything they wear is black - T-shirts, jackets, trousers and boots.

They sport dark glasses despite the gloom and a range of body jewellery that makes me wince at the thought of the pain they must have endured.

"What the hell is this, Fechner?"

The two don't say a word but stand stiff and immobile either side of Fechner's armchair. They look like characters in one of the more bizarre modern productions of Wagnerian opera.

"Horst and Dagmar are your guides," says Fechner. "They may look grotesque and terrifying and they do pack a punch if called upon to use it. But they will not threaten you, Mr Barrow. Do not ask where they come from or who they work for. Just depend on them to deliver you safely to your destination. They will now return with you to your hotel where you will pack your bags for an absence of perhaps five days from Berlin. Then the three of you will catch a late night train to Dresden where you will stay in a modest but perfectly comfortable hotel. They will pay all the bills. Later they will brief you on your various encounters. Then they will decide whether to leave you to your own devices or offer you further protection."

"They'll pay the bills, will they? That's nice to know. On whose behalf?"

"No more questions, Mr Barrow. It is time to go."

"Well, at least tell me this. Do they talk or do I have to use sign language?" I am trying hard to appear imperturbable. But this is becoming a farce.

"Horst and Dagmar are highly educated." Fechner's voice contains a trace of disdain but not enough to rile me again. "They have university degrees, Horst in mathematics, Dagmar in linguistics. She has good English, by the way. They will speak to you when they judge the time is right. You should take their advice at all times."

"This is all rather melodramatic, isn't it?" I make a last effort to extract more information from him. "We'll make an odd trio, to say the least."

I scrutinise Horst and Dagmar as if they're cattle at an agricultural show.

"I mean, the disguise is hardly subtle. The general populace will hardly fail to notice the discrepancies between us."

"Horst and Dagmar are more discreet than you suppose, Mr Barrow. You will attract very little attention."

"I don't believe it," I say. But I have no choice. And Fechner has clearly finished with me. He bids me a curt farewell and stays seated. I look at Horst who nods towards the door. Outside the picket fence, a perfectly ordinary Berlin taxi is waiting with its engine idling. Dagmar opens the door. I get in. Horst slides alongside me. The girl takes the front seat. Neither says a word to the driver. Twenty minutes later we reach the hotel. I pack and we leave in the same taxi.

# Chapter 2

My minders avoid all conversation. Any attempt at an opening gambit from me produces no response. All I get are commands. "Be ready in fifteen minutes." "Take no more than two bags." "Sit there."

The express slides out of Zoo station and leaves Berlin swiftly behind. Looking into the darkness from my window seat, I can just pick out a friendless landscape of forest and field. I have morbid thoughts about the fierce fighting that raged here as the Russians beat back remnants of the *Wehrmacht* in 1945. The books I've read describe a countryside littered with corpses, abandoned weapons and helmets, hand-carts and baggage, and human heads squashed flat in pools of petrol and blood. And now, sixty years later, German youth is ready to believe again in the Hitler myth, the nobility of the SS and insane theories of racial superiority. I am going to accost the people perpetrating these lies. I am going to ask them if they have already embarked on a killing spree, murdering blacks, punks, homosexuals and Turks, torching asylum centres and purging their own ranks of traitors and renegades. I shall ask them if their actions are designed to lead to more violence between nations, to slaughter and mayhem in cities, towns and villages, to a repeat of the

Second World War. I must be mad. Poor Axel, who believed his Brave New Germany could be built in other ways.

"A drink, Mr Barrow?"

I look up to find Horst gesturing to an attendant wheeling a refreshments trolley.

"Very civil. Thank you."

I wonder if the ice is broken. The beer is set before me. Horst pays and says no more. I drink and ponder and the rhythm of the train sends me to sleep.

I dream of an old girlfriend in Berlin. She lived in a smart flat in Steglitz, tastefully furnished with bits and bobs she'd picked up on trips to Thailand or Tunisia. She gave me tea and kept creaming her hands with some lotion from a jar set on the low table in front of us. I wanted to take her to bed but she made it plain this was not an option even though she kept planting chaste kisses on my forehead and firmly grasped my hands between sips of Earl Grey. It was a comforting reverie, a throw-back to more innocent times when flirting might successfully lead to a gentle affair.

It lasts until I am nudged awake by Dagmar, a woman in stark contrast to the lady of my dreams. But at least she speaks to me, and in English.

"I'm afraid we shall be staying in a rather plastic hotel, Mr Barrow." I am almost delirious with delight at this concern for my welfare even if it is on the brief side. "When we arrive, you will walk in front of us. Head for the taxi rank. It is well sign-posted."

I need a pee. Horst says he will follow me through the carriage to the toilet and wait outside. I hold the door handle and realise we have company. A skinhead, short and stocky, has followed us and stands a few metres behind Horst. He produces a knife and lunges. Horst swings round, knocks the weapon out of his hand and catches hold of his attacker's parka. If I have any doubts about the immense strength of my minder, they are instantly dispelled. He hauls the man towards him, lifts him up and fells him with a head butt.

"Carry on, Mr Barrow. No harm done. I'll stay here."

"I hope that's a firm promise," I say as I sidle into the cubicle.

"Where did our friend go?" I ask as we return to our seats.

"Forget it, Mr Barrow. You're safe. That's all that matters."

If I didn't know that it is technically impossible to open the door of a German Inter-City Express moving at speed, I can easily imagine Horst despatching the skinhead into the night.

But his fate isn't uppermost in my mind. "They, whoever *they* are, know I'm on this train, don't they? And they know who you are." It's a statement. I don't expect a response. I don't get one.

We arrive. I walk from the train along a crowded platform, a bag in both hands, past shops and kiosks, some of them still doing business despite the hour. I turn into the street towards a line of cabs. I keep my eyes peeled but see no sign of the skinhead. My feet suddenly feel as heavy as lead. As I hail a cab, Horst and Dagmar are standing behind me. The ride to the hotel, the process of checking in, of being escorted to my room and almost frog-marched to bed, I remember them now as a hazy sequence. I was aware of danger yet disconnected from what was happening. Did they pop something into the beer on the train? Was the rumble with the skin just a figment of my imagination?

I still have the wit to unpack, grab another beer from the mini-bar, and organise my clothes and notebooks. Then I crash and sleep soundly. No more dreams or nightmares. At eight in the morning I am wide awake and grateful for the provision of room-service and a large pot of coffee. The buzzer sounds and Horst and Dagmar slip in like a pair of well oiled seals. I decide to be nosy again.

"It would be comforting to know who you two work for," I say as firmly as I can.

"We are not allowed to say," they answer in unison.

They look me squarely in the eye and give nothing away.

"That's the answer I thought I'd get."

I may be past the point of indignation and protest but I have conceived a strong desire to rid our relationship of mystery and charade.

"So, I shall ask again. Are you, so to speak, friend or foe, the representatives of authority, or links in a chain to some nasty people? And, if I don't do as you say, will you bash me over the head and leave my body to rot on some landfill site outside this wonderful jewel of a restored city?"

Horst leans forward and folds his huge hands together. Dagmar turns away as if embarrassed by the whole procedure.

"Mr Barrow, you heard what Herr Fechner said. You are to trust us."

"Oh I heard what he said. But I don't even know whose side *he's* on, do I? Then we meet this clown on the train who tries to inflict grievous bodily harm. Are you surprised that I'm burning to get answers to some questions?"

I sip coffee and wish I still smoked.

Dagmar intervenes. "Mr Barrow, you are very lucky to have our protection. We know all about your assignment. We have our doubts about the wisdom of it. But we follow orders. You will recollect that that is something of a German trait." She waits for me to respond to this whiff of self-mockery. I resist the temptation. But she knows what I am thinking. "We have spent months, if not years," she says, "cultivating the contacts of which you are about to take advantage."

I nod, accepting the rebuke. Their body language tells me they want to get on with the business in hand. And I think I am reassured that they are on the side of the angels.

"We shall head for Gorbitz," Dagmar tells me. "It is a very unattractive suburb. It has no redeeming features, just the usual collection of high rise built by the communists."

"To house the workers," chimes in Horst. "Dagmar and I were brought up there."

"Home from home then?"

They ignore this. "We hate it," says Dagmar. "We dragged ourselves out of there. But it is home to the people you need to meet. If you went in there on your own and asked your questions, I doubt you would come out alive. So, at least give us credit for doing something that sticks in our craw."

This is said with a quiet passion that hasn't surfaced before.

"I am sorry," I say. "I am not ungrateful. And I take on board what you have said. It's just that it's not easy for me to accept reticence in my travelling companions when my stock in trade is words."

Horst gets up. "We accept your apology. Now it's time to go." I shrug my shoulders and Dagmar allows herself a flicker of a smile.

# Chapter 3

Gorbitz is the pits. The pits of East German communist planning. It was built in response to the Allied fire storms that all but wiped Dresden from the face of the earth. The people needed new housing. And they had to be kept under control. High rise was the ideal solution. Since the collapse of the old regime, the authorities have tarted the place up to hide the crumbling concrete and prefabrication. There are shops and stores and even the odd pub. But for all the cans of paint they've used and the trees they've planted, for all the playgrounds, the slides and the swings, they've failed to wipe away the essential cheerlessness, the regimentation, and the atmosphere of duress and moral blackmail.

We turn a corner and confront Willi's Fitness Parlour to the left and the Ecko Club to the right, a single storey block covered with challenging graffiti. 'Foreigners Out!' and 'Long Live The Reich!' are two of the more uncompromising messages defacing its walls. An old man with a plastic bag in each hand trudges towards us, avoiding eye contact. I look back to the main road, where the trams are droning through the rain. I want to run and climb aboard the first one heading for the city centre. But Horst is already holding the door open.

I am definitely out of place. We're in a large hall, neon-lit, lined with breeze-block, a sparsely stocked bar down one side and a couple of ping-pong tables at the far end. It smells of stale coffee and cigarettes. Loudspeakers play some indefinable rock. The place isn't crowded but there are enough customers to make it hum a little. Horst and Dagmar take me over to where a man in this late thirties with no discernible neck is furiously washing beer glasses. He surveys us with a mixture of amusement and suspicion.

"Well, look who it is! The Golden Duo - and friend."

Dagmar climbs on to a bar stool and Horst leans against the counter, almost nose to nose with our host.

"Two cokes, Jochen." The absence of any courtesies seems to set the tone for most of what happens next.

"I see we are being good boys and girls then. No alcohol before twelve? And what about our visitor? Coke for him too?" Jochen has already applied himself to the drinks cooler, fishing out a couple of bottles.

"Since you serve draught Radeberger," I call, "I'll have a large one, please."

Jochen straightens himself and beams at me with new interest. "So, a real drinker, this English friend of yours. Or is he another American who's come to gloat?"

"If you're going to talk about me," I say, "do me a favour. To my face, if that's all right with you. And no, I'm not American. I'm European - like you."

I stand back and sense what's coming. Jochen edges himself round the bar and walks towards me. Horst and Dagmar shift their buttocks almost imperceptibly.

"I know what you are," Jochen mutters. "*Das sieht doch ein Blinder mit dem Krueckstock.* I can see you coming a mile off. You're a journalist. You're going to write more lies about us, especially about these kids. You're going to call them 'neo-Nazis'."

His face is up against mine. His breath smells of warm mouthwash. I keep quiet. He backs off. But not before a small group of customers has gathered round. Horst watches every move. Dagmar watches me. Jochen goes back behind the counter. He picks up a glass and starts to wipe it. Again it's a vigorous movement as if he needs to douse stress and tension. Then he carefully draws my Radeberger. He pushes it towards me and glowers. It has just the right amount of head on it.

"We've had your kind in here before," he says.

"Well, that's nice to know. They must have got out alive. So there's hope for me."

"Don't get smart. I'll tell you what I told them, if you have the patience to listen." He waits while I taste my beer. "These are decent kids. They don't go around beating the shit out of old ladies. They don't trash the shop fronts in town. They behave themselves."

He pours himself a glass of water and drinks it in one.

"You see, the *Wessis* moved in and closed our factories. So these boys and girls are out of work." He wipes his mouth with a tissue. "With time on their hands. Restless. No jobs and no prospects. Bloody Kohl and Reunification. They come in here every day, spending their welfare on beers and 'softs'. I serve them and keep them in order."

Someone at the back of the crowd sniggers. The mood spreads until they're all cackling like monkeys. Horst and Dagmar relax a little.

"Shut up," Jochen bawls. "Get back to your ping-pong."

They drift away with a few curses. Jochen's temper subsides. But he isn't for giving ground. "And you," he says, pointing at me. "Drink your beer and get out."

I am going to protest but Horst gets in before me. "Herr Barrow wants to talk to some of them, Jochen. You can arrange that, can't you? Just for half an hour. That's all he's asking." He draws himself up to his full, formidable height. Jochen beckons to him for a quiet word in the corner. Dagmar moves alongside me.

"Not so *gemuetlich* is it, Mr Barrow? Not your average German pub where the tourists drink the best beer in town and listen to a little um-pah-pah from the band. Now you see why Horst and I were so keen to leave."

"How did you do it?" I ask

"We were lucky, I suppose." She speaks in English again. "Our families still live in Gorbitz, if 'living' is the right word. It's an endless round - work, if you have it, shopping, if you can afford it, and drinking, whether you've got it or not. You sit and watch football on television with a six-pack. Or you come in here. Some of the locals look on us as the couple that got away, made the best of our schooling, furthered our education and fled. And we did it when this part of the world was in chaos. But they're not proud of us. They're jealous. They know they've missed a chance to do the same. And they hate us for it."

"But what *made* you do it? Why did you decide to be different?"

"It was Jochen." She gives me one of her rare smiles. "Don't be so surprised. He's outspoken. With a filthy temper. And he's too honest. He spent time inside for that, as a guest of the *Stasi.* But he's wise. He virtually ordered us to go. He warned us of the mess we'd be in if we stayed. We used to come in here, just like this lot. Somehow we caught his eye. He spotted our ambition even when we didn't know we had it in us."

She lets this sink in.

"But we motivated one another," she says.

I take my cue and hope I haven't mistimed my lines. "So, are you, as they say, an item?"

"Yes. But before you probe any further, don't think love has much to do with it. We are simply loyal to each other.

We were kids in a communist school and teenagers just as the GDR collapsed."

I try to picture them in class together, soaking up the nonsense they were taught and inwardly rejecting it.

"It was difficult because our teachers didn't know how to advise us. They hadn't got a clue. They knew nothing about the rest of Germany, never mind the rest of the world. We put our heads together, got a map and picked out the places we reckoned had reputable universities. One day, without even thinking about it, we got on a train and hours later ended up in Freiburg. We took a tram to the faculty building and walked into the admissions department. Showed them our matriculation certificates - we had good grades - and talked our way in. We conjured up government grants, earned a little extra washing dishes and did our three years. We could have been perpetual students. But we wanted something special."

"And did you get it? Is this it?"

"You're forgetting, Mr Barrow. No more questions. Just trust us. Because the people you want to meet trust us, even if they don't like us."

Horst and Jochen have finished their tete-a-tete. Jochen is still scowling but his aggression is under control.

"Jochen says you can stay and speak to anyone you want. And he's got a list of names you might approach - and some you might avoid."

"Over here," says Jochen. Horst and Dagmar give me one of their collective confidential nods and we follow the barman to the far corner of the hall. A broad-shouldered skinhead in his twenties, overweight and blotchy, lounges at one of the tables. Next to him, a girl with dyed red hair and a sullen face that might have been pretty in another context.

"Hi, Horst! How's Berlin?"

Horst ignores the skinhead's greeting. He explains who I am and why I'm here.

Two pairs of eyes drill holes in me. I succeed in meeting them.

"What's your name?" I ask the skinhead.

"What's it to you?" He sniffs and chews a thumb nail.

"Don't bugger about, Matthias!" This from the grouchy girlfriend.

"Why the Nazi slogans on the walls outside?" I ask.

"What Nazi slogans?"

"Well let's start with 'Foreigners Out' and 'Long Live The Reich'. Why that flag hanging from the back wall there - the Battle Flag of the *Wehrmacht* - the cross *without* the swastika. A swastika wouldn't be legal, would it?"

"You are a clever sod, aren't you?"

"As it happens, yes. I know a thing or two about military history, especially *your* military history. Does that bother you?"

Matthias pulls on a cigarette. His ruddy face suggests he's in for an early heart attack. I expect him to blow the smoke straight at me but he tosses back his head and sends it up into the steel rafters.

"The slogans and the flag are about what we want and what we deserve," he says. "We've had enough of foreigners - Viets and blacks. They should go back where they belong. They don't fit in here. We didn't ask for them. Honi and the Reds brought them in - Marxist solidarity and all that crap."

"But they did the dirty jobs you wouldn't do." He isn't provoked.

"No they didn't. They just sponged off us - took advantage of the welfare."

He stops as if he's bored already.

"Go on," I say.

"The Viets run rackets – grow pot – smuggle cigs - sell us Western fags at a big profit. The blacks are students who've decided life here is so good they're not going back to Africa. I don't blame them. But times have changed. We don't want them. They stink and they think they can have our women."

His girlfriend snorts. "I wouldn't go with one of them if they paid me."

"And what's your name?" I ask

"None of your bloody business."

Matthias rounds on her. "Tell him." She glares back, then lowers her gaze, the pretty face twisted into captiousness.

"Klara has her little secrets, don't you, sweetheart?" Jochen tries to wind his arm round her shoulders.

"Get off, you groper! Get off."

"We're wasting time." Dagmar's voice cuts into the altercation.

Klara says she joined the Viking Youth a year ago. Maguire's bits of paper have told me this is modelled on the old Union of German Girls, sister organisation of the Hitler Youth. Its website says it aims to restore German values to German women. I doubt that Klara will soon be swapping life in jeans and the Ecko Club for the sentimentality of children, hearth and kitchen. She says she likes tagging along with the boys and having a punch-up with the Lefties every now and then.

"So you like violence?"

"Like it? We love it." Matthias cracks his knuckles, flexes his muscles and rolls his shoulders.

"Enough to kill?"

Matthias, Jochen, Horst and Dagmar rise as one.

Chair-legs scrape the floor and Klara looks terrified. I don't move.

"What are you fucking talking about?" Jochen hovers over me, eyes blazing and fists screwed tight. Horst pounces and holds him. Matthias spits.

"I'm talking about murder," I say.

I'd like to let them sweat a little but there isn't time. "I'm talking about the killing of an African in Dessau, married to a nice German woman with two kids. I'm talking about Hoyerswerda, September 1991, Rostock, August 1992, Moelln, Solingen. I'm talking about torching asylum seekers' hostels. I'm talking about the deaths of two paid-up members of The Movement in Berlin, slaughtered by their own people. That's what I'm talking about - and a hell of a lot more."

I draw breath and wait. No-one moves. We glare at each other. The ping-pong has gone quiet and no-one's concentrating on the cards in their hands.

They sit down again.

Then Matthias speaks, keeping his voice low as he leans towards me. "We know nothing about any of that. We're not stupid. Not here, in Dresden. Yes, we like a punch-up. And we use bats and dusters when we have to. But we've never firebombed a thing, not anywhere. The killings were done by kids who were drunk or on something. They lost control. And we're not The Movement. That's Berlin stuff. We have our gangs and we march. And, yes, the flag's like the one on the wall. But we're not Nazis, not neo-Nazis, not any kind of Nazi. We're nationalists. We put Germany first and Germans first - like it should be."

He looks round the table. Jochen and Karla nod energetically.

"That answer your question?" spits Matthias.

A door bursts open at the other end of the clubhouse. Six young skins stride in. They curse and sneer at the other kids. Jochen and Matthias are quickly on their feet again.

"Oh God," groans Klara. "Not this lot."

The new arrivals storm up to the bar. They grab a set of empty glasses and beat a tattoo on the counter top. "Where's that fuckin' Jochen? Where is he? We want a fuckin' drink."

They keep up the chant until Matthias gets close enough to intervene.

"OK, you lot. Enough…." Two of them rush him and punch him to the floor. Another picks up a chair. He's about to smash it over Matthias's head when Horst wades in, snatches the chair and tosses it aside. Then he lifts the skin high in the air and throws him against the concrete wall. The skin stays put. By which time we're all involved, with some of the kids from the corner tables doing their bit to defend Matthias.

Then a knife appears. One of them has spotted me.

"Who's this *Wichser*, then?" He lurches towards me. I may be less fit than when I was a member of Her Majesty's Armed Forces but I move a little more deftly than he expects. Before Horst and Dagmar can stop me, I've side-stepped him, gripped his arm and wrenched it out of its socket. He screams like a bad soprano. The knife skids across the floor. The fight subsides. A circle forms round my attacker, now on his back and writhing in noisy agony. Horst and Dagmar have three of his companions in arm locks. Two more are out cold.

"Where did you learn to fight like that?" Jochen is grinning like a chimpanzee.

"That would be telling, wouldn't it? Let's just say I once wore a uniform in Northern Ireland."

Jochen taps the side of his nose. *"Du stellst dein Licht unter den Scheffel?"*

"I'm hiding nothing. And when you've finished with that specimen, I'll have another beer, please. Horst, get an ambulance."

For once the big man is amazingly docile. He sets about calling up a number on his *Handy*. But Dagmar, eyeing me with slightly less contempt than of old, puts a hand on his arm.

Jochen goes back behind the bar and pulls another Radeberger. The three skins who are still conscious are in no mood for any more. They slink out into the rain, aiming one last chorus of abuse as they slam the door.

"Unfortunately, Herr Barrow, calling an ambulance will mean calling the police as well." Dagmar has resumed her role as the perpetual pourer of cold water on even my minor triumphs.

"Then we shall have to tell them why we're here." I look straight at her.

"You, Horst and I," she says, "will not be around when they arrive." It is as much an order as a prediction.

I throw up my arms. "Suits me. I've seen all I need to see."

I turn to Jochen. "Except for that list of contacts you promised me."

He pulls a piece of paper from his shirt pocket and hands it over. "You deserve this at any rate," he says ruefully.

I glance at the names but don't recognise them.

Jochen points to the wounded skinheads as if they're specimens under a microscope.

"These are scum," he says. "But like the rest of us, they've nothing else to do. They just drink, fight and shout their heads off. They have no work and no future."

He shakes his head at me. "Remember that when you write your words of wisdom." He heads for the men's room.

"And don't bloody well come back," he calls as he disappears.

I walk out into the fresh air. The clouds still hang low like clumps of steel wool but the rain has stopped. I am very hungry.

# Chapter 4

I have the rest of the day to myself. Horst and Dagmar go about their own, unspecified, business. If they're reporting back to Fechner, or Renate, they're not telling me. And I'm not bothering to ask. After the fight at the Ecko Club, they seem to have lost interest in me although I'm not banking on it. I use my new found freedom to wander the streets of Dresden, trying to get to grips with its geography and admire its architectural gems.

I buy the papers but there are no references today to the Berlin murders. Over another beer in the corner of a quiet bar, I summon up the energy to scrutinise Jochen's list. This time there is a name that catches my eye. Otto Struck, described as an executive member of the Dresden branch of The Movement.

How many Strucks are there in Dresden? How many in Germany? It's not the most common surname. Are they all related?

I ask the bar staff for a directory. There are ten Strucks in the book but none of them with the initial "O". I try the payphone. Only three numbers respond. They're all women who say they have never heard of Otto, although one of them hesitates before answering. I take a note of the address and think about following it up.

I pick up the papers again. All of them carry reports on the government's attempts to outlaw The Movement. These have run into technical problems. The judges in the Constitutional Court aren't keen on banning any political party, even one as distasteful as this. They're doing what lawyers always do when confronted with obstacles - stalling for time.

I turn to a report on the death of an old down-and-out in a tenement block in Leipzig. It's another unexplained killing, except that he was a foreigner - a Pole.

But the tabloids can't resist a touch of innuendo. They refer to a group of skins seen in the neighbourhood the day before the man was found beaten to pulp. The police are refusing to comment. They've learnt from their mistakes. They've been forced to release four men they accused of torching an asylum-seekers' hostel in Luebeck. They backtracked and admitted there was no evidence to support the charges. But the press is still more than ready to draw inferences and come to its own conclusions

I'm being watched. He's elderly and wears a dowdy pin-stripe suit and a Homburg. He observes me from a table near the counter. I catch his eye. He comes over.

"You are English?" I wonder what trouble I'm in for now.

"I am." I say no more and wait for his reaction.

"You are either very brave or very foolish to be in Dresden on your own." I'm not inclined to explain myself. I ask what he's drinking.

"*Kaffee mit Milch*." Just three words. No courtesies. I signal to the bar and let time pass. He doesn't speak again until the coffee is set before him.

"February 1945," he says. "The 13th and the 14th. Your air force razed this city to the ground, destroyed its treasures and killed 135,000 people." He sips, coughs and wipes his mouth with a large red handkerchief plucked from the top pocket of his jacket.

"My air force and the Americans," I say. "Yes, it was terrible. A brutal act of revenge. Churchill's pretext was that he was responding to Stalin's request for cover for the invading Red Army. But it wasn't necessary. I admit that. What else do you want me to say?"

He is looking past me at nothing in particular.

"I was five years old at the time."

"Go on," I say. "I'm listening."

"I can still hear the drone of bombers, the crash of incendiaries, the thunder of explosions. The houses shook and collapsed all around us. My mother picked me up and ran before this great wave of fire. It chased us down one street, then the next, until, for no obvious reason, it stopped and turned to devour another building. We kept going until we reached high ground where there was air to breathe. I saw the river. And bodies. My mother died a week later. She was killed by falling masonry. She'd gone back to our building, hoping to salvage some belongings." He pauses and coughs again. "You do not know what it was like."

"No, I do not know what it was like. But I have read the diaries of Victor Klemperer."

"Klemperer?" He spits. "He was a Jew. Nearly all the Jews survived the raid." If his voice wasn't so feeble, he would be shouting at me. "How do you account for that? What American-Jewish-Bolshevik conspiracy managed that little miracle?"

I let him subside.

"I'm not going to have an argument with you about the Jews," I say, "or the Holocaust, or Hitler, or communism."

He stirs the muddy liquid in his cup. "You are right," he says, apparently mollified. "We have all come through too much to argue any more." He applies the handkerchief again. "But why are you here?"

If I tell him the truth, we will not avoid another row. And I rather like him. He has a temper. But he has gentle eyes and a generous mouth. I introduce myself.

"Friedrich Kuhls," he replies and offers his hand. I shake it. His grip is firm. "But you haven't answered my question. Are you a tourist? You don't look like one."

I laugh, take a risk and relate some of my story. He listens carefully and doesn't interrupt. I tell him where I've been that morning and he frowns. But when I come to the bit about the punch-up, the frown changes to a broad grin.

"You gave them what they deserved," he says. "They are brutes."

"May I say, Herr Kuhls, that you are something of a walking paradox. A moment ago you were raging against the Jews. Now you are chuckling over the way a bunch of neo-Nazi skinheads got their come-uppance. I don't think I understand."

"I am an old-fashioned communist, Mr Barrow….."

"No, that can't be right. You just included Bolsheviks in your trio of rogues and villains."

He blinks several times, then looks attentively at his hands. Then at the empty coffee cup. Then at me.

"Yes, I did, didn't I? Language is so confusing especially when you've been educated to twist the meaning of words and deal in slogans. That's what they did to me, you know. They trained me to be a schoolteacher. In the German Democratic Republic." He emphasises 'Democratic'. "Well, there you are, you see. I had to define 'democracy' for my students. And I did. And I believed in it. I believed Walter Ulbricht when he said that everything must have the semblance of democracy but the party must have control." Again his sudden passion dies down. "And now I have to *re*-define it. Because it didn't mean what we said.....what I said it meant." He sighs. There are traces of tears in his eyes. I take another risk.

"And Jews?"

The answer comes quickly.

"They had too much economic power in the Weimar Republic. Too much for their own good. They should have seen that. They should have been wise enough to avoid provoking the mass of Germans into believing that they were thieves and spongers. If they had drawn back, Hitler would never have succeeded. They brought it on themselves."

"Herr Kuhls. You know that isn't true."

His reply astounds me. "You haven't read *The Protocols of the Elders of Zion* then?"

I consider my answer carefully. "I started to," I say, "many moons ago. It doesn't make for gripping reading and in any case it's utter drivel. And it has been discredited many times. There was no Jewish conspiracy to rule the world. The thing was a forgery, cooked up by the Tsar's secret police. But it took on a life of its own like some indestructible cancer. Hitler wasn't the only anti-Semite who thought the book could be put to good use."

He lifts his shoulders, then lets them sag. "You seem very sure of that," he says. "Perhaps you can tell me why the book is still in print."

I don't know what else to say. I deflect the conversation by ordering more drinks. But he hasn't finished.

"I suppose you have a point, though." he says. "Jews are human beings. Hitler didn't think so and look where it landed them - and him - and us. He couldn't tell the difference, didn't want to, between the Jew who profiteered from the collapse of a currency and the Jew who was as good a German as the non-Jew, the doctor, the teacher, the musician, even the soldier."

"Is that what you taught your students in the GDR?"

"We never touched on the subject. It was swept under the Marxist-Leninist carpet. Ignored. We taught only that West Germany was the successor, the heir, to the Nazi regime. It was just as aggressive and, with the help of the Americans and their allies, would do its utmost to undermine and destroy the workers' state."

"And you didn't tell your charges that it wasn't run by Jews?"

His reply is disarmingly honest. "We didn't tell them that, no."

I spread my hands in a gesture that asks for more.

"We didn't tell them that we ourselves harboured some very nasty tendencies, little neo-Nazi vipers in our collective bosom, reptiles that have crawled out of their nests and are doing what they do now. These days there are precious few Jews to attack. So the reptiles have found alternative prey, ideal substitutes - blacks, Vietnamese, Turks, whatever." The thesis is almost concluded.

"And you still hate the British and Americans for destroying your city?"

He doesn't rise to that one. "Our city has been rebuilt, with West German money." He laughs softly and sighs again. "I hate no-one, Mr Barrow. I am too old to hate. I shall die, muddled and full of doubt, but still listening, I hope, to the music of Bach and Beethoven."

He pushes back his chair and thanks me for the coffee. I don't stop him. Our meeting has run its course. He pauses on the threshold of the bar and nods a farewell. I think of it later as a half hour well spent.

I fish out the piece of paper on which I've scribbled the address of the hesitant female. There's a taxi stand opposite the bar. I'm driven to some apartments close to the Schloss Pillnitz.

It's not a single castle but a collection of summer palaces, described in the guide books as authentic and undamaged examples of the work of Matthaeus Daniel Poeppelmann, one of the most original of German Baroque architects. I'm too preoccupied to take in its charms.

I ring the buzzer on an entry phone. Then realise I haven't worked out an opening gambit. The same woman who took my original call asks, "Who is it?"

I come clean. I'm expecting her to send me away with a flea in my ear but she tells me to wait. Within the minute the apartment house door has been opened to reveal a matronly figure, bare-headed but wearing a black overcoat, older than she sounded and deeply courteous despite my intrusiveness.

"You are not the police?"

"No, as I told you, I am a journalist working for a British newspaper. I want to find out if there is an Otto Struck living at this address. I should like to talk to him."

"He died last week. Of a broken heart."

I don't move. "Shall we walk a little?" she asks. She pulls out a scarf and covers her head, trying a knot at the throat.

"You are Frau Struck?" We have turned into a street from which the Schloss can be seen in all its mock oriental splendour.

She tells me that Otto Struck was 65 when he had his fatal attack. He'd been an official in the East German transport ministry but never a communist.

"Never," she insists, "even though he had to join the party. When the GDR collapsed, he was a happy man for a while. He'd always held socially conservative views and educated our son to believe in them."

"Your son?" I brace myself to ask the question. "Is your son's name Kai - Kai Struck?"

"Oh no. Our son is Erich - Erich Andreas Struck."

"But do you know a Kai Struck?"

She puckers her brow. "I know no-one of that name."

She taps the side of her head with a forefinger. "Unless….. unless my relatives in the West, in Hanover, had a child called Kai. But I have no contact with them. They wrote us off years ago and the *Wende* has made no difference." She sniffs her disapproval.

I press on. "But I have been told that your husband was a leading member of The Movement in Dresden. On the executive of the local branch."

She stops. Courtesy gives way to anger.

"They killed him. Damn them. He gave them such a lot of his time, organised them into something like a proper political unit, spent hours in meetings, at rallies and marches. He even got involved in fights with those Leftists. I told him time and again, he was too old for that."

"Did you approve of what he was doing? Did you support The Movement as well?"

"I had had enough of politics in the GDR," she answers. "I let him get on with it." The disclaimer doesn't convince me but it's not what I'm interested in. I want to know why she is accusing The Movement of murdering Otto Struck.

"He quarrelled with the young bloods. It's always happening in these right-wing groups. They will never get anywhere. In the end they can agree on nothing. But the arguments grew so fierce. They became violent. Because they love violence, these people."

"Yes, I know they do, Frau Struck."

She isn't listening. She's burning to finish her story.

"Last week, he came home from a meeting, his face covered in bruises and his hands a bloody mess. How he drove home, I shall never know. I begged him to call the doctor. But he would have none of it."

She leads me back to the apartment house. Then she lifts her head and I see, not tears, not grief, but unadulterated rage. Otto Struck had slumped into an armchair and clutched at his chest. His body had shuddered as if he were being tortured. Then his head fell to one side.

"Is that enough for you?"

"I think....." But I get no further.

"Then go to Hell." She grabs the door handle and vanishes.

I walk back down the street and take the first tram into town. And think selfish thoughts. If her story is true, it will make great copy for Fred in London. As I sit down and look out the window, I see him again. Pin-stripes and Homburg watching me from a wooden bench next to a newspaper kiosk. A pensioner, picking up a little extra as freelance sleuth. I wave. He takes out his red handkerchief and wipes his mouth.

I want to tell Maguire about the meeting with Frau Struck. But I'm not risking a call to Berlin. I dine early and sleep well again. No nightmares. No re-runs of the Ecko Club or of conversations and encounters. Even Horst and Dagmar stay out of my dreams. And so does Renate Seelig. And I don't even notice.

# Chapter 5

The next day I meet Marion. Reception phone early and tell me there's a young woman waiting to see me. I go down to the lobby. She wears a drab blue skirt, white blouse, three-quarter length coat, also in blue, and sensible shoes. She's blond, with some of her hair tied in a traditional German plait. Her face is plain and pale and she smiles wanly through thinly framed spectacles. She speaks of important information. Can we talk, somewhere quiet?

"In that bar across the road," I say. Herr Kuhls is not in evidence.

"I don't drink," she replies.

"Not even coffee?"

We arrange that I shall walk ahead of her. She will follow in exactly one minute. I am sure we are being watched but I can't pick out the tail. When Marion joins me, she is nervous but not diffident. She accepts a cappuccino and starts to tell her story.

"When I was as young as six or seven, I flirted secretly with The Movement's youth wing. It was possible. Even in the GDR. But my parents found out. They were appalled and frightened. They were party members but only in name.

Their aim in life was to keep their heads down and hold on to jobs as administrators at a hospital in Zwickau."

She looks at me with growing confidence.

"We certainly weren't poor by East German standards. My parents' position meant we had many privileges, access to special shops and stuff like that. I had a settled home life. The idea that deprivation forced me into the arms of The Movement is crazy. It was simply that it was what I came to believe in, despite all the brainwashing at school, all that garbage about fighting shoulder to shoulder with comrades in the Third World."

I conjure up a vision of this young woman listening to Herr Kuhls in some dreary classroom, neither of them believing a word he's saying. It's a similar story to the one Dagmar told me. Not even the *Stasi* could have pried on that amount of inner scepticism.

"My mother and father were disgusted by my xenophobia. They went to ridiculous lengths to cure me. They took me to a Vietnamese restaurant to meet the staff. I surprised them because I got on well with the waiters. I said these were nice people but they should go back to where they'd come from. It was as simple as that."

There is more. It comes out as pseudo-Marxist jargon justifying a bogus right wing cause. But for a reason I can't fathom, she doesn't sound convinced by what she's saying.

"Once Germany had been united on Helmut Kohl's terms and no-one else's, our youth wing saw itself as a new revolutionary movement, with strict internal discipline, its members ready to sacrifice themselves for The Movement. We refused to conform to bourgeois thinking or give way to the desire for material possessions, for money or excessive consumption. We were interested only in the well-being of the German people."

I blink forlornly. "But you are Jewish - or so I'm told?"

"That is true, Mr Barrow. Half-Jewish at least. My mother was - is - a Jew, one of the few whose parents survived in Hitler's Germany. Yet I am a Jew brought up under communism, in a country where religion was not supposed to matter. That's why *my* parents survived. My mother rejected her Jewish origins a long time ago. And so have I. They are irrelevant."

I look at her perhaps more closely than courtesy allows. But she doesn't object.

"Later I had the feeling that there was something very wrong with the new Germany."

"And something was going to happen to put it right?" I venture.

I still get the impression that she doesn't believe what she's telling me.

"I saw our society as rotten and false," she says. "Its politics, its culture, the drugs scene, the rape of the environment, all these things made it corrupt. Big business, the major political parties, the establishment - they decide, not the people. Just because I had the vote. It meant nothing. If Germans go on electing the wrong men and women into government, then something must give way, sooner or later."

"That's the trouble with democracy," I say. "Sometimes it doesn't work the way you want it to."

"I didn't want it to *work*," she counters. "I wanted it to collapse, just like Weimar."

Now I'm hearing a different, discordant tune. "Why do you speak in the past tense?" I ask.

She avoids the question. Instead she tells me how her friends had shown her some of The Movement's more innocuous propaganda. They'd invited her to celebrations of pagan festivals - Walpurgis Night, the eve of the 1st May - six planets in line with a full moon and all the other astrological hocus-pocus. She'd sung the folk songs and danced round camp fires up in the Erzgebirge. Then came the more serious stuff - *Volk, Heimat und Vaterland* - People, Home and Fatherland - the notion that it was the country that mattered, not the state and not the government.

"Even the Left recognises the corrupting power of the state," she says.

"Political extremes have a lot in common."

She's annoyed at this.

"That was far too glib," I say. "I apologise."

"Mr Barrow, even you can't deny that if you give people bread and circuses, football and game shows, the state can do what it wants."

"I do deny it," I say. But I am not going to be sidetracked into that argument. "So, you were hooked by this idea. You'd discovered your mission in life?"

Marion takes a deep breath, drinks her coffee and assumes an air of sweet innocence.

"The young men with shaven heads," I say, "who go around beating up asylum seekers, setting fire to hostels, murdering people for no reason other than they're black or Asian - they're just a figment of our collective imagination, are they? I mean their behaviour is hardly likely to attract the popular vote."

"Look," she says, "I have been on the front row of demos. The cameras were there. But do I appear on television? No. All you see are the skins brandishing beer cans or giving the Hitler salute. Yes, they're there. But so are others, ignored by the newscasters because their faces don't fit the image of the Right which the authorities want the media to portray. In any case, The Movement's leaders regard the skins as socially weak beings….."

"Do they indeed?" I snort. "And what is the leadership doing for these 'socially weak beings'? Does it plan to find them jobs, feed them, educate them…..?"

"You can be as snide as you like, Mr Barrow. But I tell you, the state is afraid of The Movement. That's why the police and the courts are taking such an interest in its activities. They're trying to decide whether these go against the Basic Law, what Lenz and the others call that pseudo-democratic constitution imposed by the western powers after the Second World War. They *should* be interested. And they should be worried. Because The Movement is mobilising. It is growing. And it plans to take over."

I ought to find this laughable but her eyes tell me to take her seriously.

"I don't quite understand, Marion. Why are you telling me all this?"

Behind us the coffee machine splutters and cups are rattled on to saucers.

"Again I ask - why the past tense? You sound as if you're having a change of mind. Suffering a crisis of conscience."

She doesn't react so I push on.

"And why me? Why talk to me? A foreign journalist. Why not the German press or even the police, or the *Verfassungsschutz*, the men in suits responsible for defending the Basic Law? Or the *BND* and the *BKA*?"

She frowns and takes time with her reply.

"I have talked to them," she says.

There's another long pause while she composes herself. I know I must not interrupt.

"I am still a member of The Movement but I have become an informer. Perhaps this is my true fantasy. More enticing than those provided by Lenz and his friends. Much more exciting. In spite of what you see, in spite of these dowdy clothes, I like the silent thrills that make my life worth living. I like the danger. That's why I'm talking to you now."

"Did Fechner tell you to speak to me?"

Again the frown and the intense concentration. "I think you know the answer to that."

"So, what precisely have you said to the others? What have you told them that you haven't told me? Or *vice versa*?"

She observes the bar, the waiter behind the counter, the passers-by outside the window and my hotel across the street. "I have given them names, and plans for demos and future action against foreigners."

"The Movement kills those it considers traitors, Marion. I know. I have seen the victims."

She ignores this. "There is one piece of information I have not passed on to anybody." She glances over her shoulder.

"I would take you more seriously, Marion, if you'd cut out the melodrama."

I sit up, flex my shoulders and call the waiter. I order a beer and another coffee for Marion, whether she wants it or not.

"You were followed here," I say. "You know that don't you? I'm not sure who by. But I've been watching the hotel entrance and he's still there."

"Yes," she sighs. "He follows me everywhere. Could be The Movement, although they don't really have the manpower. Could be *Verfassungsschutz*."

"You aren't even scared, are you?" I ask. She rubs her forehead with the thumb and first finger of her left hand. "Is that a signal - to him - or somebody else?"

"You're the one who's paranoid. Mr Barrow." Above her half-moons I see sea-green eyes. "Of course I'm scared. But I can't turn back now. You will be the only one who knows this."

"Knows what?"

"That there's a plot by The Movement to kill the Chancellor and members of the government."

I get up, drink my beer in one, approach the bar with the empty glass and order a cognac. I wait while it's poured, staring at the shiny blue tiles above a shelf lined with liqueur bottles. I turn and amble back to our table. She pulls a tissue out of a shoulder bag, blows her nose on it and stuffs it back into the bag. I down the cognac.

"A plot? By whom? Where? When? Details, Marion, please. You can't make a statement like that and expect me to sit back and smile sweetly."

Is she going to walk out on me? Indignation is not in her make-up. "I don't know the details, Mr Barrow. All I do know is that The Movement has hired a professional killer to assassinate the Chancellor at an important public function. I don't know when, except that it will be quite soon. And I don't know where, except that it will be in Berlin."

"How do you know?"

"Think, Mr Barrow. Think. I am close enough to senior people in The Movement to have this kind of knowledge. The rank and file are restless. They're starting to ask awkward questions. Will the Great Day of Change ever happen? Is it all pie in the sky, promises that will never be met? Is the future nothing but a long, tedious succession of rallies, demos, punch-ups and a few minor successes at the polls?"

Just as Axel Dreissig had described it.

"Your Axel was typical," she says. "He asked the same questions, openly, and that's why he was killed. Lenz and company are getting desperate. They need to placate the membership. So, they're ready to spend money on a spectacular act of violence."

"What about Lenz's Arab contacts?" I ask. "You haven't said a word about the Middle East connection. I know it exists. Some foreigners actually count for something, don't they? Tell me, does The Movement have links with Al Qaeda?"

A shadow falls across the table. I look up and see Dagmar. But I am not the object of her attention.

"Hullo, Marion," she says.

The two women stare at each other, unblinking and expressionless.

"So, you two are acquainted?" I ask.

"It would be difficult to deny it," Dagmar replies.

"And I suppose some natty little device attached to your person has allowed you to hear everything we have said in the last half hour?"

She concentrates her gaze on Marion. There is something extra here, almost spectral, a wraith of a relationship to which I am not allowed to be privy. Dagmar pulls up a chair and leans towards Marion.

"The plot," she says.

"Very dramatic," I say. "So you *were* listening in?" She continues to ignore me.

"You have to find out more, Marion."

Marion furrows her brow. All we hear is the soft babble of customers and the gurgling of the coffee machine. Dagmar turns to me.

"And you, Mr Barrow," she says, "will go to Kittlitz."

"I resent your interruption," I say, as softly and as temperately as I can, letting my anger seep out like so much puss from a wound. "I was having a private and fruitful conversation with this woman. It was none of your business. And I am in no mood to be pushed around especially after the way I acquitted myself at the Ecko Club. I will not accept instructions from people who are in effect state officials, cloaking themselves in some spurious identity designed to intimidate me."

Dagmar is not impressed. "You will go to Kittlitz, Mr Barrow."

"Because you and Horst are under orders to take me there. Orders from the *Verfassungsschutz*. Orders from the *BKA*. Orders from the *BND*. It doesn't really matter."

I close my eyes, fold my hands, and sit back in the chair trying to control my rage.

"Where the hell is Kittlitz anyway?"

"It's a village, about sixty kilometres east of Dresden," Marion tells me.

She looks at Dagmar who nods at her to continue. "It has a violent history. A neo-Nazi outfit called Odin's Legion has been terrorising the district for months. They work out of a youth club."

"I don't need to visit another bloody right-wing youth club. I had my fill of that yesterday."

"But Kittlitz is special," says Marion, "because there is a man there who wants to meet you."

"Is he one of you? An informer? Who told him about me? What does he know?"

"When you go to Kittlitz, you will find out." says Dagmar, wearing me down. "You have no choice."

"I have every bloody choice," I shout. The bar goes quiet. Customers and staff look on, annoyed and embarrassed. I whisper, "I can back out of this now. I am a *free* agent."

"No, Mr Barrow!" Horst has arrived, all bulk and black leather. The women stand up. Horst bends forward and brings his mouth close to my left ear.

"This isn't the Ecko club, Mr Barrow. We aren't foul-mouthed skinheads whose arms can be broken like matchwood. So, let's leave quietly and go back to the hotel."

I am not about to test his knowledge of the martial arts. I am learning fast that the *Verfassungsschutz* may be on the side of law and order but are prone to mete out their own brand of justice to those who don't do as they're told.

"And if I resist, the saga will end, here in Dresden. With no story and quite possibly my body dumped off a bridge into the swirling waters of the Elbe?"

"Don't be so stupid," says Dagmar.

I do as I am told. But not before thanking Marion, perhaps too effusively.

"You have been very helpful," I say. "I hope that somehow I can return the favour."

She shakes my hand but says nothing. I look defiantly at my minders, stalk to the counter and pay the bill. We cross the street to the hotel where I am forced to sit through a wordless lunch in the coffee shop.

As I get up to leave, Horst breaks the silence. "We head for Kittlitz in the morning. By car. Don't wander too far. You are being watched and followed."

"Yes, by an old age pensioner who goes by the name of Kuhls. I know."

"And others."

"Therefore I shall hide away in my room and do some research." I bid them a frosty farewell.

*** *** *** ***

I drag a notebook from my case and try to recall Marion's story. I spend the early afternoon writing a piece for Fred in long hand. The fact that it flows on to the paper with consummate ease steadies my nerves and stills my irritation. But I don't want to file from the hotel's internet facility with Horst and Dagmar looking over my shoulder. I need to kill time. I want them to think that I've retired for the day, nursing my grudges and drinking myself into oblivion. I shall at least pull another beer from the mini-bar.

I need distraction and dip into a book about the *Stasi*. I bought it some time ago, attracted by the sinister black and white dust cover. It tells me how one Vladimir Putin worked as a KGB agent in Dresden, recruiting students for espionage. I turn the pages, happy to read that it was a miserable and badly paid, job.

I play with the fantasy that his recruits might have included Horst and Dagmar, or even Marion.

The book is a good read but a hundred pages later, I put it down, yawn and stretch the stiffness from my limbs. It's about five in the evening. I stuff the notebook into an inside pocket and step into the corridor. Creeping down a back staircase, I find a fire-door which yields to a quick push. I walk slowly along a dark alley towards the bright lights of the main road and turn right. My street craft is rusty but I don't think I'm being tailed. I have the *Handy* but opt for a payphone which takes credit cards. Breaking Renate's rules, I dial her home number. All I get is her voicemail.

"Phone me, Renate. Please, as soon as possible - somehow. Please."

There's an internet café on the other side of the road. It's brightly lit but not too busy. A personable young man greets me politely, charges me the going rate for an hour's use and shows me to one of the booths. I fish out the notebook and tap out the draft.

It takes me twenty minutes. With a flourish I zap the e-mail off to London, praying that Fred will see it in time for the first edition.

I am retracing my steps when I hear shouting. I peer down the street and see an overweight skinhead grappling with someone smaller and nimble on his feet. Other skins urge on their friend but stand back from the fray. The small man is Asian. He ducks and weaves and is getting the better of it. A crowd gathers. I ask what it's all about.

"Cigarettes." says a bystander. "He's probably been flogging them smuggled fags and charging too much. They're bloody thieves, these Viets. Always at it."

"Why do they buy from him, then?"

"Because he's cheaper than the shops."

"But they still think they're being had?"

"That's right. Every so often, they get together and pick on one of them."

"Part of the Dresden scene, is it?"

"You could say that." He looks at me more closely. "I'd vanish if I was you."

A trio of Vietnamese emerge from behind an *Imbiss* fast food stall. They don't wait to size things up. They simply wade in against the skinhead whose friends take their cue and follow suit. Someone draws a knife and a skin goes down screaming in pain. I hear police sirens and scuttle away, back up the alley and the fire escape. I close the door to my room and jump as the *Handy* chirrups into life.

"Charlie? Renate. Speak - quickly."

I eschew expressions of love and affection and gave her a brief rundown of everything that's happened in Dresden, including the salient parts of my conversation with Marion. But I leave out the bit about the plot.

"Charlie - you still there?"

"Shaking like a bloody leaf. I've just witnessed a very nasty street fight."

"You didn't get involved?"

"Are you joking?"

"Go to Kittlitz. I'm not far behind."

"You keep saying that."

She's cut the line. Now I want to phone Maguire and tell him about Frau Struck. But he'll be at the *Kanal.* Eavesdroppers will pick up every single word. I make do with a curse.

There's a knock at the door. I freeze and stare at the handle.

I force myself to step forward and open it. Standing before me is a meek, elfin girl wearing a white overall.

"I've come to turn your bed down," she says.

"Please." I say tamely. "Carry on."

I leave her to it and stumble along the corridor to the lifts. The hotel bar is quiet. My guardians are not in evidence. I collect the papers from a wall rack, move to a table and wallow in a very large Radeberger. Still no references to Axel Dreissig's connection with The Movement. Still no hint that his murder was a political crime.

I suddenly understand who it is I'm going to meet in Kittlitz.

# Chapter 6

Early in the morning we take the *Autobahn* to Goerlitz, on through Bautzen, and turn south east to Loebau about 25 kilometres from the Polish border. I note the preparation. The car has been rented even before I was told about this journey or expressed my reservations. I was never going to be consulted.

Marion is not with us. A council of war, with me as reluctant observer and non-voting delegate, has decided she should go to Berlin. She's again told to concentrate on the plot. There is no more dissembling. The *Verfassungsschutz* bosses need to know how far The Movement's preparations have progressed.

Kittlitz is a short hop up a minor road, one of a cluster of hamlets in a rolling landscape of ploughed fields. Pleasant enough in summer, it now wears the desolate air of abandoned tank country.

I have started to take copious notes. More stirring copy is required if I'm to sell my wares to various news desks. The hour-long ride to Kittlitz, even with Dagmar driving flat out, offers me the chance to look through what I sent to Fred last night and other bits and pieces penned at random. I have invested in a laptop but left it in Berlin. I can't type in the back of a bouncing car and I don't trust floppy disks and unreliable 'Save' commands. Jottings in old-fashioned shorthand suit me fine plus a few choice phrases scribbled and ready for use when the time's ripe.

We pull up in front of another grey concrete block with the usual graffiti drawn artlessly across its walls. This had better be good. Otherwise I am in a mood to wrench a few more arms out of their sockets. We must wait for our contact but I am not going to sit here in silence.

"Before we go any further," I say, "let's get a few things straight, shall we?"

Horst and Dagmar scrutinise me. They haven't lost patience with me yet but I can tell I'm pushing my luck.

"There's something missing in all this," I say.

"Like what?" asks Dagmar with a hint of petulance.

"In a word - Jews."

"Jews?" They look at me as if I've got the plague.

"So far in the course of our little expedition, you haven't mentioned the word. We have talked about foreigners, blacks and Asians but we have avoided the obvious. I know about Marion. But her ancestry is irrelevant."

Dagmar raises an eyebrow at that one. But I press on.

"In case you've forgotten, the Nazis did some rather reprehensible things to Jews. It was called the Holocaust. What I want to know is, what is the current bunch of right-wing spokespersons likely to say on the subject?"

During the ride, I've had a chance to wade through another clutch of newspapers. There are stories about desecrated Jewish graves, swastikas daubed on broken headstones and an arson attack on a synagogue. They're not given prominence but they're there none the less, tucked away on the inside pages, as if editors are ashamed of them. Marion hasn't mentioned any of this. Nor did our hosts at the Ecko club.

"I think the man you are about to meet will answer your question," says Horst. He's twitchy and scans the landscape as if seeking an escape route from the conversation. Dagmar pretends to be busy with the road atlas.

"Then we'd better go and meet him, hadn't we?"

I open the car door, rather more briskly than the two of them expect.

"Wait. You must wait. He isn't here yet."

Their insouciance is getting to me though I note it's increasingly tempered with a trace of anxiety. "So we have to sit in this bloody steamed up contraption - for how long?"

Another car sweeps into the parking lot. Horst and Dagmar move very quickly.

It's a silver grey Audi, surprisingly spotless given the weather. Out of it step four men, one wearing an elegant navy overcoat, a crisp white shirt with a red silk tie, black Savile Row shoes and rimless spectacles. The others are no real surprise - shiny leather and boots. But they are armed with hand guns tucked into expensive belts. All four have polished scalps and beards trimmed to the chin. Horst and Dagmar jog across the car-park. I drag myself from the back seat, close the door with exaggerated care, and follow way behind trying to look bored.

There are no handshakes, only subdued conversation as I amble over.

"And this is Charles Barrow, the English journalist who wants to know all about The Movement?" The overcoat approaches me smiling but not generously. He resembles a lawyer softening up a hostile witness.

I stand my ground. "And you are.......?"

"I am Heinrich Lenz."

The bile rises to my mouth. I moisten my lips and try to control my trembling hands.

"You did not perhaps expect to meet me in a windswept car-park in the middle of the East German countryside."

We're the same height but I get the sensation that he's towering over me, like a gaunt, black spectre in a horror movie.

"I did not expect to meet you at all," I say. I breathe the icy air. My heart thumps and my chest tightens.

"Why not, Mr Barrow? You would not have been doing your job if you had failed to make an appointment."

"That is true, Herr Lenz. But party leaders in Germany don't make themselves readily available to foreign hacks." I use the term *Schreiberling* to see if he will respond to a touch of self-deprecation. But the smile fades.

"You are all the same, Mr Barrow, German or foreign, tabloid or broadsheet, supposedly serious or hypocritical muckraker. I have little time for any of you. But you have taken the trouble to seek me out and you have come a long way. So, if you want some of my time, let's go inside."

We walk quickly towards the clubhouse. Horst, Dagmar and Lenz's bodyguards fall in behind. This is too neat and too convenient.

The interior is almost a carbon copy of the Ecko club in Gorbitz. But the building is older and shabbier, the ceiling lower, the smoke thicker and the odours more pungent. There are more customers, unattractive, unemployed, East German male youth at their most raucous and rowdy, and ready for an excuse to turn violent. The rock music is deafening. There's a long banner stretched across a wall proclaiming *Odins Legion,* the outfit Marion had mentioned. As we enter, a man in his late thirties, dressed as a bad imitation of an American cowboy, takes in Lenz's arrival and virtually collapses to his knees. Others, who've been the quickest to realise what is happening, fall silent. The music stops abruptly. They raise their right arms and bellow "*Sieg Heil*!" The rest follow in a ragged show of stunned loyalty.

Lenz barely acknowledges the greeting. He gives a cursory salute and nods his hairless head. The cowboy forges a gap through the crowd to a door at the back. We enter a room with walls of peeling paint, containing a long wooden table and cheap plastic chairs. The door closes with a bang. Lenz motions us to sit. The door opens again and the cowboy clatters in with bottles of water and glasses. He lays them hastily on the table and scuttles out again.

"Now I know who you are," I say.

"Do you indeed?" Lenz has taken off his overcoat to reveal a smart Hugo Boss suit in the latest three-button style.

"You don't disguise yourself too well, Herr Best."

He unscrews a bottle top, pours himself half a glass of water and drinks thirstily.

"Herr Hans Best," I go on. "Lawyer and counsel for groups of West German leftists accused of terrorism in the seventies. Apologist for the German Democratic Republic throughout the Cold War." Toss him a few bones and see if he bites. It's worth the risk as long as I get out of here in one piece. Horst is sweating.

"I never supported the GDR," he replies artlessly. "It was an aberration, a distortion of Marxism-Leninism."

"But you spied for them. You grassed on leading Social Democrats. You were even a member of the SPD, until they kicked you out for being too militant."

"I wasn't the only one passing on information, believe me."

"I know," I say. "25 members of the *Bundestag* were paid *Stasi* informers. All of them SPD."

"You are well briefed on some things, Mr Barrow, and badly misinformed on others."

"So I'm told," I say.

Lenz has a habit of opening and closing his hands as if testing his physical strength. I know he's been trained by the PLO as an urban guerrilla. That was in Jordan in the seventies. He fled there after copping a suspended sentence for criminal damage to the premises of a highly conservative newspaper. Even at 60 plus he looks fit and full of latent energy.

"In any case, you are not here to delve into my past," he says. "Ask me questions about The Movement and I shall have something to say."

I tell him that the most remarkable thing about him is his transmogrification - from left-wing activist to leader of a neo-Nazi party which the German government wants to ban. From Best to Lenz, in the twinkling of an eye. And this by the son of solid middle class parents.

The reference to his upbringing gets under his skin. "We are not neo-Nazis," he spits. "We are nationalists. Do you want to hear what I have to say or are you going to persist with your insults?"

He twitches his hands again. I shrug and take out my pad and biro. He accepts this tacit offer to sound off, although this time the language is so infernally esoteric that my note-taking is confined to scribbled shorthand which I hope will make sense later on.

"The generation of 1968, Dutschke, Baader and Ensslin, were right and wrong at the same time," he declares. These were people he once fiercely defended in court, self-proclaimed revolutionaries who, for all their love of terror, at least made Germans face up to the fact that an ex-Nazi called Kiesinger had somehow become Chancellor. And if that was so, the Federal Republic was a sham.

Best drones on. "They correctly rejected tradition and religion. That brought the German people closer to political maturity and enlightenment. But it also eroded their moral fibre. A sad miscalculation. What we have now is globalisation, big business and the Jewish conspiracy. Have you not read *The Protocols of the Elders of Zion*?"

"I've already had a conversation with someone about that discredited diatribe," I answer. "He seemed convinced that it was true and yet he was no supporter of The Movement."

"He will be," says Lenz, "when he understands that the Jews and the Christian fundamentalists in America still threaten to destroy us. That is why we must defend and restore ourselves as a *Volk*. We must behave as if we are at war with the state."

To the extent of plotting to kill the German Chancellor? I am tempted to put the question but I need to hear more.

"The government uses its so-called secret services, its *BKA* and its *BND*, to keep the system alive. It organises witch-hunts against us and the opposition parties go along with them. There is a politicians' consensus for this attempt to have us banned, to have us declared unconstitutional. As if the German constitution mattered a damn. Meanwhile the cowardly press we have in this country fails to speak out against enforced *Ueberfremdung* - too many foreigners, Mr Barrow. They have to go. We have to make them go."

"And is that why you and your followers firebomb asylum seekers and murder blacks and Turks in the streets?"

Lenz's minders lean forward and copy his hand movements. Horst and Dagmar stay as stiff as puppets.

"These are symptoms of a spiritual illness," he declares. "But they are also acts of legitimate violence."

He is shamelessly admitting that The Movement's boys and girls have been doing what the inmates of the Ecko club denied doing. "They are expressions of the natural, instinctive resistance of the German people against being turned into Afro-Euro-Asiatic crossbreeds - mongrels, pariah dogs eating scraps thrown down by the Americans and their Jewish friends. Fear and hatred of foreigners are essential to our survival. The pressure of immigration calls into question the very identity of Europe - of Germany - and of your own country."

"Leave my country out of this," I shoot back. "Let's concentrate on what you asked me to concentrate on - The Movement and all its works, in *this* country."

He likes riling me and isn't going to stop now. "We must take the stigma out of words like 'racist', 'anti-Semitism', and 'xenophobia'. They are not taboo. They are honest expressions of the truth."

"And do they justify a Holocaust?" I ask. "The old one and the new one you are advocating?"

I should have been ready for his answer but it still dumbfounds me. "History represents the actions of God, not of human beings. The Final Solution was just such - history. But current political correctness continues to place the responsibility for history - for God's actions - on the German people."

We might as well take this drivel to its logical conclusion. "And Nine-Eleven? Madrid? Bali? Beslan? London? Were they 'History'? Acts of God for which the perpetrators bear no responsibility?"

"Those you call terrorists have my full sympathy, Mr Barrow. They were cruel but they were justified in what they did."

He pauses to let this sink in.

"Have you thought," I ask, "what it must be like to spend ten seconds falling to your death or being burned alive?"

"The Arabs have a right to retribution against the United States and its allies including the Jewish establishment. They are fighting for *their* lives, just as we Germans must."

"So, to gain power, you will not stay within the law. You will pursue a dual strategy - contest elections and march your thugs through the streets. Indulge in violence to satisfy their instincts and ultimately try to overthrow the state by force?"

He takes off his spectacles and polishes them with the end of his tie.

"Apart from your use of the word 'thugs', I congratulate you on summing up our aims rather well."

He pauses again. "Not that you will get an opportunity to write any of this."

The stifling atmosphere of the small room is disturbed only by the muffled din from inside the clubhouse and the heavy bass of a rock band. Best allows it to linger while he rubs away at his glasses.

"I beg your pardon."

Even as I speak, Horst and Dagmar push back their chairs and make for the door. Best's bodyguards get there first. One of them draws a gun. I stay put, but only because a very heavy hand grips my left shoulder.

"Take those two away and lock them up," Best says quietly.

"I go where they go," I say.

I try resisting the pressure on my upper arm but the minder has good purchase and I am trapped between table and chair.

"No, Barrow. You stay here. I have more to say to you. I fancy you will not see this duo from the so-called *Verfassungsschutz* again."

"I wouldn't bet on that."

Horst and Dagmar have been well trained. A lightning kick knocks the gun from the minder's hand. Horst elbows the other in the midriff. He sinks to the floor with a pleasing groan. Dagmar tries the door but it doesn't budge.

By now Best is flourishing his own little automatic. "Get up against that wall - now - you two." They have no choice. He delivers a string of venomous abuse to his guards, reissues his orders and waits until they've all left the room. His gun remains pointed at my chest. I keep my mouth shut. The noises-off from the clubhouse continue. I stare at the table giving all my attention to the grain of the wood. The door lock clicks. One of the minders has returned.

"Keep him covered," Best orders. "I need the bathroom."

"So do I." It's worth a try. "Unless you want the stink of urine in your fucking meeting room."

Best sighs impatiently and nods to the minder. I follow him, with the guard behind me. We are caught up in a crowd of youngsters, smoking, drinking and yelling in time to the pulse of the band. I pick out a gap, lunge past Best and sprint for the main exit. The door is miraculously ajar. I hurl myself outside, aware of a chorus of shouts and curses and orders to stop me, trip me, get after me, whatever it takes.

I see the car. Then realise I don't have the keys.

But the engine is running with the exhaust discharging a plume of white vapour. Dagmar sits behind the wheel.

"Get in, Charlie."

I wrench the door open and fling myself on to the seat. My head hits an arm rest. I see the usual stars and hear the whine of an abused gearbox and the scream of tyres. The back window shatters.

"Stay down. Down," she screams.

I am covered in glass splinters and feel blood on my face. The car moves at high speed. My head aches and I black out. Darkness gives way to a medley of swirling colours. I open my eyes, take my time to sit up, and see Dagmar, her face pale under her short, spiky hair, watching me in the driving mirror.

"You all right, Charlie?" she calls as the wind whips through an open window.

I am more shocked by her use of my first name than the circumstances in which we find ourselves. I blink, shake my head and seize the headrest of the front passenger seat.

"Christ, Dagmar. How did you do it?"

She smiles.

"Watch that glass."

I look down at my coat and spend the next ten minutes trying to brush away the remains of the rear window. Dagmar drives as fast as the Golf will let her.

"There's precious little traffic on the roads of rural Saxony, Charlie. I want to be sure we aren't being chased by something more powerful."

This doesn't stop me from closing my eyes every time she takes a sharp bend.

She tells me how Horst had lashed out again.

"He yelled at me to run for the car while he kept them occupied."

Her smile fades. "I think they shot him." I wince. "But I don't think they killed him. Not in the car-park. They'll roast him, beat him about, try to make him sing. Then they'll finish him, strong as he is."

I open my mouth to make some inadequate noises but she shakes her head. "It's what we're paid to do - what we signed up for. No need to feel guilty."

"That's not what you said to me yesterday."

I close my eyes again as she overtakes a tractor and trailer. She breaks a long silence with the news that we're heading for the *Autobahn*.

"We'll use this road until we hit the big one near Senftenberg. And then on to Berlin."

I look at the instrument panel. We're low on fuel. Dagmar pulls into a little *Tankstelle* out in the wilds. We are cruelly exposed to anything that's pursuing us. We do the business quickly. I can't be sure the girl in the kiosk hasn't noticed something which might prompt her to phone the *Polizei*. But the Golf purrs on. Somewhere on the final stretch, ten kilometres short of the motorway, the purring gives way to the slap of a flat tyre. It is the only time I hear Dagmar swear.

The car hire firm hasn't checked the toolkit. The spare is there but the wrench and jack seem to be missing. We heave everything out of the boot, rubber mats, pieces of old road atlas, an oily rag, until we find the tools tucked into a recess where the first aid kit should be. It takes time. I work the jack frantically while Dagmar prepares to change the wheel.

We are too late. A big silver Audi roars over the crown of a hill and crunches to a halt. Four men get out, every one of them waving a gun. Open fields stretch to the horizon and the nearest tree cover is a good five hundred metres away.

They don't mess about and they know how to inflict rapid pain. Our right arms are forced up behind our backs. Dagmar grimaces but stays silent. I'm not so reticent. My reward is a clip across the face and a thump behind my left ear.

They bind and gag us and bundle us into a second Audi which has rolled up behind the chasing car. Then come the needles. The last thing I recall before succumbing to the darkness is a view of the abandoned Golf, all four doors ajar, and still jacked up. My notes float across the brown stubble, borne by a gentle wind towards Poland.

# Chapter 7

I lie on a bunk in a cell four metres by three. My mouth is as dry as sandpaper and there's a steam hammer inside my head. I still wear my overcoat. But I'm cold and my shoulders ache as if I've been carrying dead weight. A few splinters of glass cling to the lapels like diamante. I am too tired to pick them off.

The grey walls are of rough stone, the ceiling a pattern of well worn timbers which look as if they've been treated with preservative. There's a small window, a wooden frame set at eye level, like those the Russians install in their apartment houses - *fortochki*, a kind of double glazing with a cavity between the inner and outer panes.

The door is a classic. Heavy metal painted a ghastly cream with a spy hole.

There's a stool next to the bed. Someone has left a plastic tray with a bottle of water and carton of sweet biscuits. I stare at these and, for no reason, recall my meeting with Best, alias Lenz. Will I see him again? I don't relish the thought but my jigsaw is considerably short of a few pieces. I visualise Fred pounding his desk in London, wondering where the hell I've got to with my next batch of copy.

I'm trying, Fred. I'm really trying.

My watch has been taken. I lift myself off the bunk and go over to the door. I peer through the spy hole but the corridor beyond is invisible. I move to the window. Through iron bars set into the outside wall, I can look down on a well tended garden. It's a day with no sun to throw tell-tale shadows on to paths and denuded flower beds, only dull, leaden clouds, nothing to indicate time. We were taken from the Golf in the early afternoon but I have no idea how long the drug has lasted. Is this tomorrow? Or the same day?

We're approaching winter. Darkness will come early. A wind moans at me through cracks in the woodwork. Perhaps it will snow. I smile at my sentimentality.

I sit on the bunk again, take the glass, sniff it and sip the water.

The carton of biscuits is brand new, still in its cellophane wrapping. I can even read the sell-by date. I peel it away, slowly, filling the seconds with more circumspection. The biscuits taste good. I eat two and fight the temptation to take a third out of the packet. I lose.

I stare at my shoes. They're scuffed and soiled. They feel too small, too tight. I become preoccupied with a conundrum - whether to take them off and ease the cramp or keep them on and stay as warm as possible. In the end I discard them, together with my overcoat. To fend off the cold I begin a desultory jog, ten paces from door to window, ten paces back. Nothing else matters. I must restore the circulation and be ready to respond when someone barges through that door.

As I jog, I hum tunelessly, then raise my voice through a long crescendo only to let it dip into a series of staccato grunts when I run out of breath. I stop jogging, lie down again and look up. I missed it. A small camera set into the ceiling high above the window to the left. Then a light comes on. So it *must* be late in the day - five thirty perhaps. It is certainly darker outside. The wind has dropped. But the silence isn't total. My stomach protests and I think I hear a vehicle way in the distance. Something starts to tick. I raise my head and make another discovery. A radiator, fixed to the wall next to the door, is tapping out an irregular rhythm. I get up again and drag my hand along it. It's already warm and getting hotter. Then the camera whirs and turns - ninety degrees, and back again.

They are offering me sparse but relative comfort and solitary confinement. They're keeping a continuous watch. I'm being left to simmer until I lose my wits and offer to squeal.

"Lenz will want more than that," I say out loud.

I'm not banking on avoiding physical abuse. By their own admission they thrive on brutality. They have killed Dreissig and Koard, among others. And they're planning to assassinate the Chancellor of Germany. Why leave me out? And what have they done with Horst and Dagmar? I wish I had pen and paper. I remember my notes drifting across the ploughed fields. The police must have picked up the abandoned Golf by now. Perhaps they've retrieved the odd scrap of paper. There was plenty there to link me with the *Verfassungsschutz*, and with Fechner and Renate.

This is the first time I've thought about her since the drug wore off. If she's been told of my disappearance, what is she doing about it? "Behind you all the time," she said. Was that no more than empty reassurance? Was it her intention, and Fechner's, to abandon me, if the thing went wrong?

I sit up again and rummage in the pockets of my overcoat. No *Handy*. But I find a biro with a chewed end and another scruffy notebook.

The camera whirs again. Can it see me wherever I am? Or can I find a corner, a blind spot where the thing won't pry? As I move, it follows me. But its range is limited. If I tuck myself into a niche on the right side of the window, I am out of sight.

I crouch and sit on my folded overcoat. I've shaken it vigorously. It seems to have worked. No more glass diamonds. Small victories but they don't snuff out the petty anxieties.

My hand trembles as I try to write. I have nothing on which to lean and I'm afraid the ink in the biro will run out.

Now I need the toilet. No pan. No bucket. Hell. The more I think about it, the worse it gets. I bang on the door and bellow. The camera buzzes through another ninety degrees. The radiator clicks. As does the lock in the door. One of the heavies who was with Best at Kittlitz stands there with his arms folded.

"You want the WC?" He pulls me towards him, spins me round and marches me down the corridor, keeping a hand on my shoulder.

"In here," he says. "For as long as you like." He grins and bangs the door in my face.

Performing my natural functions in strange surroundings always unnerves me. But I do as he says and take my time. I curse, remembering that I've left my cheap biro and those crumpled bits of paper on the bunk-bed. Don't let him spot them. If there's one way to defeat a sense of foreboding, it's to write everything down. I have to keep doing it, before they get a chance to beat me senseless.

I hurry through the rest of the procedure and press the flush. The guard escorts me back to the cell without saying a word. I mull over the thought that he must have been close by when he heard me pounding on the door. That means they're *not* going to let me moulder. Doesn't it?

I withdraw to where I think the camera can't see me. The biro and paper are still there untouched. I write furiously. I put as much down as I can recall, starting with Dreissig, on to Renate, Fechner, Horst and Dagmar, the rumpus in Dresden, Frau Struck, Kuhls, Marion, the meeting with Best. I drag the dregs of conversations from the back of my mind, until I have ten or more pages of scrawl to hand.

The light goes out. In the glimmer of a full moon, I gather my bits of paper and stuff them into an overcoat pocket. I feel my way back to the bunk, drape the coat over me and stare at the window. I doze and am wafted into vivid dreams in which I begin to see the print on the page. At first, it's an illegible floater at the back of my eye. Then the eye focuses and the print becomes clear.

*There are nine people on duty in the crematorium, all of them certain candidates for the gas chamber. They know too much. They have to be exterminated as the opportunity arises. There are four ovens on the left side of the crematorium. The gas chamber is on the right. A room with a narrow door and no windows. We don't use gas. We use a powder which we heat to a certain temperature. It gives off poisonous fumes. It must be quite agreeable because the people never make a mess.*

I wake, shouting my own name, and leap off the bunk. I move to the window. The moon is still there, bathing the garden in a white glow. I'm sweating. The moisture slides down my neck into the hairs of my chest, running in rills from my armpits.

What have I got stuffed in the recesses of my mind that reconstructs the horrors of Auschwitz? I continue to stare into the night. Then I remember the book, an account of testimony at the Nuremberg trials. I'm terrified that, if I asleep again, there will be more of the same. But I cannot resist. I lie down and my eyes close. And the printed page is there again.

*I saw that bastard Meister chase a Jew the other day. He ran him ragged until he was exhausted. Then he asked him if he'd like some water. So he made him kneel in front of a bucket and when he bent to drink he pushed his head down under the water with his foot. He held the Jew until he drowned.*

I wake. The camera buzzes and the radiator ticks. Then the beams of moonlight fade. Now there is no need to fight against sleep.

# Chapter 8

They come for me at first light. Best's original duo of minders. I am allowed to use the toilet again and wash in cold water. They push me down a corridor and a flight of stairs into a room containing a pine table and two matching chairs. Nobody speaks. On the table are jugs of coffee, milk, sachets of sugar, a roll, a croissant and a pat of butter.

At last a single word. "Eat."

The room echoes with the gush of coffee poured into a plain white mug and the clatter of a knife on the rim of a plate. I hear tetchy voices in the distance and the thud of shoes on flagstones. I swing round as the door opens. Best enters, dressed as ever in suit, white shirt and silk tie.

He greets me politely, almost affably, and makes as if to shake hands. I decline, concentrating instead on spreading butter into a croissant. He sits opposite me and looks over a sheaf of papers one of the minders has given him. I can see them from here. They are my notes from the back seat of the Golf. I almost admire the thoroughness of Lenz's people who have chased across miles of open country to retrieve them.

I chew away and drink the coffee.

"Mr Barrow. You will have to talk to me sooner or later. We might as well make this as civilised as possible."

"I don't see why," I counter. "You don't believe in civilised values. They're too bourgeois for you. Why should I even meet you half way?"

"You have no choice. You are our prisoner and we intend to interrogate you."

"And after that? If I am in for a spell of gratuitous violence, I'd sooner know now then be caught short".

He looks at my notes again and examines his finger nails. Then, without a second glance, he rises and leaves the room.

They beat me about for most of the morning. There are two of them, tall skinheads, with the physiques of all-in wrestlers. They work on my midriff, ribcage and kidneys but spare the head and the genitals. They do it mechanically, systematically, and without speaking. No insults or threats. There is no need. The only sounds are my own groans, my coughing and retching. A session lasts about five minutes. Then a pause while I roll over in the foetus position trying to fight the pain. Then another five minutes of the same. Six or seven bouts in all. They don't ask me to talk and I don't offer them anything. Then they drag me back to the cell and leave me on the floor.

I try to find a position that will fend off the agony. But I don't weep and there is no more panic.

The words of another testimony flood into my mind.

*I asked many times why these things had to happen, why they should not be stopped. My commanding officer said he did not like this but he had strict instructions and nothing could be done about it. Like the rest of us, he suffered and none of us was really sane any more.*

I doze. More echoes of the past bombard me. They merge into thoughts of a possible rescue, the fate of Dagmar and Horst, and the likely impact of my absence and failure to communicate with Berlin. The pain comes and goes, sometimes shooting through me like hot darts, then lingering as a dull ache that consumes my upper body. They have broken some ribs and the blows to my kidneys have damaged my waterworks. When I come to, I am wet and stinking.

It is dark again but a shaft of reflected light winks at me from the bottle of water on the stool next to my bunk. I crawl towards it, raise an arm, lift my head and drink enough to moisten my throat.

The lock clicks. They're back. They slip their hands into my armpits and haul me down the corridor to the bathroom. They tell me to wash and change into clothes they've brought with them. Before I can protest that a very sore thorax will make this impossible, they shut the door on me. I don't know how much time I have. I sit on the pan and take in deep gasps of air. I set about performing a slow striptease, sluice myself down in the shower room, and do everything else I'm supposed to do. The water is hot and brings some relief. They've left a vest, blue T-shirt, boxer shorts, a grey track suit and a pair of trainers. And they've guessed my size correctly.

I manage to bundle my own clothes into a plastic waste bag and muse on the likelihood that they will never see the inside of a dry cleaner's again. It makes me laugh out loud. Ten minutes later, I face Best across the table.

"I imagine that you do not feel too well, Mr Barrow?"

He pushes a glass of Scotch towards me. I look at the surface of the table and see a small sheet of aluminium foil and a line of white powder.

"Is that for me as well? I thought you advocated clean living. Or is cocaine solely for the Big Boss?"

I grasp the Scotch and gulp it down.

"Can I ask," I croak, "if what your thugs have done to me is an expression of the natural, instinctive resistance of the German people against being turned into Afro-Euro-Asiatic crossbreeds?"

He frowns and for once fails to look me in the eye. "You have an excellent memory even in the worst of circumstances. What a pity it cannot be used in a just cause."

Before I can manage another quip, he ploughs on. "I should like you to tell me all you know about me, my organisation and our plans to kill the Chancellor."

"And what good will that do?" I ask, savouring the taste of whisky and rubbing away at two days of growth. "Especially if you are going to kill me."

"You do not deny that you know of those plans?"

"It would be pointless," I say. "But I don't appear to be in a position to stop you, do I?"

"I will put to you the obvious question. Who else have you told?"

My escape route is blocked. I can either lie my way out of this or bring Renate's name into it. Best will then call the whole thing off but be well aware of who in authority is on to him. Can I take more beatings? Will they go so far as to top me here and now? I grimace at the pain in my chest. Then I gamble.

"No one knows except my *Verfassungsschutz* minders. And you have them as well. I assume they are still alive."

"Unfortunately, no….."

"You bastard."

"The girl lives and is in a condition somewhat similar to yours. The man was shot when he resisted our people at Kittlitz. It was his own fault."

My anger subsides into depression.

"Why not confess the lot, Mr Barrow? You will not be getting out of here."

I close my eyes and try to marshal the words carefully.

"You know what I know about your organisation from the questions I put to you at our first meeting. I have done my research, visited the club in Dresden and the one at Kittlitz. I have seen what I have seen and I have interviewed your supporters. I could write a convincing article right now. I don't need any more."

"I've already told you. You won't be writing any articles."

He gets up as if to leave. But he can't resist an audience, even an audience of one.

"Listen to me. Why do I expend so much effort on you even though you're a dead man? Because I am a lawyer with a lawyer's skill to persuade you to tell me what you know. I am also an advocate with a good case to argue….."

"I doubt that very much." It is only a muttered remark but it angers him.

"Do not doubt," he screams. "Do not doubt that I - we - The Movement - have right on our side." He fights for breath and I do not interrupt.

He produces a length of plastic tube from his pocket, picks up the aluminium foil and hurriedly sniffs the cocaine.

"More of that, Herr Best, and with luck and your complexion, you might have a heart attack."

"Shut up, you silly little man."

There's a drop of liquid left in the glass. I knock it back in one.

"Germany lives," he continues. "Its people endure. They have a strong will and purpose. No amount of foreign intervention can subdue them - neither the Americans nor the Jews will succeed in doing that. Nor their proxies - the blacks, Turks and Asians they place in our midst."

"What about Arabs? I notice you continue to leave them out of the equation."

He's taken aback by the question.

"And, incidentally, you sound like that jackass, William Joyce," I add.

He's clearly never heard of Lord Haw Haw and his broadcasts from Nazi Germany during the Second World War. He blinks and pursues his theme.

"The Arabs have seen sense. They too have suffered under American and Israeli imperialism. Now they are fighting back along with their fellow Muslims in other countries."

I surprise myself by having the wit to interject. "Don't tarnish a world religion, Best. Bin Laden's campaign is backfiring on him. He's lost Afghanistan and, for all their mistakes, the Americans still occupy Baghdad, which, I might remind you, was once the capital of the caliphate." He's enjoying his high. He doesn't stop me. "Nine-eleven, Madrid, London and all the rest are the *jihad* that went wrong. There's war and chaos in Islam's heartland and all the regimes bin Laden wants to get rid of are still in place - in Saudi, Egypt, Jordan and Syria. Most Muslims want peace and quiet, like the rest of us."

"Those that think like us don't," he replies. "They help us and we reciprocate."

"How do you reciprocate?" I have put my toe in a whirlpool which might easily sweep me away, Fred, but if I get a chance to write this, boy, will you be a happy man. And I will be little richer.

"We supply safe houses where they can hatch their plots and bide their time. We have several of these - in Berlin, Hamburg, Munich, Frankfurt."

He doesn't bat an eyelid. He's throwing caution to the winds because he no longer sees a need for it.

"And we have arms."

"What sort of arms?" The whirlpool has become a raging torrent.

"Explosives, anti-tank weapons, mortars, machine guns. What do you expect?"

"Do you buy them from your Al Qaeda friends or the Russian mafia? And when do you plan to use them?"

He isn't falling for that one.

"I quote the head of the so-called *Verfassungsschutz*," he says. "'Armed violence as an option is being discussed more and more among the far right in Germany. There are right-wing extremists who are increasingly questioning their previous reluctance to use guns to further political aims'. He's so right, Mr Barrow."

"Well, you should know all about that. You and the Baader-Meinhof bunch weren't averse to lobbing the odd bomb and firing the occasional AK-47."

He spits at this reminder of his past.

"Let me put this to you," he says, changing tack. "I cannot accept that Jews and liberals should be the people who make the decisions in this country - in government, the security services, industry, law, teaching, the media."

"They don't," I say. "Until recently you had a centre right government. And judging by the way this current lot have managed things, you will soon have another one. Your press is for the most part highly conservative and so are the people running radio and television. And no-one in their right mind could call the banks, or Daimler-Benz, Volkswagen, Siemens and the rest, bastions of left-wing economic theory. The head of a right-wing government in Bavaria has made it plain he doesn't want dirty foreigners wandering all over his state. Close the borders. Send them home. That's his motto. Why don't you pal up with him?"

"They are all too soft, these conservatives." He makes the word sound like the ultimate insult. "And suppose these Jews and their allies take control of the armed forces, where would Germany be then?"

"A lot better off than when the anti-Semitic Prussian officer class, a stupid monarch, and that mad little corporal led you into two wars in which, I might remind you,

Germany was defeated and damn near laid to waste. Why don't you live in the real world?"

I feel purged and confident but it isn't the most skilful hand I could have played. I get no more out of him about Arabs and safe houses. Or about the assassination plot. He rambles on, mouthing old shibboleths about Jewish and Bolshevik conspiracies, the threat from a resurgent Russia and disgust for 'Gypsy parasites'. But my bonus is his failure to chase me on what I know about his plans for the future.

He breaks off his tirade in mid-sentence, stands up and strides out of the room without a backward glance. I am left slouched in the chair, stupidly holding an empty whisky glass and sorely tempted to blow away the rest of the cocaine like so much dust. I lean forward but the ribs issue a warning. On a sideboard to the right I see a coffee pot. I haul myself out of the chair. The pot's still warm. I raise the spout to my lips and pour the stuff down my gullet. The effort is worth it. Caffeine gives me the lift I need to feel defiant again.

The half-silence is broken by shouts and gunshots. The door flies open. A skinhead waves an automatic at me.

"Up. Follow me. Now."

He grabs my tracksuit and pushes me outside. There is more bawling and more gunfire. I can't work out what's happening. My captor shoves me down a long corridor.

"Take it easy, for Christ's sake. My chest is killing me."

He takes no notice. We turn left, hurtle through a hefty wooden door and are instantly outside in the centre of a courtyard. Skinheads are bundling other skinheads into a minibus. Two of them have hold of Best. There's a gun at his head. Someone opens the rear door of a battered saloon. I am manhandled into the back seat and gasp as my ribcage protests. We move off in a shower of gravel. I see two bodies slumped on the steps of the main entrance. And that is all

I see as they tighten the blindfold and my world turns pitch black again.

Whoever is driving this crate has no thought for the comfort of his passengers. I can sense the crazy speed and the swerving and slewing, tossing me back and forth between two heavies. I curse loudly but this only provokes earthy censure from them as they tighten their grip.

We have been going for no more than twenty minutes when our dare-devil chauffeur brakes hard. The car veers sideways, crashes into something metallic and turns turtle.

My head hits the roof but the rest of me is cushioned by the fleshy bulk of my minders. The blindfold slips. Among the hullabaloo I am aware of flashing lights. Someone rips open the door and a woman says, "Get him out of there."

I am conscious. Wounded and suffering, sound in mind if not in body. Which is more than can be said for the skinhead on my right. He is dead weight. Out cold, but probably still alive. They roll him over to get at me.

"For God's sake," I plead. I have to be twisted out of the wreck. But whoever is handling me gets the message. They lift me gently on to a paramedic's trolley. I see the needled branches of a pine tree, a white cloud and three faces.

"Charlie. Can you hear me?"

"I can hear you and see you, Inspector. And I can smell your perfume."

I turn my head. Two uniforms are handcuffing a skin. The front of the car is in my line of sight. The driver's face has been battered to pulp. I look up at floodlights and cameras. And at the sky. The cloud has passed. Renate is too well trained to smile at me.

# Chapter 9

The sun has long since dropped behind the Atlantic horizon. I still have a little wine in the bottle but I ration myself to two cigarillos per evening and I have smoked my quota. I hear the intermittent noises of the little town - the chatter in Jorge's bar below me; a snatch of *Fado* from a battered guitar and a voice roughened by tobacco. And the scooter, heading north to the beach, with Jorge's son, Joao, opening the throttle as far as it will go, his girlfriend, Amalia, riding side-saddle pillion, contemplating a night of love-making. Lucky Joao. Be good to her.

I play now with memories of such suffering as has come my way. Not the beatings and the little mental tortures that Lenz, alias Best, and his cronies inflicted on me. Those I simply add to a list of similar experiences in places as different as Belfast, Beirut, Cairo and Phnom Penh, taking cover from gunfire or dodging the blows of mutinous police recruits. Those episodes were short and sharp, nothing compared to the griping agony of the emaciated boy I saw emptying his bowels by the side of the road near Delhi airport, or the AIDS patient sweating it out on a filthy canvas bed in Bangkok. My wounds were healed by good medical practice. Theirs were permanent, or so they thought until early death brought eternal anaesthesia.

My pain is an indulgence. It is the loss of friends who have died or of lovers who abandoned me. And the solitude. I can dispel it for a while, descend to Jorge's and join in the gossip or a game of cards. That will get me through the evening until I climb back up here, down a shot or two of Jameson, and listen to a CD, perhaps Mariza singing *Menino do Bairro Negro.* I sold my precious Steinway when I left London. Now I have an old upright on which the neighbours let me play my pale imitations of Monk and Peterson.

I have only one complainant, old Monteiro who lives across from me.

"Why do you never play Bach?" he asks.

I get lost in an attempt to explain in Portuguese why I lack the necessary skill and musicality. He falls about laughing and even I weep tears of mirth.

My eyes tire quickly. I do not read as much as I should like, despite the new table lamp with the extra-strong bulb bought on a trip to Porto. So I shall sleep for about five hours and, in the early morning, drink more coffee than is good for me. Then I *shall* read, or re-read, novels and verse that bring momentary joy and a sense of well-being.

"Laugh and be cheerful," Jorge tells me every day. This from a Portuguese, who, for all his courtesy and charm, remains unflaggingly jaundiced. He smiles only when he thinks he has conned the taxman or the local police chief, or beaten the daylights out of old Francisco after six rounds of *gamao.*

"I will find you a woman," he says, "a comely widow, who will look after you."

His smile turns to a leer for which I rebuke him. I tell him I have looked after myself for longer than I care to remember, pressing my own shirts and making sure there's always food in the fridge.

Yet I would be a fool to say that I don't miss the warmth and softness of a body next to mine in the middle of the night. Which is why, as the breeze from the sea stiffens and the night air gets cooler, I give myself up to the memory of the one woman who held me in her arms as if she really loved me.

But I am expecting visitors.

# PART 3

# Chapter 1

I open my eyes after the deepest sleep I've enjoyed in the whole of my life. A table lamp sprays soft light over the sheets. I am warm and comfortable. I've been left unmolested by nightmares and ghosts, even visited by idyllic dreams. I feel buoyant and free of phobias.

Then I recall the beatings and lie quite still. I do not want to move. I don't want my body to protest and remind me of the cell, the bunk, the moaning wind and the indignity of wetting my pants.

I try to sit up and take in the room. From this angle it could be a set for a TV hospital soap, cream walls and frosted windows covered by venetian blinds. There is a faint buzz from the adjoining corridor. Otherwise the outside world does not exist.

"Charlie?"

Renate sits to my right. She wears denims and a white T-shirt which cannot hide the curve of her breasts. She bends and kisses me on the forehead. My mouth is dry and my teeth need cleaning. I look at her for ages until it dawns on me that I'm gawking. I try to speak.

"Sorry. You on your own? No superiors listening in?"

She puts a finger to her lips and shifts it to mine. "Mac will be here soon. He has things to tell you."

"And I have things to tell him - and you," I rasp. I am seized by a bout of coughing.

She pours me a glass of water. I pull a hand from under the covers. I won't let her hold it while I drink.

"You are stubborn."

"That's why I survive," I reply.

She takes the glass away, holds my free hand and presses it to her cheek.

"If I could crawl into bed beside you, I would, Charlie." She kisses my fingers. "But this is a hospital - even if you are in a private ward. And you have some nasty bruises and three broken ribs".

"That wouldn't stop me," I say. "My captors weren't very efficient, were they?"

I lie back, exhausted by this feeble attempt at humour. Then I panic.

"The plot, Renate. I must tell you about the plot."

"Calm down, Charlie. I know about the plot."

"From Marion?"

"From her and others."

"Lenz, Best, whatever you call him - he confirmed it. But I couldn't get the details - time and place and all that. Where is that bastard by the way?"

Renate accepts that I am now past the point where I simply want to rest and do nothing. She lets me go over the events of the last few days, takes notes, and asks more questions. Then provides explanations.

"Best is under arrest. We've got some of his heavies too."

"But what happened at the place where I was held? He'd just finished haranguing me when another mob roll up. There was a shoot-out and a few dead bodies and I'm being whisked off to God knows where again. Come to that, where was I?"

"You were held at a country house near Zerbst. Almost on the Elbe, not far from Magdeburg. A nice little retreat in any other circumstances."

"Could we turn it into a home for retired police officers?"

She smiles indulgently.

"As I recall," I add, "my accommodation was a trifle sparse. And it was bloody cold. How did you track me down?"

"Marion made an educated guess. She's a great asset."

"Then treat her well. Because if they rumble her, she's a dead asset."

"We've been working on the material she's given us. Not least on the splits in the far right. Best has many enemies among other neo-Nazis. That's useful to us. It means they fight among themselves. Keeps them busy."

Frau Struck said that in Dresden. But it doesn't offer much comfort .

"They've still got the gumption to organise an assassination," I point out.

"Perhaps," she concedes. "Anyway, the outfit that sprung you were paying Best back for expelling them from The Movement. We got them too."

"Where am I now?"

"In Berlin. In the Charite hospital. And not too far from my office."

"And who's paying? I don't see reciprocal agreements between the German and British health services covering the cost of this little lot."

"The German government is being very generous, Charlie. Don't worry about it."

She leans in and kisses me on the lips. We let the embrace linger.

"I am glad you lived to tell the tale," whispers Renate.

"Which is more than can be said for my *Verfassungsschutz* escort. Best boasted that Horst had been killed. What happened to Dagmar?"

"She's in here as well. But she was put through the wringer at Zerbst."

"How?"

"She was left to die. The *BKA* found her trussed and unconscious in her cell."

I curse again.

"Her wounds are bad. She's blaming herself for Horst's death and the way you were treated."

The door opens and in steps Maguire. He strides towards me and grasps my hand.

"Steady, Mac. I'm a poor, weak, invalid."

"Bollocks, Charlie. You're a tough old turkey who's had a few feathers plucked."

He sits down heavily on the edge of the bed and realises he hasn't acknowledged Renate's presence. "My apologies, Inspector. I am so relieved to see this old monster in rude health, I have forgotten how to behave in polite society."

He holds out his hand. Much to his surprise, and mine, she ignores it and plants a kiss on the side of his mottled face. He blushes and we laugh at him.

Then Renate becomes businesslike. "What's our timetable?"

"You and I have been doing the same sums," says Maguire. "Today is the sixth of November. The ninth is *der Tag*. It's obvious. The anniversary of *Kristallnacht* in 1938 - the attack on Jewish property and, in effect, the start of the Holocaust."

"Carry on," says Renate.

"The Chancellor is using the ninth to demonstrate his repugnance for the far right. He will do it in the very heart of a reunited Berlin, at the Brandenburg Gate. He will lead a procession from the main synagogue in Oranienburgerstrasse and thousands will follow him. Somewhere along that route, The Movement will try to kill him."

"So you know?" asks Renate.

"I know. And don't force me to tell you how I know." Maguire stares her out.

"The briefings say he'll have the chief rabbi, the president and the parliamentary speaker with him."

Renate scratches her lower lip and writes in her notebook.

Maguire continues. "And the interior minister. It's his policies which have stirred The Movement to such an extent they're now preparing a truly spectacular act of vengeance. They're not daft enough to threaten the Chancellor directly but they've been saying some bloodcurdling things about the government of late. It's not all bluff and bravado."

Renate gazes at him thoughtfully. "You're right about the Brandenburg Gate. But where exactly? Where in that area would you place a sharpshooter with telescopic sights?"

"I have a map," he says, opens it up and spreads it out on the bed. "The protest march will take the VIP's north west along Oranienburgerstrasse, past the Tacheles building, down Friedrichstrasse, over the Weidendammer Bridge and into Unter den Linden. Then they'll move to the Gate."

"They may alter the route," says Renate. "My information is that the Chancellor's office haven't made up their minds. They certainly haven't finalised the details with any of the security agencies. We've got to comb every building along Unter den Linden, every office block and bank and a lot more besides."

She is bundling her things together. "I must be off." She gives me a quick peck on the cheek and is gone.

Maguire throws me an inquiring look. "Sorry, Charlie. But I think the Inspector's got the jitters."

"No, she isn't that sort of person. And before you make any cracks about the two of us, the answer's 'yes', we're getting on rather well."

"I am not passing judgement," he retorts.

"But you're still asking yourself - what is she getting out of this arrangement?"

He ignores this and turns to the map. "We've got seventy-two hours to work out where these buggers are going to put their man."

We trace our fingers along the projected route.

"We have to stand on every street corner," says Maguire, "test every angle, climb a hundred stairways, look for exits and entrances or fourth floor balconies where a hired gun with high tech weapon might wait patiently for the right moment."

"Who's 'we'? I won't be out of here until well after the ninth unless I discharge myself."

"You've got to be there. You can't miss the big day."

"I'll aim for that. But are you taking on the preliminaries yourself?"

"I just might do that," he says, jaw set and eyes wide open.

"Anyone miss me at the *Kanal*?"

"Crowds of people. And they've read the papers. You don't get caught up in a shoot-out between *Grenzschutzgruppe 9* and a bunch of neo-Nazis without the hacks reporting it."

"*Grenzschutzgruppe 9*? Who the hell are they?"

"GSG9. German's equivalent of the S.A.S."

"Christ."

"Your Inspector has her fingers in all kinds of pies."

"The *Kanal*?" I ask again.

"I haven't seen Kai Struck since your bust-up. The word is, he's out for blood. But he hasn't been around to spill any so far. He's left me alone."

"Well, he can't fire you, Mac."

"But he could shunt me into some backwater, like handling 'Letters from Viewers'. It hasn't happened."

Maguire blenches with distaste at the prospect.

"Yes, I don't see you tucked away, licking envelopes for eight hours a day."

"Struck is a mystery," he goes on. "He's vanished from the building. I made a few surreptitious checks. He isn't on a foreign junket. He hasn't been seen wining and dining."

I tell him about Frau Struck in Dresden and her dead husband Otto.

"In which case, I shall have to break into a few files and see what gives. I don't think I've got time to go to Hanover and ask the family."

We pause to digest the stream of information.

"Oh, and by the way," says Maguire. "If we ever get the money together to hire a crew, we've got a contract with *Fernseh Eins*."

"That's brilliant. I just hope I'll have the stamina to do the job."

Maguire shrugs. "Of course you will." He promises to bring me magazines, books and a bowl of cherries.

"At this time of the year?"

"The Turkish 'Fruit and Veg' on Potsdammerstrasse, Charlie. They'll get you anything if you ask nicely."

He ambles towards the door in his flat-footed way and waves at me.

"Phone you later," he says and disappears. He has to go back to the *Kanal*. Thank God I'm spared that.

# Chapter 2

My highly efficient nurse lifts me up, props my torso against a bank of pillows and brings me the papers. And there I see myself, pale, eyes closed, lying on a paramedic's trolley. The banner headline reads, '*Fernsehmoderator aus Terror gerettet*' - newscaster rescued from the clutches of terror. Next to it, a photo of a wrecked car and a couple of mutilated bodies. And an announcement that Heinrich Lenz, leader of The Movement, is in police custody and being interrogated. So far, no charges.

My bedside phone rings twice - former colleagues hoping I'm on the mend. I lose track of time again. The nurse says it's around seven in the evening and dinner will be served in fifteen minutes. Do I want a glass of wine with my meal? I remind myself to ask Maguire to bring a bottle or two so that I can start a secret store.

The phone buzzes again. It's Renate. Solemn and urgent. She has something to tell me but it must be done in person. She's on her way.

Dinner arrives. A lamb cutlet, pureed potato and a salad. And that glass of wine. Followed by ice cream and coffee if I want it. I say I'd prefer another glass of wine. The nurse doesn't blink.

I open Maguire's street plan and examine the route he's outlined. I try to conjure up the shape and size of familiar buildings, embassies, hotels, shops and restaurants. A sniper could park himself anywhere within that crowded square mile.

Renate walks in. She kisses me but isn't smiling.

"I've been taken off the case, Charlie." She stares hard at me and lets the statement sink in.

"You've been what?"

It's the first time I've seen her vulnerable.

"On what grounds? Who by?"

She takes a deep breath to control her anger.

"I got back to Jaegerstrasse after seeing you and was told that my *BKA* chief wanted to see me." It's the first time she's openly admitted working for the Federal Criminal Investigation Agency.

"He said I was to restrict myself to routine criminal work. He stressed 'routine'. I'm to steer clear of the Dreissig enquiry and the wider investigation into The Movement. I am to have nothing to do with neo-Nazis. When I asked why, he said I'd compromised myself by being too close to you, especially now that your name's up in lights."

"But that's crazy. You're the one with the experience - all that knowledge stashed away in your files - and in your head."

"I've also been the subject of a complaint from Kai Struck which our 'human resources' people are looking into. I got no chance to defend myself. He said that if I even dreamed of disobeying him, I'd be in deeper water. Then he threw me out."

I'm trying to find the right words.

"Someone's been telling tales out of school, Renate."

She stalks the room. It's pointless for me to apologise. But I do. She comes back, sits on the edge of the bed and holds my hands.

"Don't say 'sorry', Charlie. Not after what you've been through."

"I just don't want it to end like this."

"It hasn't ended. I'm not going to let it end," she says.

"How so?"

"I'm going to carry on, whether he likes it or not. Someone in high places is playing a double bluff. And I can call it."

I hold a finger to my lips, grab a newspaper and point to a pen clipped to the pocket of her T-shirt. She hands it over and I write slowly along the edge of the page.

"ROOM BUGGED. WRITE IT DOWN."

She scribbles a hurried reply. She will go back to her office and check her computer. If the Dreissig file has been removed, she'll do a trace through a reliable colleague in IT Support. It might be possible to find out who's wiped the material. If it isn't wiped, she can copy it and work from there.

"DESTROY THIS," she writes. We revert to speech.

"Were you followed here?" I ask.

"Probably. But I couldn't tell you all this over the phone. I've said too much as it is. Good night, Charlie. Sweet dreams."

No farewell kiss this time. Perhaps Maguire is right. Perhaps she is starting to panic. Perhaps she has good cause. Before I can take stock, the nurse comes in.

"Are you able to go to the bathroom yourself, Herr Barrow?"

I am no longer wired to expensive equipment, not even a drip. The chest and back pains are still there but I'm determined to be independent. She helps me out of bed and I stagger down the corridor with the aid of a stick. Renate's news is buzzing round in my head. Which is why I almost miss seeing them.

At the entrance to the lifts, there's a uniformed officer in conversation with a tall man in a grey raincoat. I shuffle towards the toilet. They look up and realise I've spotted them. They turn away. I ask myself if they've seen Renate leave the building.

I do what I have to do and emerge unsteadily from the washroom. I am accosted politely by the young man in uniform.

"Herr Barrow. I am Officer Wilzel. I am here to make sure no-one disturbs you. I am on duty till dawn. I hope you have a good night's sleep."

"That's very civil." I scrutinise him. No badge of rank. No number. "Who was that man you were talking to a moment ago?"

Wilzel is not taken aback. "He is one of the senior officers who would like to interview you tomorrow morning. His name is Wels."

"Thank you for that, officer. I hope your vigil won't be too tedious."

"You are welcome," he says and salutes me.

Five minutes later I am back in bed. The nurse has given me a painkiller, an injection in my right arm. I am drifting off, still weighing up Renate's fate and hoping the nightmares won't return, when the door opens. The man in the raincoat enters.

"Herr Barrow?"

"Who the hell are you?"

"Wels," he says. "Klaus Wels."

"Representing?"

He draws up a chair and settles himself. "The *Bundeskriminalamt*, the *BKA*. I think you know who we are."

"I thought you were coming tomorrow morning."

"I've changed my mind. Time presses."

"I think I want to know why you have taken Inspector Renate Seelig off the Dreissig case. But first I want to see some identification."

He takes out an ID and holds it up. I do my best to focus but my vision is beginning to blur. He whips it away before I can check the details.

"I should like to see that ID again, please. And I should like you to answer my question."

He sighs irascibly and brings out the card. I take it from him and laboriously scrutinise the name, signature and photo. In so far as the pain at the back of my eyes allows me to read, it all seems genuine.

"Well, are you going to explain or not? If not, bugger off until tomorrow."

"Inspector Seelig is under investigation for a disciplinary offence."

"Like what?"

"She is the subject of a complaint from the chief editor of the *Deutscher Fernsehkanal.*"

"Is she indeed? Well, if you take that bastard's word against hers, you are not the professional you claim to be, Herr Wels."

"I have not come here to discuss Inspector Seelig….."

"No. You have waylaid me, knowing that I'm under the influence of a very strong painkiller which is now giving me double vision."

"I am sorry for that, Herr Barrow. It is not my intention to take advantage of your medical condition."

"That's nice to know." I retort. But the drug is taking effect. I try desperately to formulate articulate responses.

"I suppose you want me to tell you about my recent unpleasant dealings with The Movement?"

"I need the answers to two questions, Herr Barrow. And I need them quickly"

I volunteer nothing. And keep my eyes closed.

"I know a lot about The Movement, Herr Barrow. But I also want to know why you are so interested in it."

I can just about manage this. "I am a journalist, Herr Wels. I have been asked to write a series of articles on the rise of neo-Nazism. I like to get my information first hand. So I took a train to Dresden to talk to the people that matter. I met the leader of The Movement himself and he kept me incarcerated in a country house where I was beaten up by his thugs. It was a situation from which, thankfully, Inspector Seelig rescued me."

"The plot?" He has moved close to the bed, bending low to pick up my slurred speech.

"What plot?"

"Don't fool around, Herr Barrow."

"A young lady tipped me off. She's a *Verfassungsschutz* mole. But you know that, don't you?" This was getting harder. I was losing contact with my limbs.

He brings his mouth up to my ear. "You are a former British intelligence agent who keeps in touch with his old employers, Herr Barrow. Your journalism can be construed as a cover for work which even the authorities in a friendly European Union country find unacceptable."

I hear the room humming somewhere behind him

"Inspector Seelig has seriously misjudged you," he adds *sotto voce*.

"I don't think I believe what I'm hearing. You have me down as a British spy who's seduced a German police officer?"

I manage to cackle out my derision.

"I hope that's a bad joke, Wels."

But he hasn't finished.

"You are supplying your people with material that could discredit the German government in certain important negotiations in Brussels."

Even under the influence of the injection and two glasses of wine, I snort enough disdain to make him recoil.

"You have a wild and vivid imagination, Herr Wels," I croak. "Unless of course the Chancellor and his ministers are so paranoid about British intentions that they don't want their failure to crack down on the far right out in the open."

A siren sounds at the back of my head. Say no more. Whether his stated reasons are genuine or not, he's going to throw the book at me. I'll be tossed out of the country. No more copy for Fred.

I'm still aware of his presence, of his bulk, and his footfall. But I can't ward off the inevitable. My head spins and the painkiller takes charge.

# PART 4

# Chapter 1

We sit here, on a small balcony, looking westward at a vast red sunset. We sip wine and the sea rolls in, the Atlantic breakers pounding the rocks at the end of the bay. Maguire and the others stay silent while I try to empty my mind of black memories.

"I'm going to be melodramatic," I say. "I'm not expecting death just yet but I know what it will be like when it comes," They smile in unison and let me ramble on.

"There'll be no pain. I'm in credit with pain. I have more than enough in the bank to pay off what dying can demand of me. Beatings, solitary confinement, killings and forced marches; hunger and thirst."

They listen to my tale of woe and survival. They haven't heard it in full before.

*** *** *** ***

The first thing I notice as I come round is the cold. And the howling wind. It isn't completely dark. I can see that I'm lying on a parquet floor, the blocks warped and loose from neglect. They have wrapped me in a sheet and a blanket smelling of disinfectant. Whoever they are, they've done it again, forced my body into a tracksuit to which they've added woollen socks and a V-neck sweater. The thought that they must have stripped me makes me angry.

They have drugged me, abducted me and dumped me, left me for dead. Why not lie back and let it happen? Die, for God's sake. You're no use to anybody.

Depression and fatigue. A potent cocktail for inducing surrender. So stay angry, Charlie.

*"And you did. Didn't* you?" *says Maguire. "Your rage kept you alive."*

*"Don't interrupt."*

*"Shelley will interrupt. 'He lives, he wakes, - 'tis Death is dead, not he'."*

*"Beautiful." I pour him another glass. "Now shut up."*

I lift myself on to my left elbow and rest my chin in a hand. I peer into the gloom and become aware of the size of the place. I pick out an exit. It must be thirty metres away and it's the source of the light that's reaching me. There is no door. It has been wrenched from its hinges and discarded. Beyond the exit, I can make out panes of glass and dancing shadows from trees blown by the gale outside. The wind moans and the rain hisses but there is another sound in the far corner. Rats? My mind wanders back to a car lot off Oranienstrasse where I stumbled across Jens Koard's dismembered body. I recall the comfort of Renate's apartment and a lot of other things besides.

I give in. I cry like a little boy lost, letting my body shake until I'm choking on my breathlessness. I sneeze and cough and wipe my eyes on the sleeve of the sweater. I lie back again. I can't bring myself to throw off this bedding.

I have no food, no water and no shoes. I laugh out loud.

"How the hell are *you* going to stop the assassination of the German Chancellor?"

It's set for the ninth. But I don't know whether this is the $6^{th}$, the $7^{th}$, or the $8^{th}$. I have no idea of time, no watch, no mobile and no money. Am I suppose to expire, die of hypothermia, or just plain boredom? Why the clothes and the blanket? Why here?

"Where am I, for Christ's sake?"

I don't want to move until I can see more of the room. Waiting will make the time drag but exploring this place in the half light courts disaster. I'll probably put my foot through a rotten floorboard and bring the ceiling down. I'll be trapped.

Unless somebody is coming for me.

My head is clearer. The light is changing. I see that my bed is nothing more than a worn mattress placed on a platform extending from one side of the room to the other. I crane my neck to look behind me. There are windows half hidden by drapes, stained and torn, hanging from a long horizontal pole. My chest feels as if a rugby scrum has used it as a practice ball. I run my right hand round to the small of my back. I start from the pain. The flesh is tender. But there's no trace of blood. I stand up and brush the woolly sweater with my hands.

There is a mirror propped against the wall to my left, a huge plate glass monstrosity in a gilded Louis Quinze frame. I walk towards it and gasp when I see my reflection. My hair is wild and filthy. My chin bristles and my eyes stare from blackened sockets. I glower at this image, nod my head, lean on one foot, smile crazily and push my shoulders back.

I look in the mirror again. I see him standing behind me. He has a gun. I swivel round.

"Stay there," he says in English.

"Who in God's name are you?"

"Don't blaspheme, Barrow."

He is thick set, powerful, wears jeans, trainers and a black parka. And sports a luxuriant beard. Arab, Turk, Kurd, Iranian? I can't tell.

"Go back to your bed," he says.

I don't move.

"Fuck off." I want to see how he'll react.

All he says is, "If you don't do as I say, I shall shoot you here and now."

I move back to the platform.

"Sit with your legs crossed and your hands behind your head."

I comply.

"You are remarkably resilient, Barrow. I think they thought you would perish in here. Fade away like some forgotten ghost. They were very stupid."

"Who are *they*?"

"Those fools in the *BKA* who want you out of the way."

"Did they bring me here?"

"I ask the questions, Mr Barrow."

I ignore this. "And who are you?"

"I said I ask the questions." He waves his automatic in a way that suggests he's not used to handling firearms.

"Will they really be questions - genuine questions - or will I be subjected to another harangue, like the one I got from Lenz?"

"I could lecture you on the oppression of Arabs and Muslims by the United States and your country but it would be a waste of time."

"Thank God for that," I mutter.

"I told you not to blaspheme."

"I didn't."

"Do it again and I shall pull this trigger."

I smell his discomfort. The weight of the gun makes him nervous.

"Lenz's people were incompetent," he says. "They should have killed you at Zerbst."

"How did you trace me?"

He can't resist telling me.

"I kept watch on the hospital."

I nod in comprehension.

"We knew you'd been taken there after you were rescued by GSG9. They weren't very good at concealing your whereabouts. We have people working in the Charite. When Wels's men abducted you last night, I simply followed..."

"Wels's men?" I raise an eyebrow. I'm not sure why I'm feeling so confident. "Why would he want to abduct me and leave me here to rot? He intended to question me and then throw me out of Germany."

"Your naivety is astonishing," he replies. "The German intelligence services are riddled with rival factions. Some do the government's bidding - like cracking down on the neo-Nazis. Others have their links to the Far Right. Some are even ex-*Stasi* who slipped through the vetting procedure. They protect people like Lenz."

"But they've failed. Miserably. Lenz is in custody."

"They've failed - but only for the time being," he says. "Lenz will be freed. But you - you got in their way. Or, more accurately, you were used as an obstacle to block them. And us."

"Them? And Us? You revel in mystery, don't you? Am I right to assume that you and Lenz are on the same side?"

"Lenz has been useful. He is a lawyer, a member of a perfectly legitimate practice in Cologne. The money we give him for providing safe houses and other services is laundered through that practice."

He still holds the gun. But he's forgotten about it.

"It's known as *hawala*, Barrow. An alternative to conventional banking."

He licks his lips and launches into an explanation. As I listen, my mind wanders to Fred again. If I live, this story will be better than ever

"You transfer cash without actually moving it."

"And how do you that?" I ask.

"No records are kept. Brokers in Asia and the Middle East send messages to contacts in Germany. Innocent e-mails. They say - go and deliver so many thousands of euros to X who will pass them to Y. And Y delivers bundles of notes to one of Lenz's minions."

Like Axel Dreissig or Jens Koard?

"*Hawala* is normally used to move cash from immigrants in Europe to families back home. In Lenz's case, it works the other way."

He's flushed with enthusiasm at the beauty of the system he's describing.

"It's cheap. No bank charges. Efficient, reliable and quick. No bureaucracy. No paperwork. No taxes. All based on trust."

"You trust Lenz?"

"No. But he has to trust us."

I take a risk.

"Are you telling me that Al Qaeda uses *hawala* to finance The Movement?"

"Who said anything about Al Qaeda?"

"I'm not quite as naïve as you suppose."

"Then draw your own conclusions, Barrow. It won't do you any good."

He waves the gun, steps forward and slips on the twisted parquet. I jump. The weapon skids out of his reach.

Ignoring my aches and pains, I grapple with him and find the energy to pin him down. But he's strong and we roll off the platform crashing into a line of chairs. I see the gun close to my right hand and reach for it. He strains to hold me back but I feel its shape tight in my grasp.

The shot echoes round the room. He lies across my thighs like a sack of coal. I wait. He doesn't move. Then I see the hole in his chest. And the blood staining my tracksuit.

I push him off. I'm still holding the automatic, staring at it, still deaf from the report, not quite believing what I've done. I look around for a place to hide the body. Then it dawns on me. I know where I am. On the back wall is a large emblem made of plywood, fixed above a makeshift proscenium arch. It displays a gold hammer and sickle against a red background. It's surrounded by torn posters, Cyrillic advertisements for uplifting films and musical evenings, and dire warnings against life's temptations. A woman wearing a head scarf holds a finger to her lips.

"Don't gossip," she advises. "Don't fraternise. Don't give away our secrets."

A self-righteous man in a suit rejects the offer of a glass of vodka.

"No," he exclaims. It's a relic of Gorbachev's hopeless campaign against alcoholism.

This was a theatre where the men and women of the Red Army were entertained with concerts and movies. It was inside a Soviet base. Since the Russians pulled their troops out of East Germany, it's been left to decompose. But where is it exactly? North or south of Berlin? How far from Berlin? Or am I close to the Polish border?

The daylight is getting stronger. I look down at the corpse and realise I never knew his name. I riffle through his clothing. All I find is a dog-eared train ticket. I stuff the gun into the waistband of my tracksuit and drag the sheet and blanket off the mattress.

I cover him quickly. He's not the first man I've killed. But I was in uniform then. I'm not going to think about the consequences. All that matters is the discovery of where I am and his explanation of *hawala*. And the need to get out of here before more visitors arrive.

I stagger out into the lobby. Stacked in a corner is a pile of boots, worn and grubby but, as it turns out, serviceable. I try sorting them into pairs. I feel like a tramp picking through rubbish but if this is what it takes to get me some decent footwear, so be it. They're standard Soviet issue, knee length, black leather, the infantryman's best friend.

I unearth two that look as if they'll fit me. I'm even far-sighted enough to shove my hand inside. I don't want my toes bitten by some angry rodent whose slumbers have been disturbed. I lean as far forward as I can but the boot slips out of my hand. I curse and try again. I stamp the boot into submission. And the other one. They're loose. But they'll do.

I blunder into the wind and rain. Gibbous clouds move fast across the sky. I look to right and left and choose the latter. There's an asphalt path running round the side of the building towards an access road for vehicles. When I reach the corner, I turn. My prison, with the theatre inside, is a three-storey block, with lines of broken windows and concrete walls streaked with grime. Zinc drainpipes hang from rusting brackets. Some have broken away from the main structure.

The sight of them rings a bell. I need water, a wash, and if my luck's in, a bottle of some sort. I walk back into the lobby and try the staircase to my left. I can't tell if the boards are sound but I take a chance. It leads me safely to the first floor where I have a choice of corridors. I pad down the one on the right and find a washroom. Water trickles from a tap covered in verdigris. A metal canister stands on the window sill. I rinse it out. Then sniff it and fill it up. Its screw-cap still fits. I splash my face and hands.

The wind has subsided and the washroom is as still as a tomb, except for the echo of the tap, releasing drops of water like a ticking clock. I hold my breath and listen. Behind me linger a row of evil-smelling lavatories. I enter and relieve myself.

I walk back down the corridor, peering into rooms as I pass. More dereliction. Abandoned desks and broken chairs, the legacy of a frenzy of destruction.

Someone has left a camouflaged combat jacket hanging from a hook. I grab it and give it a cursory inspection. The sleeves are torn but it has a hood. It's padded and warm. It's a plus.

Outside again, I keep to the very middle of an unwaveringly straight road. My commandeered footwear makes surprisingly little noise on the tarmac. Over to the right more derelict buildings squat like rotting carcasses, two and three-storey barracks in the style of Soviet prefabricated *Khrushchoby*. They must have housed thousands of Russians, ready and able, if not too willing, to defend the German version of a Marxist-Leninist paradise. Beyond lies the forest, a mix of conifers and deciduous, dense and uninviting.

I trudge on, trying to work out where the sun is above the clouds. South or west must be a better bet than north and east. That way I might stumble across a village, a farm or even a signpost.

A car turns on to the road, about half a kilometre away. I could wait for it and wave it down. But I choose caution, crouching behind a pile of concrete that might once have been a blockhouse. It roars towards me, a sporty saloon, with adverts for Kawasaki and Michelin stuck to its blood-red bodywork. It flashes past and vanishes round a bend.

The roar dies. I hear only wind and the croaking of rooks and crows.

I strike away from the road, walking through sodden thickets of fir and bracken, across a maze of paths, over ditches and culverts blocked with debris. To stop will leave me stranded and confused when I need to stay focused and angry.

There it is again, the throaty revving of high-powered engines, like the start of a Formula 1 race. It's incongruous, incredible. But it's happening none the less. I linger in the hollow of a copse and swig my water.

Pushing aside the branches of a small oak, I see a wide open space, a massive expanse of tarmac, bounded to left and right by aircraft hangars built into embankments covered with earth and grass. In the distance, a control tower. Soviet and East German Migs once scrambled from here to scour the skies for intruders from the West. Now there isn't a plane to be seen apart from a smart, little Cessna, parked near one of the hangars. Four cars, red, blue, green and black and plastered with adverts, are being hurled round a stretch of runway made wet and greasy by a line of sprinklers. They skid and swerve through a set of chicanes. After fifteen minutes they stop and line up nose to tail before heading in procession towards the control tower.

I screw up my eyes to decipher the hoardings attached to the distant buildings. Again I read 'Kawasaki' and 'Michelin' and see the symbol of the rubber tyre man. Another sign says 'Restaurant'. Before I can work out what this is all about, the cars are replaced by a posse of motor cyclists who try their luck on the skid-pan. Shattering the peace of the day, they race across the runway, negotiating the chicanes at madcap speeds. I stand transfixed and forget that they might see me.

*"Did you want them to see you?" Maguire asks. "Rescue you? Question you?"*

*"I might have had a secret wish, yes. But I didn't trust authority, or anyone, to take me at face value. They'd have looked me up and down and decided I was a mental case."*

I slink back into the trees.

I'm ravenous. It's a long trek round the airfield perimeter. Again I push my way through brambles and young saplings.

Their branches whip my face and shred more of the combat jacket.

After twenty minutes I find myself at the back of the control tower and inhale the smell of cooking and freshly baked bread. There is an open door which looks like the rear entrance to a kitchen. I creep forward. Piled on the threshold are bagels and *Broetchen* in cellophane wrapping. Next to them, bottles of mineral water. I hide behind a large, green wheely-bin and cock an ear to the chatter of those inside.

It's useless to wait. I make a dash for the door, grab a handful of rolls and a single bottle of water and sprint as I've never done at my age, stumbling into a clearing about fifty metres from the building. I stiffen and listen hard for any cry of protest. Nothing. I fill my lungs with air and eat, not like a beggar on the run, but deliberately, chewing every mouthful until it's fit to swallow. It might be blandly baked dough but it tastes like the lightest croissant.

I drink a little water, stuff the rest of my booty into the pockets of the combat jacket and wander back into the undergrowth. I feel like a schoolboy who's robbed an orchard. The wind blows in gusts again but the rain is holding off. The sun breaks through the clouds. So the south is over there. If I retrace the route used by the hot rod, it must lead eventually to a highway. I keep to the verge and work my way back to the barracks. There's a car parked outside. Not a rally car. A very sober black Mercedes.

I slip behind another pillbox and finger the gun. Two men, one in police uniform, the other wearing a black car coat, emerge from the block carrying a body. They open the boot and toss the corpse inside. They look up and down the road.

"Are we dumping this or burying it?" the uniform asks.

I don't hear the muttered reply.

"Your Englishman is smart. No trace of him in there."

This time I do hear the response. And I recognise the voice.

"We'll find him," says Wels. "He's not that smart."

"Smart enough to kill," says the uniform.

They get back into the car. It does a respectable three point turn and moves off.

I wait another ten minutes. No one else comes out of the building. There are no more cars and no more search parties. They've lost me. I want it to stay that way.

I walk on. I'm getting tired. My chest pains have returned. But I must keep going.

Then suddenly, a T-junction and a signpost. To the left, Grossdoellnersee. To the right, Zehdenick.

*"Suddenly, you know where you are," says Maguire. "Slap bang in the middle of the Brandenburg forest about fifty kilometres north of Berlin."*

*"Yes. But I don't know how to get to a main road. I sat on a bench which the Schorfheide Nature Park authorities had thoughtfully provided for hikers."*

*"Now, wasn't that lucky?"*

*"Shut up."*

*"Which way did you go?"*

*"Left. The name, Grossdoelln, rang a bell. But I couldn't think why it was important."*

It's early afternoon now. The road runs through more thick woodland, the trees forming a dark tunnel with no end in sight. I dredge up memories from my German studies, of landscapes full of foreboding, where Goethe's *Erlkoenig* deceived an unsuspecting father and fatally bewitched the son lying in his arms. A car engine jerks me out of these morbid thoughts. I have just enough time to scuttle into the long grass.

The Mercedes flies past. I lie very still. Have they seen me? Are they going to stop? I half hope they will. Then this crazy adventure will be over and damn the consequences.

The road stays empty and silent.

I took a wrong turn at the T-junction. I know I did. I'm getting nowhere and I'm dead on my feet. Which means finding a nook and cranny, with shelter from the wind and the rain that's bound to return. I stagger into the brush and fall flat on my face.

# Chapter 2

It's pitch black when I wake. I fumble for the bottle and the *Broetchen*, chew on the bread and sip tepid water. I check that I still have the gun. Heading back to where I think I left the road, I'm tempted by a path that takes me deeper into the forest. I crash through the damp undergrowth defying whatever is aware of my presence to do its worst. The trees rustle perpetually and drop water on to my hood. There's the odd grunt and the hoot of an owl, a subdued cacophony of squeaks and moans from creatures I've always assumed slept silently in the depths of the night. I plunge on, making as much noise as I can.

The forest thins out and a full moon appears. I trip and fall to my knees. I'm face to face with an enormous animal that squeals and snorts its outrage, a wild boar with a curlicue set of tusks, plainly sharp and far too close for comfort. Light glints in the blue-grey pearl of its eyes. It crouches and rotates its head, trying to bring me into focus. I watch and wonder whether to keep still or spring up, yell and bawl, and run like hell.

The boar blinks and blinks again. I expect it to paw the ground like a bull in the ring, presaging a headlong charge. But, with a flick of its bristly snout, it executes a frantic pirouette and rushes off into the gloom howling its protest at this disturbance to its nightly routine.

I let time go by, drink more water and force myself to breathe more regularly. The same question. Which way to go? I am completely lost.

The moonlight has picked out a circle of half-rusted metal. At first I think it's a beer can discarded by some untidy hiker. But I know what landmines look like. I stand up slowly and scour the ground around me. Who planted this one? East Germans? Russians? The *Wehrmacht*? And how many more of them are there in these woods?

I stride along a path lit by shafts of silver penetrating the forest canopy. I'm starting to see metal canisters every few yards, mirages that persuade me to adopt a ludicrously evasive gait.

So far the ground I've covered has been roughly level. Now it dips and rises again until it falls away into a depression. A stream gurgles away to my left. Through the sound of its waters, I hear singing and strange martial music. It comes from somewhere up ahead. I stop and listen.

*Oh, raise the flag and close your ranks up tight!*
*SA men march with bold, determined tread.*
*Comrades felled by Reds and Ultras in fight*
*March at our side, in spirit never dead.*

I'm hearing the 'Horst Wessel' song in the deepest part of a German forest on a raw November night, seventy or more years after it was composed by a Nazi thug, shot by communists and later dubbed by Goebbels 'a martyr for the Third Reich'.

I take to the undergrowth again and discover a broader clearing to my right. It serves as a parking lot for a dozen or so cars. I recall seeing two of them at the motor club. And there are bikes, stacked with helmets and assorted gear.

I move towards the source of the singing. The clearing glows red. A motley group of men and women are holding torches and fervently rasping their battle hymn. At the end of every verse, they roar *Sieg Heil.* Not all of them are skinheads but most wear the usual black jackets and boots. The chanting dies down and an older man speaks, but softly, so that his words are lost in the night air.

This is no Hitlerite harangue. The group bow their heads as if in prayer. The torches crackle and the flames draw monstrous patterns on the bare branches. I beat a stealthy retreat into the thicket behind me.

There is no more singing and chanting. Just chatter and busts of laughter. But they're not for leaving. I watch them gather round a makeshift barbecue, swigging beer and wine. The smell of roasting meat tortures my taste buds. I settle down to watch.

There's a rustling beside me. Not a boar this time. Just a wizened furry face with a fine set of whiskers. I smile idiotically at it and am fool enough to raise a finger to my lips. Will it cry out and give me away? It examines me, decides I'm harmless and scurries into the rough grass.

They start to decamp. Cars and bikes are revving up. And suddenly they're gone. But I wait before creeping into the clearing. The embers still glow. I speculate on the risk of a brush fire and curse them for being so careless in spite of the damp ground.

I move in closer and stumble into a boulder. It bears a carved inscription. *Karinhall.*

*"Good God," says Maguire. "So, now you knew the reason for the shindig. Hermann Goering's grand villa, the one he built for himself as* Reichsmarschall *and head of the* Luftwaffe. *You were standing on the spot. And they were paying homage."*

I know all about *Karinhall* from histories of the Third Reich. Goering named it after his first wife, Karin von Fock Kantzow. He stored his loot here, stuff pilfered from art galleries, museums and private collections in occupied Europe. There were Flemish tapestries, Rembrandts, altarpieces, ancient manuscripts and masses of jewellery.

*"He fooled himself into thinking he was Nazi Germany's Renaissance Man," says Maguire.*

*"And it was where he planned the formation of the Gestapo?"*

*"And the Holocaust."*

I stand by the boundary stone oblivious to the possibility of being seen and recaptured. I imagine what this fantasy palace must have been like, with Goering enjoying immense parties thrown in vulgar splendour, his guests consuming mountains of caviar and gallons of champagne He would stalk the rooms and corridors, their walls decked out with the heads and antlers of poor, dumb beasts shot in the forest. He spent hours admiring his booty, holding trysts with the Third Reich's most beautiful women, and imbibing drink and drugs to relieve the pain and humiliation of the Luftwaffe's failures.

I leave the glowing ashes behind and become aware of new source of light, white shading to yellow. In another clearing, hundreds of candles have been placed on what remains of a thick, granite wall. Tonight's gathering was a pilgrimage by a new generation of Nazis to the ruins of Goering's vanity. Which was why, after the bombast, their leader had spoken quietly and they'd offered their silent, unwholesome praise to some strange deity.

"Karinhall *was blown up on Hitler's birthday, April 20*$^{th}$ *1945," Maguire tells me. He loves relating the history he knows. "The Russians were closing in on Berlin. But Goering thought it would be wise to attend a bizarre celebration in the bunker at the Reich chancellery. In the morning, with the sound of Soviet guns ringing in his ears, Goering ordered troops to load as much of his treasure as they could into trucks. He told them to head south for Bavaria where he'd catch up with them. He was going to double-*

*cross Hitler and start negotiations with the Americans. The whole place was wired for a sensational act of wanton destruction."*

*"Goering pushed the plunger himself, didn't he?* Karinhall *was blown to pieces, almost. The advancing Russians finished the job a few days later."*

*"But his plans failed," says Maguire. "He ended up in court in Nuremberg and killed himself with a cyanide capsule before the Allies could carry out the sentence they'd passed on him - death by hanging. Goering asked to die before a firing squad. They refused his request."*

The candles are still flickering. I see a wreath with a swastika at its heart. A card has been pinned to one of the laurel leaves. It reads, "The victors may murder me. But they have no right to judge me. I deny them that. Hermann Goering."

*"Those were virtually his last words before he committed suicide," says Maguire.*

I get out fast, sliding down a muddy path through the undergrowth. The trees part and there is the Grossdoellnersee, with the moon reflected a hundred times in its rippling surface. I look across the water to a long line of darkened conifers. All I hear is the soughing breeze and the lake lapping against the shoreline at my feet.

# Chapter 3

I delve into the combat jacket and find a *Broetchen*. Sitting on a rotting tree trunk, I eat and weigh the gun in my hand. The forest behind me echoes with an explosion, muffled by distance and the thickness of the brush. Perhaps the boar has sacrificed himself. Or, perish the uncharitable thought, some young neo-Nazi has blown his leg off. I'm not staying to find out.

I see the boat, a skiff with oars laid bow to stern. It nestles in a patch of reeds, its painter tied to a branch. Tucking the gun back into my waistband, I undo the rope, push the boat away from the shore and clamber aboard. As it drifts towards the middle of the lake, I take each oar and place it in a rowlock. I haven't done this since childhood and find the whole business awkward and comic. But I settle myself and start to make progress. The Plough and the North Star shine from a clear sky. I head west.

It's cold out in the middle, made worse by a stiff breeze. The oars are heavy and I handle them clumsily. But the wind's behind me, lessening the strain on an aching body. Rounding a small headland, I glimpse a light. Which means a house and possibly a landing stage, and a road beyond.

The skiff slips smoothly under the spar of a wooden jetty. I ship the oars, leaning out as far as I dare to stop the gunwale banging against the supports. I haul myself out and run, forgetting to tie the painter and make fast. I stop, look back and watch the boat drift away from the jetty.

A path leads from the lake and meets a country road close to a small, trim cottage. As I pass, a security light flashes into life and a dog starts barking. I run on again but my lungs are protesting.

The forest is fenced off from the road. In any case, hiding here won't make sense. But soon I must rest. Yet the memory of what I've seen back in the forest keeps pumping the adrenaline. How many of these small groups of Nazis come to pay tribute at *Karinhall*? They didn't disguise what they were doing. Why don't the local police take action? And who owns the land round here now that the communist state is defunct? Some well-heeled supporter, ploughing money into The Movement? Or provincial officials who sympathise with them?

I haul myself over the fence and stagger back into the brush. I find another clearing, a glade with a carpet of dry leaves. I'm getting used to this. I lie down with my head against the bole of a pine and drift off.

Then it's daylight and raining again. My clothes are soggy and my limbs ache as if I've succumbed to 'flu. I can't see the helicopter but I know it's hovering directly above me. I've been up in one of those things. Eurocopters, supplied to police forces all over the world. Two pilots and an operator and a pod under the fuselage full of surveillance equipment. Searchlights, loudspeakers and digital maps. An observer in a chopper can spot things on the ground which the naked eye will miss. If it's red and white, it belongs to the Air Rescue Service and might even be friendly. Black and marked *Polizei*, and I'm in trouble. If it's green, I'm in bigger trouble. The fact that it's where it is means its crew are suspicious.

It stays aloft, rotors sputtering. I keep perfectly still and sweat it out. After a protracted quarter of an hour, the engine note changes and the chopper turns to fly south. The skies are suddenly quiet. There's no way of knowing if they've registered my presence and are calling up forces on the ground.

I push on. Another kilometre and I'm in luck. A main road at last. How have I missed it before? There are signposts proclaiming Zerpenschleuse and Berlin.

I'm going to risk it, move into the open and thumb a lift. My appearance will definitely deter the smarter cars and the average *buergerliche* in his Audi or Passat. I have a scraggy beard, my hair is lank with grease and grime and my clothes are soaked through and filthy. In any case, there isn't a lot of traffic at this time of the morning. Rural Germany doesn't go in for rush hours. But a truck might take pity on me.

I wave hopefully at the heavier stuff. No luck. It's an unforgiving road, absolutely straight as far as the horizon. Every hundred metres there's a gravel track running into the forest. Out of which, without warning, wheezes a dun-coloured IFA truck, chassis and cab high off the ground.

The driver sees me, pulls up and opens his nearside door.

"Morning," he calls over the clatter of the engine. "And where do you think you're going?"

"Berlin, if I'm lucky."

"Good thing I found you then. Get in."

"Wait a minute." He knows I'm suspicious but the door stays open. "Where are *you* going?" I ask.

"Berlin." He laughs. "If this contraption doesn't fall apart."

I climb aboard. He shuffles the ancient gears, lets in the clutch and we groan our way forward. We hear a protesting blast from a slick BMW as it overtakes.

"*Scheisser*," he says. "They think they own the bloody road. New rich with new cars and soft jobs in the city. They should try getting their hands dirty."

I'm not inclined to disagree and keep quiet. At least it wasn't a black Mercedes. After his outburst, he too stays silent. But he can't resist shooting the odd glance at me as we pick up a modicum of speed.

The cab has filled with the noise of an overworked engine. The struts rattle and the rain has returned, beating its tattoo on a cracked windscreen. But I'm going to put him out of his misery.

"You wouldn't believe it if I told you," I call out.

"Try me," he says.

Before I can launch into an explanation, he drops his bombshell.

"You're the bloke the radio's been talking about. You see, I don't pick up many hitchhikers speaking German with an English accent at eight o'clock in the morning."

My jaw drops and he flashes a trace of a smile, just enough to show he's enjoyed his little victory.

"They said you were some sort of agent posing as a journalist." He pauses. Then without taking his eye off the road, he says, "If you've got a gun, you'd better shoot me now. Of course if you do, we swerve into that ditch and bugger up your chances of getting to Berlin."

I produce the gun and lay it on the sill below the windscreen. He stretches out a hand but leaves the gun where it is. Then fumbles under the dash, pulls out an oily rag and covers it up.

I root in my pockets again.

"Not much else," I say. "Just a stale roll and a water bottle."

He nods and concentrates on his driving.

The obvious question is nagging at me. How come radio stations know I'm the object of a police search in the Brandenburg forest? He won't have the answer. But he might be inclined to tell me what he's going to do with me, now that he's got me in thrall. When we reach the outskirts of Berlin, I suppose I could jump for it. Or kill myself in the attempt.

"It's none of my business," he says. "But your face is famous."

"I beg your pardon."

"It's been plastered all over the front pages - *Bild*, *BZ*, you name it. And that outfit's no disguise."

"So, what else do you know about me?"

"Not a lot. They said you worked for some TV network we don't see in Germany - that you'd quit because your cover had been blown - you'd got mixed up with those *Arschloecher* in The Movement - the police had rescued you - you were badly wounded in a shoot out - but you did a runner from the hospital."

The wipers slap furiously, to little effect.

"That's pretty accurate," I sigh. "Except for the bit about the hospital. I didn't run. I was snatched and left for dead."

I turn to look at him. He's in his fifties, stiff grey hair and a Bismarck moustache. He wears the standard blue overalls of a million German workers, a check shirt and a black wind-cheater.

"And your name's Charlie."

"Charlie Barrow. Charles Wilson Barrow. At your service."

I lean over and offer my right hand which he shakes without hesitating.

"I'm Hansi. Hansi Kohl. Like the Chancellor that was, before he was rumbled for doling out loose change to his friends. They're all the same, these *Wessis*. Plain, fucking greedy." He pulls out a large red handkerchief and blows his nose. I notice his hands for the first time. They're rough but clean and manicured.

"Well, Charlie Barrow, what are we going to do with you?"

Is this when he tells me he's really another *BKA* plant?

"You hold all the aces, Herr Kohl."

We sit in silence as the IFA rolls on. The trees are thinning out.

I dip my toe into the water again. "You talked about those 'arseholes' in The Movement."

He doesn't react. He's waiting to hear the rest of my story.

"I got into this mess, because I've been investigating your neo-Nazis for a couple of newspapers in London. I met their leader at some miserable youth club in a dump called Kittlitz. His goons detained me and thrashed the daylights out of me. Then another lot of goons took charge of me. At which point the cavalry arrived in the shape of a very comely female police officer with whom I have fallen in love."

"That's quite a confession." He grins and wipes his nose again. "Here's mine then. Once upon a time, I was a communist. A true believer in the workers' state. Then I watched while they fucked up. Cocksure and greedy. And the *Stasi* didn't help."

"As bad as the Gestapo?"

"No," he says. "The *Stasi* could be very nasty. But they were nowhere near as thorough as Hitler's boys. They got themselves bogged down in red tape. In the end they strangled themselves with it."

"And what were you doing all this time? Keeping your head down - trying not to be noticed - like thousands of others?"

"It was all we could do, if we didn't want to get pulled in for a nice little chat. Don't tell me you haven't compromised on occasions. Even in freedom-loving England."

He tosses me a look of mild disapproval.

"In the GDR, I did what I do now. Forest warden. Twenty years at it. Looking at trees. Trees don't complain. They don't answer back. Whoever's in power, they'll always need people like me. The pay's gone up - a little. And I don't spend a lot. Got a little cottage in Klein Doelln. Wife and two teenage boys. And this bloody truck." He laughs again.

We roll into Zerpenschleuse. "Need juice. You got any cash?"

"Not a bean," I say.

"Thought so. I'll get us a couple of coffees and some *Broetchen*. There's a bog here. You look as if you need it. And by the way, if you do a runner on me, you take the consequences." He eyes me up and down. "But I don't think you will."

"And if I see you using the phone in there, what am I supposed to think?"

He gives me another old-fashioned look. "When I've filled up, I'll tell you more. And you'll do the same."

The *Tankstelle* is nothing out of the ordinary except for two remnants of the East German motor industry parked on the forecourt like trophies. A red Trabi saloon with a white roof and a Wartburg in similar livery. They're in good condition. Enthusiasts buy them, *Ossis* nostalgic for a strange past in which they never had to make painful decisions, letting Big Brother do it for them in exchange for a not indecent standard of living. But I don't think Hansi longs for the past.

He emerges from the kiosk and hands me a coffee and a roll. "I'm pulling the truck over while we scoff this lot." He gives me his little transistor. "The IFA doesn't run to a sound system. Switch on and we'll hear what they're saying about you."

Hansi parks the truck. We walk to a quieter corner of the forecourt and tune in. It's smack on the hour. The station jingle cuts through the morning air. Then come the smooth tones of the newsreader.

But I've been dropped from the agenda. "They've blue-pencilled me, Hansi."

"Or they've been told to," he retorts. "You must be valuable. Let's get out of here."

As he bends to turn the ignition, two green patrol cars swing into the *Tankstelle.* I crouch in the seat but Hansi doesn't flinch. "Don't think they're looking for you. Just want breakfast like the rest of us."

The IFA stutters into life. With the first of the five forward gears giving off a high pitched whine, we lumber back on to the highway.

"So, what were you doing in my neck of the woods?" he asks. It sounds like an innocuous question and I have to answer it if I'm to keep him on side. I decide to bring him up to date. I tell him about my abduction, about Wels and about killing the nameless Arab. He listens in silence until I get to the bit about *Karinhall,* the torchlight parade and the 'Horst Wessel' song.

"They'd have slaughtered you if they'd found you," he says. "You'd have been beaten senseless and flung in the lake. They're up there all the time. Weekends mostly, rain or shine. Not just for rallies and such. They're bounty hunters, looking for spoils in the ruins. Some say they've unearthed bits of jewellery, stained glass, chinaware, that sort of thing. The keen ones have been digging tunnels into the old foundations."

"They're mad," I say.

"And dangerous. I go in there only when I know it's quiet."

I tell him about the landmines.

"Yes, some stupid bugger got his foot blown off not so long ago. Serves them right. They're *Abschaum* - scum. But the police turn a blind eye. I've been of a mind to report them but I don't want trouble."

He meets my gaze.

"I know what you're going to say," he says.

"Do you?"

"Yes, you're going to tell me that doing nothing got our parents' generation into a big mess - keeping their mouths shut when they should have spoken up."

"I'm not judging, Hansi."

He changes tack. "Funny thing is, right opposite where Goering had his place, on the other side of the lake, there's a posh hotel. Know what it used to be? The Central Committee's holiday home where Honecker entertained foreign visitors. Gorbachev stayed there when he was telling Erich the game was up. They say even Brezhnev spent a few days shooting boar - just like Goering. Now they serve *Schweinfiletmedaillons* at ten euros a time. The Rotary Clubs meet there. Very up market. What a laugh."

He hauls a packet of cigarettes out of his jacket and lights one with a small blue Bic. He offers them to me but I decline.

"Why are you going to Berlin, Hansi?"

He blows smoke at the windscreen and shifts his backside in the driving seat.

"Got people to see and one or two things to buy," he says.

I make it obvious that I'm expecting more.

"For the job," he says. "And the wife wants a new fridge. I know where I can get one cheap."

We're still out in the countryside. But I'll have to ask him soon where he proposes to drop me. The best bet would be the first S-bahn station. Then I remember I've no money. And he's good at reading my thoughts.

"I've got a mate who owns a warehouse in Pankow," he tells me. "He's converted a corner of it into a snug, an apartment, all mod cons."

"Sounds good."

"You're going to need a shower, a shave and a change of clothes. If you walk the streets looking like that, they'll have you inside in no time. They tell me the cells in Moabit are bloody uncomfortable."

Warning bells are starting to ring again. Was it a chance encounter? Or had he been waiting for me in the IFA? Had the guys in the chopper tipped him off? I begin to imagine an array of sophisticated communications equipment hidden under the IFA's stained tarpaulin. Is it time to jump at the next red light?

He's way ahead of me. "Listen, you clown. I am what I am and what I said I was. Nothing more, nothing less."

I grip the door handle with my right hand. "I've been through too much to take people I've only known for five minutes at face value," I say.

"I can believe that," he says as we slow down. He pulls into a lay-by and makes a performance of pulling on the handbrake.

"If you want to slip out now, go on. I won't stop you. Only hear me out first."

He turns off the engine.

"Yes, I was a *Mitarbeiter*, a *Stasi* informer. I passed on tittle-tattle about my neighbours to the goons in Berlin. And they informed on me. It wasn't hard to do if you wanted to keep your job. But I'll tell you what else living in the GDR did for me. It gave me an abiding hatred of the old Nazis who clawed their way back into authority and used people like me. When it all came tumbling down, as we knew it would, we also knew the past would come back to haunt us."

He lights up again, lowers the window and wafts the smoke into the open air.

"I've got good credentials, Charlie. I lost my father to the Nazis. He was sent to the eastern front and left to freeze to death by the SS. My mother went mad and died of dementia."

I say nothing, take my hand off the cab door and unwrap a bread roll.

"I promised myself that one day, if I got the chance, I'd avenge them. So, Mr Charlie Barrow, having allowed you to walk into my humdrum life, I'm going to stop being a fucking ostrich and do something about those *Scheisser* in The Movement."

"Like what?"

"Like helping you to find your nice lady police officer again so that you can tell her what you saw back in the woods." He punches the air. "It's a small contribution to the creation of a better world. And it'll ease my conscience."

"Hansi, there's more to it than that."

I tell him about the assassination plot. He grips the wheel and looks daggers at me.

"Shit, Charlie Barrow. You're full of surprises, aren't you?"

He abuses the gear box and we're back on the highway. The IFA groans on.

Rural Brandenburg gives way to suburbia. The neat little villages are expanding as *Wessis* move in, build new homes or buy up property for a song and spend the rest of their cash on renovation. The locals resent them. But this is the new Germany. Hansi doesn't like it but he knows he can't do much about it.

"What's the date?" I ask.

"How the hell do I know?" He's still angry. "It's Thursday."

"It's happening on the ninth. If this is the eighth, we're as good as fucked."

There's another *Tankstelle* looming up.

"I'll pull in and buy a paper. Stay in the cab. Get down in the seat. Keep your face hidden."

He steers the IFA into a slot beyond the pumps and trots back to the kiosk. Within the minute he's climbing back in and tossing a copy of *Bild* at me. "Thursday the 8$^{th}$ of November," he says. "And your picture's on the inside page."

They've used that photo again, the one taken when Renate rescued me after the shoot-out. Eyes closed, hair dank and dishevelled. I read the copy that goes with it. I'm still a wanted man. A dangerous fugitive. And members of the public should not approach me.

"Bugger. Look at that," shouts Hansi. A hundred metres ahead of us, the police have coned the highway and erected a red and white barrier. We're about six vehicles back from the one at the front of the queue.

"Just like the old days," moans Hansi. "Take off that jacket. And put this on." He fishes out a battered baseball cap from under the seat. "Now slide over here and take the wheel."

He jumps out, runs round the back and clambers in again on the near side.

If the patrol have seen him, they're sure to ask why. But we've gambled and we have to live with it. Hansi pulls out his smokes again and offers me one. I break a rule and accept. We build up a fug and wipe away just enough condensation to watch what the police are doing. They take their time. I try the gears and gently ease the clutch pedal back.

"Rev her a bit." urges Hansi. "A touch more."

We jerk forward, until there's a green and white cap level with the window on Hansi's side. He winds it down half way.

"What's all this about?" he asks.

The cop tries to peer into the cab. "Your licence, please."

Damn. How are we going to get out of this one?

"With pleasure," says Hansi. He fumbles in a shirt pocket. Then says casually, "Your mate there wants to talk to you."

The cop turns round and sees his colleague questioning the occupants of an Audi in front of us. He beckons to our friend, who throws up his arms in despair.

Turning to Hansi, the cop says ruefully, "As if I hadn't got enough on my plate. On your way then."

I don't dare look at Hansi's face. I concentrate on the gear lever and get it right this time. We drive another five hundred metres, round a bend and can't contain ourselves any longer.

"Pull in, Charlie, for God's sake, before we hit something." We're in hysterics, like two kids who've cheated in the exams and got away with it.

"How the hell did we do that?" he asks, as the tears roll down his cheeks.

We calm down after a couple of minutes and swap seats again. There's a little *Imbiss* on the other side of the road.

"Come on," Hansi splutters. "We need more coffee and a *Wurstbrot*."

He adds *pommes* and ketchup to the order, pulls out a hip flask and pours a little schnapps into the coffee. We lean happily against the greasy counter. It's pelting with rain. But junk food has never tasted so good.

# Chapter 4

We enter Berlin's northern suburbs, trundle under the Outer Ring and over an urban *Autobahn* at Schoenerlinderstrasse. We pass dilapidated workshops, allotments and neat little bungalows, like Fechner's at Kolonie Paradies. Then come the old apartment blocks spared by Allied bombing and the newer high rise. Hansi stays clear of the motorway and tucks us up into the narrower streets of Pankow.

The IFA bucks and sways, rattling over surfaces neglected by communist planning, cobbles, sets and potholed concrete. We stop in front of a factory gate. Hansi gets out and pushes a button on a security phone. A voice squawks back at him and the gate swings open. We park in a small and cluttered yard among a motley collection of containers, vehicles and fork-lift trucks.

"Come and meet Udo," he says. We trek to the far corner and through a door marked 'Trade Only'. The warehouse is stacked with packing cases, some open, with the contents on display - microwaves, cookers, TV's and fridges. A wooden staircase leads up to a platform and a line of windows. We see two men apparently in the act of washing dishes. One of them spots us and waves. We climb. Through an open door comes the sound of a football commentary.

I follow Hansi into a small kitchen-diner where he embraces a stout middle-aged man wearing almost identical clothing.

"Hansi, you old bugger," he shouts. "Long time, no see."

"Can't you turn that thing down a notch, Udo? How come you're watching on a Thursday?"

"He's an addict," says a younger, slimmer man.

This is David, tall and fresh faced, Udo's son, wearing an expression of abused tolerance. "If Hertha go down at the end of the season, we'll never hear the last of it."

"It's a video of last week's game against Schalke," Udo explains. "The idiots lost 3 - 1 at home, for God's sake. In front of fifty thousand. Believe me, I could run a football club better than that lot." Udo looks over Hansi's shoulder. "Grief. It's the wild man of Borneo. Who's your friend then?"

Hansi introduces me. "Can we all sit down with a cup of coffee and I'll tell you what's up?"

The video flickers on, with the commentary muted. Udo can't resist the odd glance every now and then. But both father and son listen solemnly to Hansi who then asks me to tell my story.

"Especially the bit about a plot to kill the Chancellor."

"I beg your pardon," says Udo.

I spin through the events of the last four days as fast as I can and watch their faces. I have to remind myself that these are *Ossis* who have lived their lives under a bunch of suffocating communist non-entities. They almost regret the collapse of the Wall, find much of what the West has brought them unpalatable and hold firmly to the view that economic hardship brought on by reunification is spawning some very unhealthy attitudes among the young. On the other hand, making a bob or two on the black market is not to be sniffed at. Capitalism has its points. And this particular Chancellor's not such a bad bloke, when all is said and done. The notion that he might be killed by an assassin's bullet comes as a bit of a shock.

David says he knows a few of those who get mixed up in neo-Nazi marches.

"They're not nice boys and girls."

"I'm sorry," I say, "but interesting as all this is….." I look pointedly at the clock above the TV. "The Chancellor is going to be at the head of that march tomorrow evening. If I don't re-connect with my contacts pretty soon……"

Udo and Hansi run their hands across their faces and scratch their noses.

"Look," mutters Udo. "I don't want to get mixed up with the *Bullen*."

"I agree," says Hansi. "All I'm asking, Udo, is that we kit Charlie out with some clobber and send him on his way after he's made a few phone calls."

"I don't want to drag you in any further," I say. I know this doesn't apply to Hansi but for now we're both keeping quiet.

"Well, you certainly need a shower and a shave." Udo pointedly looks me up and down. "Phone's in the back. So's the bathroom. Help yourself. Somewhere out there," he gestures towards the warehouse, "I can probably find you enough bits and pieces to make you respectable again."

Who to call first? Renate or Maguire? I dither over the decision and choose ablution. I have never relished the touch of stinging hot water, soap suds and shampoo as I do now. I let steam and moisture draw the worst out of me and revel in the sight of rivulets of grime vanishing down the drain hole. When I emerge from the washroom, Hansi's standing there with a pile of clothes in his arms topped by a pair of shoes.

"You're transformed," he says with a wide grin. The clothes fit, more or less. Trial and tribulation in the Brandenburg forest have thinned me down and I need a belt to hold the slacks up. But the shoes are a dream after the Red Army boots, brown suede with tassels. I might have been wearing them for months.

I dial Maguire's number. His line beeps back at me.

"Answer for Christ's sake."

My hands are shaking. Someone picks up at the other end. I hear atmosphere and heavy breathing. A voice full of sleep says, "Who the hell is this?"

"Charlie," I say. There's a lot of scuffling and a crash.

"Hell, that's another bloody glass. Where are you?"

"I'm going to give you an address, Mac. Just get over here as fast as you can."

I look up at a calendar pinned to the wall.

*UDO BAUER*
*IMPORT-EXPORT-LAGERRAUM*
*WACKENBERGSTR 15*
*13127 - BERLIN*
*TELEFON UND FAX: 473 3233.*

"Got it." The line goes dead.

"Can you trust him?" Hansi stands there with a look on his face that says I'm too naïve for my own good.

"He's my mate. I used to work with him. He knows what's going on. He's as involved as I am."

"I don't think that's quite true, Charlie. He hasn't been kidnapped and beaten up. He hasn't schlepped through the forest and witnessed a neo-Nazi torchlight rally. And he hasn't got the cops looking for him."

"I can trust him as much as I trust you."

He shrugs. "Nice to hear you say that at last."

Udo appears with more garments, a black parka and a blue sweater.

"I thought you sold domestic appliances," I say.

"These *are* domestic appliances. I go in for all-embracing definitions for the sake of the tax man." He beams at me. "Go on. Put them on."

Hansi has vanished. It worries me that I haven't convinced him about Maguire.

"He's picking out a fridge for his missus," says Udo. I watch him fill an electric kettle. He turns. "Hansi is the best man in the world. We've known one another for years. I sent crap about him to Normannenstrasse and he returned the compliment. That's what it was like in those days. We took a risk but they never twigged. And we got some quiet satisfaction out of it." His face is suddenly sad. "He also kept me afloat when my wife died."

"How do you know *I'm* not conning you?" I ask. "How do you know that I'm not someone else on the run from the *Bullen*?"

He takes a step nearer.

"I can see it in your eyes. If you've lived as long as I have in a society full of liars, you just need to look at somebody, watch their face, the way they sit in a chair or stand at the tram stop." I don't move. "You're not a good liar, Charlie Barrow. You're too scared to tell lies."

I'd like more time to absorb this piercingly accurate analysis of my character, but the buzzer sounds.

"Could be your mate. What's his name again?"

We move to a desk where Udo has installed a videophone. There's a small CCTV screen up in the corner.

"That's him."

I see Maguire in all his shambling glory, arms swinging in frustration because no one has answered his call. Udo tells him to push a small gate set within the bigger one.

Maguire isn't one for bear hugs. He just stands there and smiles through his pebble glasses. Hansi has followed him upstairs. David is back. I do the introductions. We sit and

Maguire retrieves a large bundle of paper from his jacket pocket.

"Read that lot," he orders. "You are a lucky man."

"Lucky?" I protest. "I've been snatched from Berlin's finest hospital, drugged to the eyeballs, tossed like a sack of spuds into the corner of a derelict building in the middle of nowhere, extricated myself by indulging in self-inflicted forced marches, witnessed a crowd of Nazi thugs paying homage to Goering in the wee small hours, and rowed a boat to freedom. And you have the gall to say I'm lucky?"

"You're lucky," says Maguire severely, "because you are still able to make friends and influence people."

He looks round at the other three who are enjoying this dressing down. "Do you know what turmoil you have caused out there? Police all over the shop, not to mention *BKA, BND, Verfassungsschutz,* and GSG9, sirens blaring, helicopters rending the skies day and night, statements from government ministers about British spies creating an unfortunate lack of trust between allies. Not to mention a scandal brewing over agents inside The Movement, blowing their cover and completely undermining official attempts to get the organisation banned by the Constitutional Court. Good Grief, Charlie. You should read a newspaper occasionally."

"I was off the news agenda this morning." I look at Hansi who nods at Maguire.

"Yes, that is very interesting."

"Well, don't keep us all in suspense. Why is it interesting?"

He doesn't answer the question. As if it's irrelevant. He's ploughing a furrow of his own.

"The *Kanal* hasn't uttered a word about you. Its own newscaster, or former newscaster, is chief suspect in a major story. Totally ignored."

Maguire coughs. "Of course I haven't pushed for it. Discretion and valour and all that. But I'd like to know which of my bosses gave the order to stay *schweigend*."

"Is Kai Struck back yet?"

"No. It's all very curious."

Maguire looks at Udo. "Please can I have that cup of coffee while Sir, here, does his homework?" David is already handing round steaming mugs and a tin of biscuits.

"What do you know about Renate?" I ask.

"Nothing. And I'm answering no more questions until you read that lot."

The pile of paper in front of me consists of Maguire's gleanings from the press and the wires. The first report covers the expulsion from a major opposition party of one of its members of parliament. He'd given a speech described by the government as anti-Semitic.

"What's this got to do with us?" I ask sullenly.

Maguire explains. "The man accused the Jews of having committed crimes quite as bad as the Holocaust. They threw him out because they're embarrassed by the fact that even the respectable political mainstream harbours views as nasty as those perpetrated by Lenz and his mates. Got it?"

He sips his coffee. "It goes into our film, Charlie. All good background when we go public on the great adventure you're currently experiencing."

"Thank you, Mac. That's very comforting."

Hansi, Udo and David have retreated to the kitchen-diner. They have their own gossip to swap.

I read on. There's more on the Constitutional Court's decision to throw out a government demand for a ban on The Movement. The rise in racially motivated murder and general mayhem has persuaded them it's time to take action, but the judges aren't buying it.

"On the grounds," says Maguire, "that informants placed inside the organisation by the interior ministry, who, we were meant to think, were leading lights in the party, have made provocative public speeches inciting racist violence. Tainted evidence. The government's screwed up."

I thank my stars that Marion is not tempted by the limelight.

"And as an officially recognised political party, The Movement can go on receiving state funds and staging its rallies when and where it wants?" I ask.

"You reason correctly. Thank you, *BND*. And thank you *Verfassungsschutz*." Maguire frowns. "What I want to know is, who on the inside planned this farce."

I see the face of interrogator Wels again. And I remember him lifting that body into the boot of the Mercedes.

I read too about a ruling from a court in Hamburg. Months ago it imposed a fifteen year jail sentence on an Arab charged with helping the 9/11 hijackers. He was accused of handling funds for a group of North Africans who'd studied at a local technical college. They're supposed to have passed on a lot of what they'd learned to the men who flew the planes into the World Trade Center and the Pentagon. And for all its bungling, the *Verfassungsschutz* had uncovered evidence which seemed to show that the Hamburg cell contained several of the 9/11 gang.

"It is a cause for concern," said a much chastened interior minister, "that we did not recognise what these men, *who had resided in Germany for some time,* were concocting."

I dig back into the recent pass. "When we met at Kittlitz, Lenz talked about how The Movement supported the justice of the Arab cause with safe houses and cash."

"Safe houses and cash for a select bunch of foreigners who were never singled out for vilification," observes Maguire.

"In return The Movement got arms."

"So there is a connection?"

"The man I shot, back at the Soviet base....."

"You did what?"

"He came for me. Had a gun. Said he was going to kill me."

"What did he look like?"

"He looked like a thousand and one Arabs, Kurds, Turks, Chechens - what have you. Swarthy. Beard. Mid-thirties. Spoke English though. And spilled the beans about links between The Movement and Al Qaeda."

I tell him what happened.

"You realize you could be charged with murder."

"I could. But I don't think I will be." I fill him in on Wels and the removal of the body.

"They dumped you and expected you to die," says Maguire. "But you didn't."

"He was sent to finish me off. He blew it. They take the body away. I'll lay good odds they want to keep it quiet."

"I wonder what the *BND* have managed to get out of Lenz."

"I'll lay another bet. They've done a deal with him."

"And the Hamburg court has quashed the original conviction. Terrific."

He picks up a piece of wire copy. "Lack of evidence. Retrial ordered. There's a lot of it about. Shilly-shally and cock-up. It's become a national disease."

"Which brings us back to Renate."

"I haven't heard from your lady friend. I've made three attempts to get in touch but she seems to have vanished from the face of the earth. When did you last have any dealings with her?"

"The night I was sedated and dragged off into the wilds. Just before it happened."

I describe how Wels had tried to interrogate me. "But when was that? Two - three nights ago?"

"Let me adjust your clock," says Maguire. "Today's Thursday. I saw you last in the Charite on Tuesday night. You were snatched soon after. We still don't know why and we don't know who did it. You've been incommunicado for the best part of two days while the authorities and the media put on a spectacular display of searching for you and accuse you of all kinds of nefarious deeds. For most of Wednesday you were hacking your way out of the Brandenburg forest. You witnessed the *Karinhallfest* last night. Hansi picks you up this morning."

"If they're so bloody brilliant," I point out, "they must know I phoned you."

"They might," says Maguire. "But they can't monitor everything."

He changes the subject, starting a slightly surreal discussion about where a determined assassin might position himself in the vicinity of the Brandenburg Gate. He unfurls his map again and outlines the route he thinks the Chancellor and his retinue will take. I'm reminded of the way he did the same for Renate.

"I think they'll start at the New Synagogue, turn into Friedrichstrasse, right into Unter den Linden near the British embassy, then head straight for the Gate."

He looks hard at the map. The rest of us peer over his shoulder.

"Word has it they might take a different route," says David.

"How do you know that?" I ask.

"I have a friend in Traffic Police. He's been told that they'll work their way past Montbijou Park, along the left bank of the river opposite Museum Island. They'll enter Unter den Linden near the old Prussian arsenal - the *Zeughaus*. And then on to the Gate."

"I smell a smokescreen," says Maguire.

"It's a hell of a long walk, that's for sure," adds Hansi.

"Oh, I don't think this Chancellor will take that much exercise," I say. "They'll use cars for most of the way. When they get to within a hundred metres from the Gate, they'll start a symbolic march which the public will be allowed to follow at a safe distance."

"So," muses Udo, "that gives your assassin the Adlon hotel, and a whole row of shops and banks to choose from."

"He could be on the other side of the Gate," Hansi points out. "In among the trees at the edge of the Tiergarten."

I slump into the armchair, confused and disconsolate. We're stabbing in the dark. Hansi says he has to go but assures me I'll see him again.

"Hope the wife likes her new fridge."

"She will." He grins and pauses in the doorway. "Do I keep quiet about all this?"

"I don't see why, Hansi. The more people know, the better. But you might have a hard time convincing them it's true."

Udo goes to buy food. David, in whose contacts with the Traffic Police I have a growing interest, says I'll find him in the warehouse if I need him.

Maguire points out that he has to work a shift at the *Kanal.*

"When do I see you again?" I ask.

"Early tomorrow. I assume you're staying here."

"I don't have much choice."

I'm instructed to sleep. But I can't. I should be out there looking for something. The problem is - I don't know what it is.

"Don't be daft," Hansi had said. "Those clothes are no disguise. You've had a shave and shower. You look too much like the real Charlie Barrow. You can't risk being spotted by the *Bullen.*"

"Then what am I supposed to do?"

Hansi had shrugged, patted me on the shoulder and was gone.

Phone Renate, you fool.

I shoot out of the chair and hear steps on the wooden staircase. David rushes in.

"There's a woman at the gate. Look."

We gaze at the CCTV monitor.

"That's her. That's Renate. Let her in, David."

"You sure about this?"

"Of course I'm bloody well sure."

He takes the handset and asks Renate to identify herself. She's not in uniform. I watch through the window overlooking the yard. She wears a blue parka over jeans and a sweater. She doesn't hurry. David goes to meet her. She's startled when she sees him but he lifts his hands in mock surrender. Then she follows him into the warehouse and up the stairs.

"Oh, my God," she cries when she sees me. "What have they done to you?"

"What do you mean?" I ask. "I've had a shower and combed my hair. I look beautiful."

"Yes, you do, Charlie. You do." Even though David's still standing there, she takes me in her arms and tries to kiss me. I move my head to one side.

"What's the matter? Don't I appeal any more?"

"Same phobia as before," I say. "I must have the worst case of halitosis in Germany."

She laughs. David withdraws muttering something about refreshment.

"You are a dunce, Charlie Barrow." She kisses me again. This time I don't resist.

"You taste of coffee and *Wurst.*" She draws back and scrutinises me. "But you look all in. You've lost weight and you haven't slept much."

"That doesn't matter. I have a hundred things to tell you and there isn't much time."

"And I have things to tell you."

"How did you know where to find me?" I'm scowling and I shouldn't be.

"Maguire phoned me. How else?"

"How long ago?"

"Twenty minutes. Why so suspicious?"

I don't want to remind her that, even if Wels has taken her off the case, she is still a police officer, with access to every known device for tracking down wanted criminals. Who else has she told? And has she left a trail others can follow?

David brings beers. I look at him. He knows his reference to the Traffic Police is bugging me. But as he leaves, his face is the picture of good-natured innocence.

# Chapter 5

"I left the Charite on Tuesday night in a taxi," she says. "Wels has barred me from using police vehicles. When I got home, I was so angry, I stalked up and down the apartment for half an hour trying to calm down. I didn't cry. I didn't shout. But I drank a stiff Scotch and even thought of dashing out to the *Tankstelle* for some cigarettes."

She smiles with obvious satisfaction that she resisted the temptation.

"Then I sat down and worked it out. I'm assuming I'm expected to stay out of sight for the foreseeable future. If they think I'm going to report in for the routine jobs, they can think again. I'll play poker for as long as I can and put the time to good use."

"I expect you already have," I say.

She stares at me, mouth open, tongue playing along the bottom row of teeth.

"I have my laptop at home," she says patiently. "It's still linked to the main *BKA* computer. I think they'll be so preoccupied with whatever it is they doing out there, they won't notice their own sloppiness."

"Did you know I'd been snatched from the Charite?" I want to watch her face as she answers.

"Not until late on Wednesday. I was a little busy during the day delving into websites and files. I switched on TV news at eight and there was a man telling me about a frenzied search for 'a renegade British journalist suspected of espionage', I kid you not."

"So who leaked the information and why?" I ask.

"I don't know, Charlie."

"Wels?"

"I said, I don't know."

"If you say so." She either fails to detect my doubts or she's deliberately ignoring them. "Go on."

"I got into The Movement's website. It's only too happy to parade itself as the party of choice for all true Germans. But I didn't find much that I didn't know already. There was the usual tasteless propaganda, anti-foreigner diatribes, falsified data about immigrants and asylum seekers. Extracts from Lenz's speeches - peons of praise for Hitler and so forth."

"What did you find that was new?"

"Songs, Charlie. I downloaded them. Machine-gun fire and a guttural voice roaring, 'You've got thirty seconds to run for your life, nigger - oh, that feels good - to kill a nigger'. And 'When Ali is swinging from the oak tree / when Mehmet staggers from the gas chamber / when the swastika is decorating our streets again / that's when Germany will be worth living in.'"

Renate swigs her beer as if she wants to clean out her mouth and curls her lip. I've not seen her like this before.

"Then almost by accident, I find *Recent Events Concerning The Movement*. And there's a paragraph in which two names appear."

"Axel Dreissig and Jens Koard?"

"They're described as martyrs to the cause murdered by the so-called security services. Dates given but no place names."

"So, we ask ourselves, who inside The Movement knew so much about the murders, when the first information made available to the media didn't refer to their membership. Or who gave additional information to the website?"

"Moles like your friend Marion?"

"She could have been playing one side off against the other. So could Dagmar and Horst. But I doubt it because they didn't have that information." Again she fails to react to my scepticism. There's a moment's silence when I'm wondering whether she's going to tell me any more.

"I tapped into files I knew were for certain eyes only," she continues. "Fascinating stuff. The personal habits and quirks of senior politicians - in Germany and elsewhere. Did you know that a member of the British government is a heavy user of cocaine?"

"Nothing surprises me. Go on."

"Details of their income and wealth, legitimately acquired or otherwise. Their connections with a host of organisations, past and present, like the Catholic *Opus Dei,* the Freemasons, even the *Stasi.*"

"Above all, the *Stasi,*" I interject.

"Lenz and other senior members of The Movement were given extensive entries, some of them referring to Combat 18, named after Adolf Hitler's initials in the alphabet. That's the outfit that does most of the dirty work. There was a file on a closed settlement of exiled right-wing Germans in South America suspected of paedophilia. Another on links with far right groups in France, Belgium, Britain etc. etc. One of Lenz's lieutenants gets his money from the Sicilian Mafia."

"Is all this well sourced? Or just speculation?" I ask.

"Pure gold," says Renate. "Our researchers are nothing if not thorough. It occurs to me they could be accused of learning from their predecessors."

"That's a chilling thought," I offer. "Did you see anything on Al Qaeda?"

"There are links," she says.

"Indeed there are." This is the moment to tell her about the man I shot at the Soviet base, about *hawala* and the arms-for-safe-houses deal between Lenz and his Arab contacts.

"Then you know what I know, Charlie. Those 'dirty foreigners' Lenz bangs on about are supplying The Movement with the wherewithal to mount a campaign of race hatred and anti-Semitism inside Germany."

I drink from the beer bottle.

"Will you charge me with murder?"

"I'm not in a position to charge you with anything, am I?" She leans forward and pulls me towards her. We stay like that for a couple of minutes, listening to a backdrop of indistinguishable noises from the warehouse and the street outside.

"What else did you find on that computer of yours?"

"Oh, oddities that tell me the far right likes to work in mysterious ways which our courts can't cope with. Like the case of the British student, apparently killed in a traffic accident. He was Jewish. He'd come to Germany to attend what he thought was an anti-war conference. Then he discovered it was a front for The Movement. The press said he rang his mother in London telling her he didn't realise what he'd got himself into. An hour later he lay dead on a main road. The police here said it was suicide - he'd thrown himself in front of a car. A coroner in Britain doesn't agree. I don't think we'll ever find out."

"So now you're telling me that there are police officers in this country willing to cover up for The Movement?"

"I could introduce them to you, Charlie. I'll tell you something else I found tucked away on the internet."

The sheer quantity of her information is beginning to get to me. I shake my head in an effort to concentrate. I'm thinking of Fred again.

"There's an organisation here in Berlin called the Anti-Racist Initiative. It hands out leaflets accusing the police of pouncing on young blacks and Arabs in public places - like Alexanderplatz and Breitscheidplatz, the square in front of the *Gedaechtniskirche.*"

"Yes, I know. I've had one of those. They want people like me to send protest notes to the city government."

"The offenders are hauled into anti-riot vehicles for questioning. Ostensibly the police are looking for drugs and dealers. Most of them are quickly released but a few are locked up in places like Jaegerstrasse, where they're given the once-over. Then they're told to get out of town and out of the country."

"What do you mean by the 'once-over'?"

"Usually a cold night in a cell with the air-conditioning turned up. Nothing physical. Maybe a bit of sleep deprivation."

"You say all that as fact, Inspector?"

"Yes, I've seen them myself. And if you're asking me if I've taken part in any of this, the answer is 'Yes' again, when I was young officer. I was ordered to do it. I know. That's no excuse. I'm not offering one."

There's a knock on the door. David and Udo walk in. I introduce Renate.

"You're police?" queries Udo.

"I am a police officer," she says with a smile to dispel his anxiety.

"Don't worry," I say. "She's not after your VAT returns, Udo."

"What VAT returns? Don't have much to do with the *Bullen* if I can help it."

Suddenly David is making signs for us all to keep quiet. He douses the lights. There's no mistake. Regular flashes of luminescent blue skip across the walls. We peer at the CCTV screen and see a green and white VW Kombiwagen and a posse of uniforms heading for the gate.

# Chapter 6

"Christ," whispers Udo. "Have you brought reinforcements or something?" He can't take his eyes off the screen.

"Far from it." says Renate. "We've got to go, Charlie. And fast."

She tugs at my sleeve and I haul myself out of the armchair.

"There's a back way," says David. "But if they've got the place surrounded it won't be much use."

We follow David along a narrow passage, down another flight of stairs and meet a steel door. David listens and squints through a spy-hole.

"You're in luck."

He pushes the bar and we stumble out into a dimly lit street. We hear sirens screaming from the other side of the building. The door slams behind us.

Renate has a sense of direction. I run with her like a trusting dog until we emerge into the half light of a square then follow a path taking us through a small park. They're not chasing us.

"Slow down," she commands.

We needn't worry. No-one takes a blind bit of notice. It's almost an insult to our sense of crisis.

"The S-Bahn, Charlie." Renate takes my hand and we stroll like a middle class couple trying to look younger than we are. The sirens have stopped. Now I'm worrying about what's in store for Udo and David. Will they be pushed against a wall, frisked and questioned, even detained? I know they've got the guile to face down their interrogators. But they'll need to get rid of evidence - styrene cups, beer bottles, and my old track suit.

We walk the best part of a kilometre before reaching the S-Bahn, And there they stand. Uniformed *Bullen* in a long line stopping everyone entering or leaving the station.

"Over the tracks," says Renate.

I don't take in the implications of this until she pushes me through a gap in a wire fence and leads me along an embankment close to the S-Bahn.

"We have to get across. Over to those rail-yards."

I gaze at what lies ahead. Eight separate tracks, S-Bahn and main line, points, ballast and floodlights.

"We won't make it, Renate. Even if we dodge the trains, they'll see us."

She doesn't wait for me to weigh up the odds. We drop down the embankment and crouch while a train rattles past, its red tail lights vanishing round a bend.

"Now," she cries. She's fit. I'm not. And I'm dog tired. We hurdle over track and sleepers, forgetting that we could be fried to death by thousands of volts from the conductor rails. I hear the whirr of an electric motor and see headlights, their reflection shimmering on the cold steel.

"Run, Charlie, run." I can't run. I'm hypnotised by the approaching train. I have no thoughts of self-destruction or premonitions of my maimed body flung like detritus to one side.

The motorman has seen me. The repeated rasp of his klaxon stabs into my skull. I'm suddenly aware of what's in store. I throw myself on to the ballast and see the wheels of the train skim past me, metal on metal, screeching its way into the night. Renate grabs my hand and hauls me towards a clump of shrivelled bushes.

"How many times are you determined to dice with death, Charlie Barrow?"

My chest is heaving and I feel residual pain from old wounds.

"Don't answer," she says. "Just rest. We've got this far." She cocks her head. No shouting. No sirens. No pursuit.

"He saw me. Why didn't he stop?" I ask feebly.

"I don't know and I don't care. But he's sure to report it. Let's get out of here."

Before us stretch abandoned sidings, relics of East Germany's rail network, home to decayed railcars, scarred with graffiti. It's dark and filthy with grime and grease. But it offers good cover. We take off again, duck and dive between wagons and coaches until we reach a patch of starved couch grass and another barrier of rusted wire netting. Renate kicks it. A section gives way and we are through.

"Keep walking," she orders.

We reach a main road and head for a taxi rank. Renate taps the window of the first cab in line. The driver's been taking a nap but he doesn't object when she gives him directions. Nor does he raise an eyebrow at my weird attire as I slump into the back seat.

Renate sits up front. Every now and then she utters precise instructions. The driver says nothing, just glances at her occasionally and gets on with it. We twist and turn a series of corners, cross thoroughfares and then I know where I am. Back at Kolonie Paradies.

# Chapter 7

Fechner unlatches his dusty door and we enter his tiny domain. The room is as dismal as ever with heavy curtains drawn against the night and the throbbing city beyond the wicket gate.

"He's exhausted," Fechner observes as I flop into the nearest chair.

"He's been through hell and high water." Renate smiles at me from the kitchen doorway, dextrously holding two mugs of coffee and a bottle of schnapps.

"Can we stop talking about me as if I wasn't here?" I nod at Renate and Fechner copies me, acknowledging the complaint. "I may be an object of curiosity but I claim the right to take part in any conversation concerning my future, and, more pertinently, that of your head of government."

Fechner settles his spectacles on the bridge of his nose.

"I apologise, Mr Barrow. Meanwhile, I have some interesting reading for you."

"Not you as well?"

He doesn't understand and Renate is not about to explain Maguire's predilection for handing me stacks of wire copy. Instead he pulls a piece of paper from the pocket of his corduroys and hands it to me. It's another cutting, a report from one of the tabloids extolling my virtues as a latter-day Scarlet Pimpernel and lambasting the security forces for failing to find me. Instead of vilifying me, it lauds my ingenuity.

"We now have to decide how to keep you hidden." Fechner has lost some of his hubris.

"I'm flattered," I say. "Perhaps you would tell me what's happened to Horst and Dagmar, and, for that matter, the girl Marion?"

"Horst is dead," says Renate. "There's no mistake. Lenz's thugs shot him in cold blood in the car park at Kittlitz. Dagmar is nursing severe injuries."

Fechner elaborates. "We have managed to extricate her from the clutches of suspect medical staff at the Charite. They're probably working for Wels."

He's angling for a response that shows I've understood his meaning.

"I think I'm beginning to get the hang of this," I sigh.

"Dagmar has been moved to a secure clinic elsewhere in Berlin. She will recover in time and eventually return to duty. Right now she's in deep depression. Marion has vanished."

He says this as if death, debility and disappearance were normal aspects of the human condition.

Renate and Fechner withdraw into the corner where he has his desk and computer. I notice it's switched on this time. He makes no effort to hide the screen showing a *Verfassungsschutz* logo. Renate taps in a few commands. Both of them study the results. Then he turns again and tosses me some files which, tired as I am, hold my attention. They cover some of the cases he's been investigating. The first concerns an octogenarian politician, one of a panel of wise persons who elect the country's president. It turns out he was a military judge during the Second World War. Now he's now accused of having ordered the execution of

*Wehrmacht* deserters in 1945. The document goes on to call into question the denazification of top officials in the months after Germany's defeat.

Next, the MP mentioned in material Maguire had shown me, who compared 'the culpability of the Jews for crimes committed during the Russian Revolution' to Germany's responsibility for the Holocaust.

The compiler of the file asks why Germans are motivated to talk like this half a century after Hitler's death?

"My people think it's time to bring these issues out into the open," says Fechner.

"Your people?"

"It is also time to come clean, Herr Barrow." He shoots me a quick smile. "Yes, I am a *Verfassungsschutz* agent. I use my cover as a down-at-heel academic to run a team of neo-Nazi look-alikes who have infiltrated The Movement. I also co-operate with Inspector Seelig and other police officers who, as you will have gathered by now, are assigned to flush out racist sympathisers at the heart of government."

"Thank you for that," I say. "And Wels?"

"Wels keeps his distance from us. And frequently works against us. He has an agenda which troubles us. It may be why you have fallen foul of him."

"I think you can put money on that," I say. "And Inspector Seelig too?" Renate says nothing. Her face is a complete blank. And she isn't looking at me.

"Are you investigating Wels?"

He ignores this and says, "I should like you to recall your meeting with Marion."

"Before I do," I counter, "explain one thing. When you sent me to Dresden with Horst and Dagmar, you told me I'd meet a girl who was both a Jew and a neo-Nazi. You thought you'd shock me. When you did that, did you know that Marion was a double agent? If you didn't, why would she pick me out? Why would she tell me, of all people, that there was a plot to kill the Chancellor?"

I've hit a nerve.

"Escorting you to Dresden and Kittlitz cost us one of our best people, Barrow."

"I wasn't responsible for that, Fechner. If Dagmar and Horst set up the meeting with Lenz, they must have weighed the consequences. In any case, Dagmar told me not to feel guilty about Horst."

He waves this aside. "I was against your escapade. But Inspector Seelig persuaded me that you would find things out that we had missed. You would get answers from Lenz and others that would incriminate them. You did. And I have to admit, reluctantly, that the Inspector has been vindicated."

He's angry. But he won't concede.

"You wanted to go, Barrow."

"I admit that but…."

"I knew what Marion was." He drops his voice. "I didn't set you up. But I miscalculated. I hope you're satisfied that she saw something in you - in that melancholy face of yours that tempted her into telling you about a conspiracy we were already trying to foil."

"You already knew about it?" I'm in a mood to punch his face in. But Renate steps between us. So far she's deferred to Fechner. Now she exerts herself.

"I don't think Mr Barrow deserves that, Fechner. He's more than met his side of the bargain."

She turns the knife a little. "We all recognise that you're brilliant at deciphering and analysing information. But when did you go out there and get shot at? He got results. And it cost him."

Fechner grunts, rises and creeps into his kitchen.

"Thanks for that," I say. "Look, we have less than twenty-four hours to crack this."

"Yes," she says. "And if those on the side of the angels are going to fall out among themselves, then we've all wasted our time."

Fechner comes back into the room. He's lost the initiative and he knows it.

"I shall not apologise for my outburst but I take your point, Seelig." He moves over to his desk again. "I asked you to recall your conversation with Marion. Please do so."

"Her sources are good," I say. "She's sure of them. And so am I."

He watches me closely. It's taken me this long to realize that Fechner's skill is in imbibing information from conversation and body language rather than bits of paper and computer print-outs.

"They've told her it'll be a solitary gunman. The place, Berlin. And we've all come to the reasonable conclusion that it'll happen during the anti-Nazi rally tomorrow."

I have half a mind to hold back on the next bit but think better of it.

"My colleague, Maguire, has speculated usefully on where the assassin might position himself but the options are numerous. We don't know the exact route of the Chancellor's procession. If your lines of communication are that good, Fechner, then tell."

That grunt again. He isn't telling. But I bet he knows. I'm also betting he hasn't told Renate.

"And there is Otto Struck," I add. I give him a full account of my meeting with the widow in Dresden. "What do you make of the surname? Coincidence? Or do you have more surprises for me? Don't tell me you have information that links the late Otto to my former chief editor."

He lets a brief scowl skitter across his face. "This is one case where you know more than I do. Kai Struck has disappeared and nobody knows why."

"And you have no evidence to suggest he's connected with The Movement?"

"Since you have told me what you have told me, I shall follow it up. For now we have to keep *you* safe and sound overnight."

I was suddenly afraid that he might have a fit of generosity, offering me a sleeping bag on the hard floor of his sitting room.

"It's fixed," says Renate. "We stay in the *Grethe*."

"What's the *Grethe*?" I ask.

It turns out to be a small, secluded hotel in a dark and grubby suburb of east Berlin. But its exterior belies what's on offer. The man at the desk is Wolf. He may project an air of dishevelled indifference to our arrival but the glint in his eye tells me this is no ordinary doss-house. The elevator moves swiftly and silently to the first floor. The room to which Renate has been given the key is spotless. It also contains a large double bed. We look at it and laugh out loud.

Wolf produces a meal which wafts away all memories of the last twenty four hours - a sizeable steak, *saute* potatoes, tender green beans, a creamy sauce and a Greek feta cheese salad with the right amount of olive oil and garlic. Not to mention a bottle of Rhenish red. I've heard of safe houses but I'm wondering if the sense of security conjured up by this one is a mirage that will vanish if I make a false move.

Renate watches me while I eat.

"You were ravenous, weren't you?"

"Aren't you?"

"Strangely, no. That meeting with Fechner took my appetite away."

"The whole thing was pointless," I mutter over a post prandial beer.

"No it wasn't," she retorts. "First, it was the best place to rest after our little adventure. You needed that rest. And don't deny it. Second, he had to know you were in one piece. Fechner's an arrogant man, Charlie. But he knows his job."

"How long have you been working with him?"

"Three years," she says. "I'd produced some good results from investigations into crimes committed by neo-Nazis and he approached me."

"Did Wels know about this?"

"I assumed so. But he never said anything and I just got on with the job. He seemed satisfied with my work. I should have realised something was wrong. I've been stupid and I'm paying for it," she says bitterly.

"Something's aggravated the rivalry between Fechner and Wels," I say. "I don't know what it is. But you might." I lay a hand on her arm but she pulls it away.

"Don't fish, Charlie. If you don't trust me now….."

"Yes?"

She does something I've never seen her do before. She pouts like a spoiled teenager. I yawn and change the subject.

"Are you staying the night?"

She glances over the rim of her glass. "Let's put it this way, Charlie Barrow. It wouldn't be wise for me to show up at my apartment."

"So, Wels is watching the front door?"

"And I have nowhere else to go."

# Chapter 8

I wake around three, stare at the white ceiling and watch the reflection of flickering lights from the street. The heavy hi-tech windows shut out the sounds of the city. All I hear is the mini-bar murmuring in the corner. I let my mind run back to memories tossed about in periods of loneliness, in restaurants and bars and spare moments in the canteen at the *Kanal.* Life was going nowhere. Now it's moving like an express train.

Renate sleeps peacefully at my side. Her face is turned towards me and a smile plays across her lips. We have made love just once. I wallow in the thought that I have been able to do it at all. This relationship is my lifeline to a better future. Make a mess of it, Barrow, and you will sail into old age unfulfilled.

She stirs. I lay a finger on her nose. Then I stroke her eyelids back to sleep. But she's coming out of a deep slumber. She moves again and seeks me with her hand.

"What time is it?"

"Time to stay where you are," I whisper.

She mumbles a protest, opens her eyes wide and sits up in a single movement.

"Charlie. We must phone Udo. We must find out what happened to them."

"Is that wise?" I ask. "At this time of the night? If they answer, you won't be able to tell whether they're free agents or speaking under duress. Suppose there's no reply?"

"We must try. Don't use the hotel phone. Get my *Handy*."

I need to find the slip of paper on which I jotted down the warehouse number. I stagger out of bed and see my jacket draped across the back of a chair. I delve into every pocket and find nothing. I try the trousers Udo procured for me. There it is. A survivor of the dash across the S-Bahn. Crumpled but legible.

I tap in the number but there's no reply. I try again and a weary voice says, "Yes?"

It's David. "Just answer - yes or no," I order. "Are you on your own?"

"Yes." I worm it out of him that he's managed to dodge the *Bullen* by hiding in a part of the warehouse they overlooked. Udo has been roughed up a bit and taken away for questioning. They've gone through his papers and confiscated some of them.

"Do you know where they've taken him?"

"No."

"Are you OK?"

"Yes. Hansi's coming back. Don't phone again." He cuts the line.

"Wels has got Udo," says Renate. "Probably holding him at Jaegerstrasse. I hope the bastard sticks to the rules." I want to ask her again what she means by that but I don't think I want to know the answer.

"What do we do now?" I ask.

"Do what you English always do at a time like this." She's serious. "Make a cup of tea."

I busy myself with an electric kettle, cups, tea bags, sachets of sugar and homogenised milk. Then we sit, propped up against the pillows like a staid married couple and sip the brew in the half light.

"I've never felt so useless," she says.

"Nor me." I contemplate a deep fold in the duvet cover. "If we drink any more of this stuff, we'll never get back to sleep."

"I don't want to sleep. I want to think."

But I can't hold back from speculating out loud.

"I keep asking myself the basic questions. What motivates people to hold these crazy views? Why do they hate foreigners, Jews, blacks, Turks, or whoever? Why crave another *Fuehrer?* Do they really think an all-powerful dictator will sort it all out, create jobs, impose order and make the country great again? Why do they want to be told what to do all the time?"

"I'll tell you a story to add to your collection." She moves nearer and lays her head on my shoulder. "There was a rabbi in Rostock. He went away for a few days. When he got back, he looked through his postbag and found some nasty letters - anti-Semitic hate-mail. To calm himself, he went for a walk. When he passed the local launderette, the manager ran out and embraced him. The rabbi said *that* was the real Germany, the greeting, not the letters. Jew-haters were a minority. The press paid them far too much attention." She sighs. "The rabbi was wrong, Charlie. He was too generous."

"Are you Jewish, Renate?" I say it before thinking of the consequences.

She doesn't hesitate. "My mother was Jewish. Like Marion, I'm half and half. She died. My father is a good, solid German gentile. Old but healthy. Sensitive, kind, liberal. He's proud of me too."

She frees herself from my embrace. "I think Marion told you how her mother's parents were among the few German Jews to survive Hitler. There was a handful the Gestapo missed. They had fair hair and rosy cheeks - had their papers doctored - for a fee - thought it was worth taking the risk. My father knew all about my mother. But if you fall in love, who cares where people come from?"

"Did that apply to your marriage?"

"Yes, at first," she says. "But it wasn't my parentage that drove us apart."

She has a faraway look in her eyes.

"It was his job. And mine. He was - is - an airline pilot. Always away. Or so it seemed. And when he admitted having sex in virtually every capital in the world and didn't look forward to coming home, we knew it was time to go our separate ways."

Now it's Renate's turn to contemplate the folds in the duvet cover. We listen to the half silence of our room. The duvet rustles. I feel her head on my shoulder again, bend to kiss her, until we both want more.

# Chapter 9

The bottle is empty.

"Unwise to open another one," Maguire observes without much conviction. "Tempted as we are to drink ourselves into oblivion, Charlie, I personally do not want a thick head in the morning."

He goes back to Berlin around noon. I doubt I shall see him again. My other visitors are down at Jorge's place, sampling the local cuisine.

"I don't want to go to bed," I say. "The night is too kind. The sea too musical."

"You're getting carried away again."

"I shall try to read." I saunter over to my shelves. "Do you know, I often just look at the spines of these books without opening them."

"A very fine collection," says Maguire. He's risen from his wicker chair to cast an eye over my library. "You've got novels, verse, history, a whole library on Germany and the Germans. Books on Hitler, the SS, the fall of Berlin, Nazi propaganda. You have an unhealthy obsession with the grisly past."

"Relics of our research, Mac. Don't you remember?"

"At least we got it to air," he chunters. "Was it worth the effort?"

"Of course it was."

We never made much money from our documentary but I did quite well out of Fred and the printed word. And Maguire was taken on by another network who were more generous than the *Kanal.*

He peers at the shelves again. "Let's see what else you've got."

He pulls one down.

"I remember this when I was a student. 'Modern German Short Stories', selected and edited by H.F.Eggeling, lecturer at the University of Edinburgh. First published in, of all years, 1933. Look at this. Gothic script. Eight stories from eight authors, copious notes and a huge vocabulary." He leafs through the pages, eyes bright with sudden enthusiasm.

"My goodness, Charlie. I've found three ways of saying, 'I plead guilty', 'I'm falling in love' and 'I wish to die a natural death'." We laugh. "The ability of the German language to skate round the obvious has always amused me."

He puts the book back in place.

"It's a treasure," I say. "But it has the habit of stirring up unpleasant memories."

"Like what?"

"Those stories are about injustice. I still ask myself, why does it happen. Why do the rogues and villains get away with it?"

"They don't," says Maguire. He turns to me, eyes hinting at tears behind those pebble spectacles. "You are a curious mixture of the naïve and the sceptic, Charlie. You have a well developed sense of humour. You appreciate the absurd and the downright ridiculous. Those are the weapons that have helped you to beat betrayal and disappointment. Don't lay them aside."

He stalks up and down the flat, trying to suppress the intensity of his emotion. Then he launches into Shelley again.

*"To suffer woes which Hope thinks infinite;*
*To forgive wrongs darker than death or night;*
*To defy Power, which seems omnipotent;*
*To love, and bear; to hope till Hope creates*
*From its own wreck the thing it contemplates;*
*Neither to change, nor falter, nor repent……"*

"To undermine the pompous, the brutal and the cruel?"

"Shelley didn't write that."

"No. I did."

Maguire isn't listening any more. He heads for bed. We never mentioned Renate. I return to the balcony and stare into the night. My melancholy subsides. I open another bottle.

# PART 5

# Chapter 1

They arrive at five thirty. Three gunmen in black, hooded and brandishing machine pistols. They smash the door down, drag the duvets off the bed and push us up against the walls. We're both naked. They poke the barrels of their guns into our navels. If they fire, they'll leave a nasty mess. When I risk a mild protest at their treatment of Renate, the gun is pushed further into my paunch. And it hurts.

I look into the eyes of the one in charge of me. There's a surprising lack of triumph in them. No ogling of my flaccid penis. No lecherous smirks at the marks on Renate's shoulders where I've bitten her in the ecstasy of lovemaking. Just a robotic stare.

I'm half expecting them to beat us to pulp. But there's an odd pause in proceedings when the only sounds are heavy breathing and the buzz of a fluorescent ceiling light.

A silhouette in the doorway reveals the presence of Wels in dark grey suit. He eases himself through a gap between the gunman and the shattered jamb.

"Get dressed. Seelig," he orders. The gunman relaxes his weapon and steps aside to let her reach the wardrobe. She says nothing, sustains a non-committal expression as she slides back the panel, retrieves her clothes and locks herself in the bathroom.

"Give him a blanket," says Wels, pointing to my torso.

"Where are you taking her, you bastard?"

The cold steel of the gun is jerked into my solar plexus.

"Easy," says Wels to his man.

I double up, with my backside against a hot radiator and my forehead buried in a blanket.

"That was unwise," I hear him say. "Your body has taken enough punishment in the last few days. Why ask for more?"

"Because," I splutter through the wool of the bed-cover, "I think I'm entitled to know what this is all about."

"You're entitled to know nothing right now." This is such a statement of the obvious that I let my body shake with muffled hysterics. Then I lift my head and see Renate emerging from the bathroom, spruce and businesslike. Not an hour ago I made love to this woman. She moaned when I entered her and pleaded with me to stay inside. I close my eyes, recalling the line of her breasts and the dimples in her buttocks. When I open them again, she merely glances at me, turns away and walks out of the room, escorted by one of the heavies. I stare at Wels like a trusting spaniel. My props have been knocked from under me again.

Wels tells his men to leave.

"You and I will talk over coffee," he says.

"How bloody civilised," I rasp as I grab my clothes and head for the shower.

Under the hot water, I agonise over Renate's behaviour and find myself quietly weeping. I try to control this. I don't want Wels to see my weakness. But as I pull on the clothes bequeathed to me by Udo, the weeping returns. We were winning, damn it. Now we're stuffed.

"I propose….." Wels pauses and stirs a sachet of sugar into his coffee.

"Propose? Why not explain first? She just did as she was told, did she? Ice cold. No surprises. Go on. Explain, Wels."

"I propose….." he begins again.

"No, wait. Seelig brought me to this hotel for a purpose. The *Grethe*. That's its name, isn't it? I presumed it was a safe house, safe from the prying eyes of her enemies inside the *BKA*, or the *BND*, or in the *Verfassungsschutz*. People like you. So, I got it wrong, did I?"

"I have to disillusion you, Barrow. You guessed rightly that this is not a conventional hotel. But you are mistaken if you think there are rival cliques within the service who use certain establishments to hide their trump cards from one another."

"Does that piece of bombast mean that Inspector Renate Seelig has been working for you all along? Taking me for a ride? It was all a big act. She's nothing but a crisp version of Mata Hari. She can fake orgasms like the best whore, can she? Fake emotion and sensitivity? And now it's time to haul her in. I don't believe you, Wels."

He's letting me ramble on. Like a professional counsellor.

"I mean, it was a bit over the top, wasn't it? You and the goons. Do I look like the sort of man who's going to hole up in a small hotel room with an AK-47 while you lay siege?"

"You killed a man."

"In self-defence. He was about to shoot me. Did you send him? Or was it Lenz?"

"It may surprise you to learn that I don't know who sent him. We had no idea where you were."

"That's a lie. I heard your uniform say how smart he thought I was. And I heard you say I wasn't smart at all."

"But *we* didn't abduct you. We picked up your assailant's trail and he led us to the Soviet base."

"And you took his body away. I saw you. Did you give him a decent funeral?"

He isn't fazed. I shake my head.

"Who did take me from the Charite? It happened pretty soon after you questioned me. When I was woozy from that painkiller."

So woozy, I tell myself, that I shouldn't rely on my memory of that conversation.

"Look. I am what I say I am, a bona fide journalist trying to investigate the far right in your country. Nothing more, nothing less. I *was* a soldier - once. I am no longer. Nor have I been for many years. And I am not an agent of the British government. The very idea makes me sick."

"I believe you now, Barrow. But there are others who don't. So I am taking you into custody for your own protection. You may have to stay that way until after tonight's ceremony at the Brandenburg Gate."

"Then you'll chuck me out of the country?"

"Perhaps. Meanwhile, nearly every police officer in this city, including me, is on duty with one aim - to protect the Chancellor and hunt down the sniper paid by Lenz to assassinate him."

I raise my eyebrows.

"Yes. You seem to have forgotten what you told me in the hospital, Barrow. We all know about the plot."

"I have to be there."

"At the Brandenburg Gate? Why? Think about it. The odds are that someone will try to shoot you as well."

"Thanks a bunch."

"Look, I'll put you out of your misery," he says. "Seelig did it."

"Did what?"

"Abducted you, of course. You were drugged either by her or the nurse acting under her orders. I should have spotted that when I came to question you. I should have realised you'd been given more than the prescribed painkiller. I thought you were just very tired. Which is why I didn't persist."

"But you did. You pushed me to the limit."

He wears an air of injured innocence.

"Not so. I asked you a few questions and left you to sleep, assuming that the guard I'd placed in the corridor would be enough to protect you. But he was distracted. They came for you around two thirty, sending the boy on a wild goose chase. He thought he was obeying orders from another senior officer. It wouldn't have taken them long to bundle you into a perfectly legitimate ambulance and drive to Grossdoelln along empty roads in the early hours. They left you in the old Soviet base thinking you would stay unconscious just long enough for them to cover their tracks. Then they'd have sent a bunch of heavies to beat it out of you, even though you had nothing to tell them."

"They? They? Who the hell's 'they'? *You* knew I was there. You came looking. In a big, black Mercedes. You took the body. Who the hell are *you*, Wels?"

"You know who I am."

I can't continue up this blind alley.

"Seelig has her own contacts in The Movement," he says suddenly.

"Seelig is half Jewish, for God's sake. Every move she's made up to now is proof positive that she wants to damage The Movement. Not protect it. You're talking crap."

"So she's tried that one on you. Does she look Jewish?"

"Who *looks* Jewish, Wels?"

For once he's stunned.

"Tell me," I say. "Tell me why they, or you, didn't come back for me until late Wednesday morning."

He pours more coffee and regains his composure. He's good at that.

"I wandered round that place for ages," I say, "trying to find a way out. I saw no-one except the motor sport people and the bikers. I'm asking you again. Who were they - these captors you find yourself unable to identify?"

"They misjudged you," he says. "They underestimated your stamina. They assumed you were so demoralised that you wouldn't move."

"Don't flatter me, Wels. I was demoralised." I sit with my head in my hands trying to make sense of this. "And who sent the chopper up? Who spread it about that I was on the run? I was a page one lead, for Christ's sake."

His message is - I'm an innocent abroad, a real mug in a world of clever shits.

"Don't say it again," I plead. "It was Seelig - part of the big show she laid on at taxpayers' expense."

He makes no move when I rise to stretch my back and shoulders. I swing round on him. "She rescued me from those neo-Nazi thugs in Zerbst. Why would she do that if she wanted me rubbed out?"

I might have expected it. Of course she rescued me. She reckoned it would draw suspicion away from her. And from Fechner.

"Her problem was, Barrow, she fell in love with you. Genuinely fell in love."

I think I am expected to admit that. But I'm not going to give him the satisfaction of hearing me say it.

"Don't deceive yourself," he says. "You won't be seeing her again."

"What the hell do you mean by that?"

"Inspector Seelig is under arrest while we prepare a case against her."

"So much for her civil rights then."

"She is not interested in civil rights, Barrow. Either hers or anybody else's. Her aim is to….."

"Yes?"

"It doesn't matter," he says. He's top dog now. That's all he's worried about. Being there and staying there.

But I need to start from the beginning again, to think it all through from Axel Dreissig's murder to the confrontation with Struck at the *Kanal*, my resignation, Renate's offer to set me on the track of a good story, our relationship, my capture by Lenz, my rescue, my wanderings in the forest, Hansi and Udo, and the second session with Fechner. All of it.

"Take me to Jaegerstrasse," I say. "I'll write a long statement for you."

Wels looks almost relieved. He's had enough of me. He'll be happy to let me stew in front of a computer screen, while he deals with the bigger crisis.

# Chapter 2

The minister looks up from his terminal, leans forward, shakes my hand and proffers me a seat. His twelfth-floor office is sparsely furnished in the way only the prominent and powerful prefer, to demonstrate they're running the show efficiently and without fuss. The only books are sets of law reports stacked neatly in discreet shelves to the left of an enormous desk.

I sit in a comfortable black leather armchair but can't help craning my neck to take in the view of a reordered Berlin. Beneath us, the narrow River Spree, and beyond, the tall, gilded column commemorating Prussian military victories over the French.

"Quite something, isn't it?" he says. "Come and take a closer look."

We walk over to the picture window and scan the rooftops. I pick out the snaking S-Bahn line, the bulk of the recently completed Chancellery and the restored Reichstag with its glass cupola and well scrubbed walls. Even from here it's possible to read the words - *Dem Deutschen Volke* - to, or for, the German People.

"A defiant use of the dative case," says the minister, "which neither Nazism nor the Soviet army were able to erase. That should tell us something about ourselves."

The Reichstag has a new, glittering companion, the *Paul-Loebe Haus*, a block of offices for members of parliament, a German version of Capitol Hill.

"It's built above an underground rail terminal," he tells me. "Politicians can be whisked to their constituencies in express trains or to European capitals as far apart as Stockholm and Athens, Madrid and Warsaw."

He preens himself. Then escorts me back to my armchair. Before he speaks again, I try my luck.

"So, what Hitler and Albert Speer failed to achieve by conquest," I say, "post-communist Germany is managing by high-tech stealth. I used to fantasise about that at two in the morning, Minister, during the cab ride from the *Kanal* to my hotel. The drivers always liked going through the new government quarter, past the Soviet war memorial and into the gloom of the Tiergarten."

The minister clearly thinks I'm slightly demented.

"I thought that if Christ had been taken up into the desert and offered the whole world by the Devil, perhaps Adolf Hitler's accursed soul was similarly shown the grandeur that could have been his if he'd had the patience to wait."

He frowns. Wels, who is sitting to one side, coughs behind his hand. He's doing his best to avoid looking like a gun-dog that's procured  wounded prey for its master.

I'm trying to work out why I'm here. I've tapped out my statement and snatched a couple of hours sleep in Wels's office. Then he tells me I'm summoned to the presence of a man with a colourful past. For this minister was a left-wing activist in his youth, a militant Green, even, for a time, an ally of Hans Best, alias Lenz, not averse to throwing the odd brick at police cars. In middle age, he moved into the political mainstream and is now landed with what many think is the worst job in government.

"I am trying to control immigration," he tells me, "keep a careful watch on asylum-seekers, oversee changes to the nationality laws and rein in the far right. I want a ban on all neo-Nazi parties including The Movement. Now, post 9/11, the War on Terror has been dumped in my lap. So I should be interested to know what you have discovered, Mr Barrow." Another smile is not enough to put me on the defensive.

"You have my report. I spent the early hours tapping it into Herr Wels's computer."

He doesn't reply.

"I have also had the dogs of war at my heels for the last forty eight hours. I have been hunted by every branch of the German security forces. Your press have labelled me a British spy. I've been beaten up by some very nasty people, injected with drugs and left to rot. And I've killed a man who threatened to kill me."

"For which you could receive a long jail sentence," he reminds me.

I look at Wels who meets my gaze with a cryptic smirk. The minister juggles with a fistful of pencils and lays them out on the desk like pick-up sticks.

"I don't exactly feel an obligation to do more, to help either you or Herr Wels," I say. "Such information as I've gathered is intended for British and Australian newspapers, perhaps a television talk show or two. Who knows where my good fortune may lie."

There is another uncomfortable silence.

"In any case," I add, "You already know that I am aware of a plot by members of The Movement to kill the Chancellor...."

He raises a hand. "Calm down, Mr Barrow. Herr Wels has brought you here so that you can give me a personal perspective. Your report will be read, believe me. But, unlike you, I haven't had the privilege of confronting my enemy at first hand. I can't walk into youth clubs in Dresden or obscure villages in the East where skinhead gangs rant and rave to the sound of poisonous rock music. I have not been able to discuss wild theories and anti-foreigner sentiment with the likes of Heinrich Lenz. Nor have I endured his interrogation techniques and his torture chambers. Perverse as this may sound, I sometimes wish I had. But ministers don't do that kind of thing. Which is why I need to hear you at first hand."

In the end we bargain. My story in exchange for an interview, which, he says, I can use in anything I write or broadcast.

"I want that on paper," I say.

"You will get it. But you go first." And he's not taking 'no' for an answer.

So I give him the lot. Events and opinions. The important and the trivial. I tell him how Lenz's thugs administered their beatings. How he twisted logic to justify 9/11 and other atrocities. And I tell him how I purloined bread rolls and a bottle of water and came face to face with a wild boar.

"Nobody was willing to tell me the truth," I say. "Neither Inspector Renate Seelig, nor Herr Fechner. And certainly not this gentleman." Wels sits impassively staring at the crease in his trousers. "Who is working for whom inside your security forces? We have the police, the *BND*, the *BKA*, and the *Verfassungsschutz*. I have singularly failed to work out which of these is trying to double-cross the other and play me like a ping-pong ball. But when it all leads to charges of espionage against me, and when I have to behave like a criminal on the run, then, for all my naivety and simple-mindedness, I get very angry. And, by the way, I should like some coffee, a notepad and a pen."

My hands are trembling. I can't disguise my loss of temper. I don't want to.

The minister nods at Wels who leaves the room. He abandons his desk and walks slowly round to my side, occupying the chair Wels has just vacated.

"Your indignation is justified," he says grandly. "And you are owed an explanation."

"That would be nice."

"Your tale of woe almost convinces me to do a U-turn."

I have no idea what he's talking about.

"Ten years ago, when, incidentally, we were not in government, the *Verfassungsschutz* came very close to unmasking a group of Arabs living in Hamburg."

I raise an eyebrow to show I'm concentrating.

"We now know that later on they were among the perpetrators of 9/11. But the *Verfassungsschutz* couldn't make evidence of terrorist activity stick, because the state prosecutor's office in Hamburg wouldn't let them. They had trodden on his toes. He was having none of it. The power of the states in this, our Federal Republic, is considerable, Mr Barrow."

He goes back to his desk, fishes in one of the drawers and hands me a pad and biro.

"If this country had had a centralised intelligence service at the time, we might have nailed those people. We might have prevented 9/11. That's a lot to have on your conscience. The Americans, not surprisingly, don't have a high opinion of us. Which is why I spend most of my time trying to do something about it."

He tosses a pencil from hand to hand.

"And it's partly their fault. When the Occupation Zones became the Federal Republic in 1949, the Allies made sure there was no single German intelligence service. They didn't want another Gestapo. So we've ended up with the

*BND* based in Berlin, while the *BKA's* headquarters are nearly 600 kilometres away in Wiesbaden and their counter-terrorism unit is in Meckenheim near Bonn. To cap it all, the *Verfassungsschutz* are in Cologne. Suppose, therefore, we have to respond to an emergency - like the Madrid and London bombings - we're fucked."

I sit up at this sudden lack of elegance in his delivery. He peers down his nose. He's indignant. And I am going to be told why.

"Even in these days of instant electronic communication, for God's sake. In the 21st century, we're still worrying about the consequences of the Second World War."

Which is no bad thing, I think privately.

"Why can't you amalgamate them?" I ask. "Bring them all to Berlin? You've been in power long enough."

"I told you. History's to blame. We now have a situation where the German police are actually banned from gathering intelligence on anyone - German or foreign - *anyone* living in the country. So, every federal state has its own intelligence agency which reports only to the state government. If the states don't feel like passing on information to the *BND*, they don't. So everybody is scrabbling around trying to pick up what they can. It's virtually impossible to co-ordinate a counter-terrorist operation. To do that stirs the pot, provokes rivalries of which, I fear, you have become the victim."

The door opens and Wels arrives with coffee.

"But your story has set me thinking. Perhaps after all we should leave things as they are. If you were so confused about the identities of those you were dealing with, it might suggest the system works better than I thought. Perhaps we should go on tying ourselves in knots in the hope that our enemies will trap themselves in the cat's cradle."

"I assume that's meant as a joke," I say.

"Not entirely."

Wels pours while we sit quietly, conversation suspended until the first shots of caffeine enter our bloodstreams. It's time to try my blockbuster.

"Both Lenz and the man I shot up in Brandenburg made it fairly obvious that The Movement and the far right are tied in with Al Qaeda and other Muslim militants."

The leather of Wels's chair crackles as he shifts from one buttock to the other.

"Are you confirming that for me?" I ask.

"Of course I am," says the minister without blinking. "You can't escape the connection, Mr Barrow."

"You mean, you open Pandora's box and you get the lot?"

"Exactly. Your account of conversations with Lenz tells me his fight is against more than just the political establishment. His obsession is the Jews. He wants to eliminate the Jewish community just as it's starting to find its feet again. He's prepared to do deals with Arab gunmen, precisely because they hate the Jews, even though they're Semites themselves, 'scurvy foreigners with swarthy non-Aryan skins, speaking an uncouth language and worshipping a different god'. I think that's how he put it to our interrogators. Articulate and disgusting at one and the same time."

He returns to his desk, and draws his fingers together like the struts of an unfinished building. He's seen the light in my eyes and the way my back has stiffened. He looks at my hands and the pencil poised over the notepad. And he smiles.

"We can talk forever about disenchanted youth in the East, the restless and the unemployed, looking for a chance to beat up blacks and Vietnamese, fodder for Lenz's little protest marches. They're easily dealt with. They're not what it's about, Mr Barrow. What we have to do is distinguish between two kinds of anti-Semitism - that of the leaders of the far right as focussed on the secular Jews, seen, wrongly of course, as all-powerful, rich and influential - on their organisations, their synagogues, and their spokesmen on TV chat shows. For Lenz & Co the Jew remains a parasite, what Himmler called the sub-human, a plague virus to be eradicated from the body politic......"

It's *The Protocols of the Elders of Zion* all over again. My mind's eye sees a flash of Herr Kuhls in the bar in Dresden. But the minister hasn't finished.

".....And on the other hand the anti-Semitism of the Muslims in our midst."

"The Turks? The *Gastarbeiter*?"

"And the Arabs. Their numbers here are growing. And their hatred is aimed differently - at the outward and visible signs of orthodox Jewry, the costumes, the hats, the curly hair, when these are paraded in our streets and the departure lounges of our airports. That hatred is prone to manipulation by Lenz. But its target is not his prime concern."

It's a fine distinction but it makes sense.

"The government now has to take into account all kinds of ramifications. There *is* a rising tide of anti-Semitism in Germany. Jewish graves are desecrated, Jewish children are set upon at school and certain politicians - not all of them on the far right - say silly things on television. A lot of this stems from hatred of Israel, or more accurately the Israelis' treatment of the Palestinians. The Palestinian cause has been taken up by the liberal left too. It's a fashionable prejudice."

"You mean, they don't actually go to the Middle East and get their hands dirty."

He sips his coffee and draws a long breath.

"It produces strange alliances," he says. "Socialists and Greens support the Islamists and tell us they understand why desperate people become suicide bombers. Talk like that and any criticism of the Israeli government are then labelled as attacks on Jews in general. That in turn persuades

Israeli leaders to invite all European Jews to emigrate to the Promised Land. And if I contend, as I do, that many of these arguments are provoked by Jewish communities for their own purposes, I am also accused of anti-Semitism."

I'm scribbling furiously. I only wish I had this on tape.

"If I talk of Holocaust fatigue," he goes on, "if I warn my fellow Germans to be careful about how words are used, I am told I am trivialising the activities of the far right and even the significance of the Nazi era. I can't win."

He throws up his arms and laughs bitterly.

"But the kids I met in Dresden hardly mentioned the Jews," I say. "They were simply anti-foreigner. Germany for the Germans and all that."

"I repeat, Mr Barrow, it's all connected. The racism of skinheads *is* directed against blacks, Turks and asylum seekers. But it's *Ersatz* protest. The skins are scapegoats for Lenz, for the violence he wants to develop into a revolution against Jews and, thereby, a revolution against the German state as presently constituted."

"Isn't that what you and some of your radical friends in the sixties wanted - the overthrow of the state?"

"Trying to catch me out, Mr Barrow?"

"No. But I am intrigued by the way you and others have espoused respectability."

"Yes, it was what we wanted at the time. And we were wrong. We mustn't fall into the trap of attracting that kind of sentiment again by allowing the state to stagnate. We became too comfortable, too fond of the material benefits provided by our Economic Miracle. But absorbing a former communist state and ten per cent unemployment show us there are no real miracles. And they certainly don't allow for stagnation. If we let that happen, Lenz and those who think like him will become a real threat. "

He lets the quiet of the room linger over us. I have lost track of time. The sky beyond the windows suggests more winter rain. Wels coughs again and looks at his watch.

"My commissioner of police is telling me that the hour approaches, Mr Barrow. I too have to join that anti-Nazi rally this evening. If your gunman misses the Chancellor, he might get me instead. That would sensationalise your journalism, wouldn't it? 'Conversations with the minister before he was shot'."

"I don't deal in sensationalism, minister." It sounds fustian but I am sufficiently rattled to let it out. "Can I just get this right? Everything you have told me is on the record? No 'ifs' - no 'buts'?"

He looks at Wels who rises from his chair and hands the minister a thin green file.

"This contains the order for your release," he says. "I'm not sure you were ever formally arrested in the first place but better to be safe than sorry."

It calls for a witty rejoinder but he's already brought out a pen and is scratching a signature on the document. He hands the file back to Wels who turns on his heels and leaves the room.

"Is that the last I'll be seeing of him?" I ask.

"Whether you like him or not, Mr Barrow, he is the guarantor of your safety."

"That didn't work too well when I was in the Charite."

He doesn't rise to the bait. But he does have more to say.

"Lenz and his Movement are our al-Qaeda, just as the IRA were yours. And I know you spent many years dealing with them."

I frown at this reference to a past I prefer to forget.

"But, as if we haven't got enough on our plate, the Americans want us to get involved in a war in Iraq which has no justification, simply because they want revenge for 9/11."

Without warning, we have moved on to new ground. I'm not ready for this.

"I want you to add this to anything you publish. We have had the same intelligence from Iraq and Afghanistan as the Americans. But we do not draw the same conclusions. The material is weak and unreliable. A lot of it comes from discredited anti-Saddam exiles. There is no link between Baghdad and al-Qaeda. But the Americans want the luxury of a costly diversion, testing their high-tech weapons in Iraq when they should be concentrating on the caves of the Hindu Kush. Unfortunately, they're not about to do us any favours. The President of the United States hasn't even bothered to telephone our Chancellor simply because he knows how we feel. And we are all going to suffer for it."

He slams his pen down on the desk, stands up and offers his hand.

"Thank you for what you have done, Mr Barrow. I am sorry *you* had to suffer. Incidentally, I am sure you would like to know that your friends at the warehouse in Pankow have come to no harm."

This is tossed in to take the edge of whatever rancour is left in me. I want to ask about Renate but he is leading me to the door, mouthing the courtesies of farewell. He hesitates. Then he shakes my hand again and marches off through the ante-room leaving me stranded like a child at the school gate.

# Chapter 3

I walk out of the ministry building unmolested. There is no sign of Wels. It's around noon on another day of low cloud, with a cold north wind and rain turning to sleet. I need to walk and clear my head. It's crammed with enough information to keep Fred happy for weeks.

I pass over the river and thread my way into the Tiergarten, along tree-lined paths covered with fallen leaves, a soft, damp, pungent carpet deadening the footfalls of those with the time and leisure to be there. I take a familiar route, past ponds and waterways and the little island that's home to a statue of Rousseau. The beer garden near the Spanish embassy is closed for the winter but the café stays open. The ducks on the boating lake quack querulously hoping for handouts. A blackbird scurries into the undergrowth chased by a rat. I am reminded of the car park near Renate's apartment, a memory I can do without.

I leave the Tiergarten and cross the road into Stauffenbergstrasse.

The entrance to the anti-Nazi Resistance museum is half way down on the right. Young trees have softened the harsh lines of these reconstituted barracks but not enough to erase painful reminders of the past. It's not a place many Germans choose to visit on a day off.

Yet as I walk into the courtyard, I see an old man contemplating a plaque set into the granite wall. He holds the hands of two small children, a girl and a boy. I wait in a corner near the iron gateway.

"Why are we here, *Opa*?" pipes the boy.

"Because this is where a brave man died. And we are here to pay our respects to him."

"Who was he?"

"His name was Claus Schenk, Count von Stauffenberg. He tried to kill Adolf Hitler."

"I know about Hitler, *Opa*."

"What do you know about Hitler?"

"He was a cruel man who ruled Germany when you were a boy."

"Yes. When I was a boy," muses the grandfather. "Remember that. It isn't so long ago."

They contemplate the plaque again.

The old man explains. "On July 20$^{th}$ 1944 - see the date there - Stauffenberg planted a bomb at the Wolf's Lair. That's the name Hitler gave to his command post in what used to be eastern Prussia. It's part of Poland now. The bomb exploded but Hitler survived. He was shaken and wounded and wanted revenge. Stauffenberg and some of his friends were caught and executed on this spot."

"Why here?" asks the boy.

"This building was the headquarters of the German army. In those days, the street outside was called Bendlerstrasse. They renamed it in honour of Stauffenberg."

They turn and see me. As I join them, the man nods and I respond in kind. The children stare at my clothes. I am still wearing the outfit given to me at the warehouse. I approach the plaque.

"When he faced the firing squad, Stauffenberg shouted, 'Long live our sacred Germany.' Remember that too," says the old man as much to me as to the children.

I resist the urge to tell him that there is another plot to kill another German leader but by those who want a facsimile of Hitler back in power.

I could ask him if there are latter-day Stauffenbergs willing to challenge them.

The old man gently prods the little girl. She steps forward and places a solitary carnation at the foot of the memorial. She turns to me and hands me another carnation.

"Thank you," I say and lay the flower next to hers.

We wait in silence. It's disturbed by a posse of sparrows wheeling round the courtyard.

"Goodbye," says *Opa*.

He turns. The children follow. And the yard is silent again.

# Chapter 4

I walk again, along the Reichpietschufer, the road that forms the northern bank of the Landwehrkanal, over the Potsdammer Bridge, and turn left into Bissingzeile, a narrow street of granite sets, hemmed in by buildings housing the purring generators that supply Berlin's energy. At the far end is a small oasis, my hotel, innocent, comfortable and unpretentious. I half expect it not to be there, as if what has happened in the last few days might have moved me into a different dimension, wiping out familiar objects and places.

But Margit is still presiding over Reception with restraint and efficiency.

I approach the desk

"Herr Rastrup wishes to see you," she says curtly.

Herr Rastrup is the owner, who is doubtless going to tell me to pay up and check out. Margit dials a number and Herr Rastrup pops out of his office, bidding me a cheery, *"Guten Tag"*.

"A moment please, Mr Barrow." He escorts me to one of his red leather armchairs at the far end of the lobby. "You have become famous," he whispers, as Margit brings coffee.

"Infamous, I think, Herr Rastrup."

His face lights up and he chuckles like a child who's been given a new toy.

"You would like me to leave?" I ask. "I assume I have become something of an embarrassment." Better to play the role of the penitent. It might mollify him into letting me stay on.

"On the contrary," he says. He still speaks softly but he is plainly excited by what he's about to tell me. "You are a special guest. With, I might add, some very special friends."

"You do know, Herr Rastrup, that I walked out of my job with *Deutscher Fernsehkanal* the other day. They told me that if I wanted to keep my room on, I would have to pay for it myself. Since when, I have been rather busy, spending most of my time outside Berlin. So, I have come back to collect my things and settle up with you."

"No, Mr Barrow. There is no need. You may stay as long as you like. I have received e-mails and faxes from…."

He pauses, straining to keep his voice low.

"…..from the Ministry of the Interior….."

He pronounces the words with exaggerated care and a look of feigned surprise on his avowedly honest face.

"We are to give you a bigger and better room. And you do not have to pay the bill."

Herr Rastrup hands me the key to my new room.

"I think you will find everything in order. If not, please let me know immediately."

He drinks a little coffee and rises as if to leave. But stays standing.

"Herr Rastrup?" He fidgets with a file he's holding. I suddenly realise what's worrying him. "If I utter the word 'security', would you be able to tell me more?" I ask.

"Ah, yes." He swallows hard. "Certain gentlemen were here this morning. My impression was that they were not about to search your room or riffle through your personal possessions. They were more concerned to ensure that your room was…….safe."

"Safe? Safe from what?"

"I am to tell you in the strictest confidence that a guard has been put on the hotel."

"Oh dear," I say. "I hope he won't frighten your residents away."

"I am assured he will be discreet. He will not be present inside the hotel. But should you see the odd yellow shirt and khaki trousers wandering up and down Bissingzeile, Mr Barrow, do not be alarmed. They told me he would have….. back-up."

"I am sorry you are being put to this inconvenience. Perhaps it would be better if I did leave."

"I don't think you and I have much choice in the matter, Mr Barrow."

It's the only time I see a trace of annoyance in his face. It passes very quickly.

"I am, in any case, being amply recompensed." He flashes a smile and retreats to his office.

I look at the clock behind Margit. There are about six hours to go before the Brandenburg Gate rally. I take a mouthful of coffee, heft the key I've been given and make for the lift.

5th Floor. 503. I turn the lock. The room is almost a carbon copy of the one I've vacated but larger, with a double bed and a view over the rooftops towards what was once the boundary between East and West. I see yellow U-bahn trains gliding through Gleisdreieck station and the shrinking plots of another *Kolonie* in the shadow of buildings close to the ruins of the Anhalterbahnhof. It's all changing so fast. Out of the garbage of the Cold War springs trendy high-rise, car parks and children's playgrounds.

I turn and slide back the doors of the wardrobe. There are the remnants of my clothes - four shirts, a jacket, two pairs of slacks, hanging clean and neatly pressed.

I open the drawers. The same story - underwear and socks, immaculate and tidy.

My second pair of black loafers shine like polished blocks of ebony from the depths of the cupboard.

Loafers. Yes, Axel. I remember what you said. And I remember how Kai Struck flaunted his footwear in front of my nose just before I flounced out of the *Kanal.*

My small library has been stacked on a shelf over the bed-head. Notebooks, two paperbacks and old newspapers, all arranged with disconcerting precision. On a desk near the window, my transistor radio and laptop, disconnected and closed.

And two envelopes. The first bears the logo of the Berlin S-bahn. Inside is a short note apologising for the conduct of a certain ticket inspector and cancelling the forty euro fine he imposed on me.

The second is addressed simply to 'Charlie'. I know who it's from. She's supposed to be in custody. Isn't she?

I slide my thumb inside the flap and draw the letter into the light of day. It's written in long hand on two plain sheets of paper. No letterhead. Nothing official.

*My dear Charlie,*

*I did not betray you. I took you to the* Grethe *in good faith, believing that you and I would be free from prying eyes. So, why, you ask, the knock on the door and the melodramatic raid by Wels in the early hours? The obvious answer is that someone did double-cross us. And the only people who knew we were there were Fechner, the hotel manager, Wolf, and David, after we put the call through to him.*

*I rule out David because of the way he reacted when the police showed up at Udo's place. David got us out of there.*

I pause, thinking of David's 'friend' in the Traffic Police. But Renate is adamant.

*I don't see a sinister link between David, Udo and Hansi. Give me credit for experience. I can tell a 'plant' from a long way off.*

*I'm also sure it was just chance that Hansi picked you up in Grossdoelln. Hansi doesn't talk or think like an ex-Stasi. He may have been a* Mitarbeiter *but that's as far as it went.*

*As for Wolf, all I can tell you is that when I was being escorted from the hotel, he was standing in Reception and caught my eye. His look said, "Not me." I can vouch for his record. He's never let me down. He could have a rotten egg on his books. But he's a genius at vetting those who work for him. He was out in the field a lot. He does that job simply because he was badly wounded in a shoot-out during a drugs bust last year. He's rock solid.*

*I sent you to Fechner because I knew he had contacts in The Movement. He was once a member but ten years ago offered himself to the* BND *if they would keep his past under wraps. He's intelligent but frightened. He knows that if Lenz and his thugs got to him, they'd torture and kill him. He's lived on the edge for months. He's also rich. He owns a small engineering firm in Stuttgart. He uses some of his money to pay private bodyguards like Horst and Dagmar who have never been members of The Movement. Nor were they formal or official agents.*

Wrong, Renate.

*But we knew about them and did our best to protect them.*

Your best wasn't good enough in Horst's case.

*But Fechner has been showing signs of rebellion. He knew I was involved in internal feuds with Wels. And he let me know that, if his part in sending you to Dresden and Kittlitz went sour, he would take it out on me. He thinks it has. He thinks the whole thing backfired and he'll be hung out to dry. He didn't say what form his revenge would take. Now I think I know. I haven't proved it yet. But I shall. And I shall take my own revenge.*

*My relationship with you, Charlie?*

Here it comes. The worst bit. This is shifting sand. And I'm going to feel like shit when I read the rest of it.

*I didn't dissemble. I fell in love with you. I fell in love with what you are. An honest, clumsy, beautiful man. And I let it cloud my judgement.*

I don't know whether to laugh or cry. I don't want to read any more. I don't want to be told that Wels was right about her. That for all his smarm, he's the genuine article and she isn't.

*I don't know what will happen now. I was hoping for a kind of justice, exposure of the bastards who killed Dreissig and Koard. Lenz and Co. aren't a genuine political movement. They're just chancers who take advantage of others' grievances and prejudices.*

No, Renate. I don't want your analysis of society's ills. I wanted to know about us. I wanted to know - if I buy a couple of one-way tickets from Tegel to London, will you be in the seat next to mine?

*I can't go anywhere. I'm being held at Jaegerstrasse. They won't even let me take part in the security operation at the Brandenburg Gate. If they don't charge me with something soon, they'll fire me.*

*Think of me, Charlie.*

*R.*

She was interrupted. I can tell from the way she folded the two sheets of paper. How the hell did she get them to me? Who brought them to the hotel?

The phone. I don't pick it up immediately. But whoever it is is insistent. I count to ten then snatch at it.

"Charlie?" It's Maguire. "Thank God."

"God has nothing to do with it, Mac. I'm in control of my own destiny. Where the hell are you?"

"In the 'Greek'. Get here. Fast. I've a lot to tell you." I can hear the restaurant chat and one of Kyriakos's CD's belting out George Dalaras.

"Mac, we haven't got time to get pissed over *slouvaki chirino.*"

"If you want to stop what could be the worst crime in German history since the Second World War, join me now. Now, damn you." He keeps the line open and lets the background work its magic. I promise to be there in five minutes.

I take fifteen. Now that I have my worldly possessions again, I need a cash dispenser. The thrill of inserting the card into a machine that'll give me crisp twenty-euro notes makes me feel a little less naked in this big, bad world.

Maguire sits in our usual corner by a huge picture window.

"Aren't we a little exposed?" Before he can answer I have to run the full gauntlet of an overwhelming welcome from Kyriakos and Dmitri the head waiter. How am I? They've seen it in the papers. Heard all about it on radio and television. So, it's drinks on the house and *ouzos* to start with.

"What about a more discreet table - like that one in the alcove?"

Maguire already has a very large Veltins in front of him. And he isn't for moving.

"If they're going to shoot us, they can do it out in the open and not in some piddling hidy-hole. Now sit down and listen."

"Wait. What happened after Renate and I left the warehouse? I've been told the boys there are OK. No problems with the police."

"Not exactly," says Maguire. "The *Bullen* searched the place thoroughly. They went through drawers of documents, opened packing cases, crawled all over Udo's vehicles. Udo swore at them as colourfully as he could. The officer in charge kept asking about David. Udo said, yes, he had a son who helped him run the business. But he didn't know where he was. Which was true. They took Udo to Jaegerstrasse and let him stew for a while. But they didn't ask any more questions and eventually released him."

"How did you find this out?"

"I phoned. And Udo answered. He was pretty relaxed about it actually. He said the police had put everything back where they found it. The place was in good order. He still doesn't know where David is. He's not frantic. Says the boy knows how to look after himself."

"Probably drinking with his mates in Traffic."

"That's your nasty suspicious mind at work again."

The table is filling up with more food and drink - *slouvaki* and *moussaka* and carafes of fruity Greek red. It's impossible to stop Kyriakos.

"Udo said Hansi were questioned by the *Bullen* up at Grossdoelln. He told them all about picking you up, about your escapade in the woods, the motor sports club, the torchlight rally at *Karinhall* - and the brooding presence of the helicopter."

"Yes, that's always bothered me," I say absentmindedly.

"Hansi said the police had raised their collective eyebrows at his reference to the chopper - looks like you were right about more than one agency taking an interest in you. They were over the moon to get a description of the rally and the man who'd spoken to the bikers. Graphic stuff. Let's hope no-one else gets to know about it before we tell the tale."

"Did Udo see Renate at Jaegerstrasse?"

"Not a trace. Why?"

I tell him about the raid at the *Grethe*, about Renate's behaviour and Wels's allegations against her and about her letter to me.

"You still sweet on her?"

He doesn't need an answer from me. He smiles benignly and shakes his head.

"I think Wels is right, Charlie. And I think you have to forget her."

"By the way," I say, desperate to change the subject. "I've been cleared."

"Officially?"

"Oh, yes, very officially." I give him the details.

"The minister?" he gawps. "*The* Minister of *the* Interior?"

He makes this an excuse to down his Veltins and follow it with a glass of wine. "I can't trump that. But I do have more to tell you."

"How goes it at the *Kanal*?"

"You anticipate my very thoughts. Curiouser and curiouser. I keep my job, which I never expected to, largely because, I think, Kai Struck still hasn't come out of hiding. In fact, he's been replaced. For the time being, you understand. At least that's what the notice on the board says. What it did not say was why our beloved chief editor had been removed, where he had gone, how long this splendid state of affairs would last, or when he might return to his ivory tower on the eleventh floor."

"But you haven't let it rest there, have you?"

He waves a sheaf of papers at me. "Read these," he says.

"Have I got time?"

"Just read them." For once Maguire's normally benign countenance has deserted him. He's giving me orders. Practically threatening me.

"You're always making me read things, Mac."

"Read, for God's sake."

They are printed e-mails, internal messages extracted from the *Kanal* computer, messages from the director to the deputy director and from them to other senior staff, and back again. They cover one topic. Kai Struck, editor-in-chief, missing but not missed.

"You have been a very naughty boy, Mac. How did you get into the system, or shouldn't I ask?"

He huffs and puffs and says it's not important.

*From: Director, Programmes and News*

*To: Senior staff restricted list*

*Date: 07.11.20XX*

*You will be aware that Charles Barrow, senior news presenter in the English Section, has been dismissed. This follows an argument and an almost violent altercation involving Barrow and Editor-in-Chief, News, on the afternoon of Wednesday 06.11. XX in E-i-C's office. I was only made aware of this incident this morning when E-i-C failed to attend the daily editorial conference. As some of you know, my subsequent enquiries have revealed that E-i-C has not reported for work since the incident; and that, according to his wife, he has not been at home in the period covered by my investigation.*

*In short, his whereabouts are unknown. I have instituted further enquiries with members of staff, the police and intelligence services but no-one has been able to provide any information on E-i-C, other than that he was seen leaving this building at about 1700 hours on 06.11. One of the staff at Reception says she saw him in his car driving at speed away from the building at about that time……*

I look up. "How much more of this is there?"

"A lot. There's stuff on the measures Director, Programmes and News, is taking to fill the gap, dishing out temporary promotions to other editorial staff. You'll find more e-mails from senior underlings on what to do about keeping the show on the road. And there is a particularly unctuous memo expressing sympathy for Struck 'in his obvious distress'."

"Which is a dig at me, I assume?"

"You aren't the only one. There's another e-mail from a senior editor, the wording of which might give both of us grounds to sue for libel."

"Remind me to take advantage of that," I say. "Anything I can wring out of those bastards will give me great pleasure."

Maguire leans towards me and points to a sheet on which he's scrawled a red star.

"This has the juicy stuff," he says.

"Juicy?"

"Think back to your meeting with Frau Struck in Dresden and then tell me what you make of it."

Maguire sinks another glass of red. He's trying hard not to look too pleased with himself. I try to ignore George Dalaras and the lively chat at the bar.

*From: Director, Personnel and Administration*
*To: Director, Programmes and News.* *Date: 07.11.XX*
*HIGHLY CONFIDENTIAL*

*In view of the urgent necessity to discover the whereabouts of E-i-C, I feel I must bring to your attention the following information contained in his personal file. It may or may not surprise you to learn that this concerns his political affiliation and occasions on which he has expressed political opinions at meetings of senior staff.*

*As you know, he has held membership of the party which is currently in opposition for ten years. At the change of government in 1998, the parliamentary committee responsible for overseeing our activities decided that his record as chief editor merited his retention in the post notwithstanding this membership. While his reputation in the post has been enhanced by his handling of our coverage of major political events and by his own performance on screen as anchor for special programmes, it has been noted by me and my colleagues in this department that he has been less than discreet in comments made at editorial and other meetings on the subject of the far right in general and The Movement in particular.*

*It is well known that E-i-C is a vigorous and energetic person who demands a similar approach to their responsibilities from his staff. He can be forceful in the expression of his views and often aggressive and irascible towards his colleagues. Although he has been warned by me on a number of occasions to control this aspect of his conduct, his overall record as a professional broadcaster and highly competent manager has precluded any action against him.*

But...... I can smell it on the page.

*Nevertheless, I have been especially disturbed to hear his views on the government's efforts to seek a ban on The Movement in the Constitutional Court. He has made no secret of his vehement criticism of, and opposition to, those efforts, using terminology to describe ministers, notably the minister of the interior, which I would view as unacceptable in polite company.*

I burst out laughing. "Pompous ass. This man can't bring himself to say straight out that Struck has defamed members of the government in official meetings."

Maguire goes on eating and drinking. Kyriakos is prodding a copy of a Greek newspaper and arguing with Dmitri about some esoteric aspect of domestic politics,

*This has occurred on several occasions and I have considered them frequent enough to pursue my own enquiries into why E-i-C behaves in this incautious manner in front of his colleagues.*

Maguire is watching the broad grin spread across my face.

*This has caused me to uncover details of his record before he was appointed to his post in this organisation which I find more than a little disconcerting. My own contacts at branches of the security and intelligence agencies in Hanover, E-i-C's place of birth, where he also completed his secondary education, have told me that they have an extensive file on him which shows that he took part in demonstrations and street rallies staged by far right groups when he was a teenager. But there is no evidence that he was ever a member of any of these groups at that time. However, police records also show that when E-i-C moved to Bonn in*

*19XX, eventually graduating from the Institute of Public Law, he did enrol as a member of The Movement.*

"And kept in touch with his uncle in Dresden, no doubt."

"What?" Maguire stammers.

"Nothing. Just thinking aloud."

*He became a prominent speaker at their public meetings. The language he employed in setting out the aims of The Movement is described as 'moderate and persuasive'. These aims included seeking an end to all immigration into Germany from whatever source and the eventual repatriation of those non-German immigrants already living and working here. I understand that police informers attended those meetings and witnessed these speeches at first hand.*

*Another file compiled by the* Verfassungsschutz *absolves E-i-C from the charge of making 'inflammatory or racist statements' or 'statements liable to cause a breach of the peace'. Instead he is said to have made out the legal and economic case for The Movement's policies with some skill and to have called for responsible action by its members in order to attract support at elections to the state and federal parliaments. But it is also worth noting that throughout his time as a student, E-i-C joined various rifle clubs and is reportedly an expert shot. He has frequently made off-the-cuff references to his fondness for firearms and hunting.*

"In other words, Struck was a member of The Movement and he's potty about guns."

*This file also shows that, when he left university in 19XX, E-i-C announced that he was severing all connection with The Movement and applying for membership of a mainstream party. A subsequent* Verfassungsschutz *file states that he was probably aware that they were already observing his activities which was why he persuaded a reporter on the* Bonner General-Anzeiger *to run an article on his change of allegiance.*

At this point, the e-mail swerves away from fact into speculation.

*My contact in the* Verfassungsschutz *has commented on the ease with which E-i-C effected this transition, stressing that the vetting procedures used by the three principal parties in Germany are normally very thorough and that senior party officials can hardly have missed seeing at the very least an outline of his previous career. These officials have their own contacts inside the security services who must have known every detail of E-i-C's activities as a student in Hanover and Bonn.*

*I am therefore inclined to doubt that his political conversion was genuine and ask whether The Movement has perfected a device for planting 'moles' in the ranks of its rivals and in important posts in public organisations. Strictly speaking, all this is irrelevant to the narrowly focussed task we face of trying to trace E-i-C and make him accountable for his absence from duty. But in the light of what has happened, I am sufficiently alarmed by my discoveries to request an early meeting with you on their implications for everyone involved.*

"Including me, I hope," I say. "Although I bet I won't be afforded the privilege."

"What?" Maguire says again. "Have you finished?" He has his nose in another piece of paper.

" 'The implications for everyone involved', Mac."

"Ah yes. I remember that bit."

"Mr Human Resources is a very frightened man."

Now it's my turn to eat and drink. I'm conscious of the hour. It's gone dark outside.

"I have one more thing to show you," says Maguire. He draws a sheet from under the pile in front of him and hands it to me.

It's a replica in German of the SS hierarchy.

*LIST OF RANKS FOR PROPOSED MILITARY ARM*

*Oberstgruppenfuehrer* (General) at the top, down to *Schuetze* (Private) at the bottom with eighteen ranks in between.

*Proposal submitted to Our Leader, Heinrich Joachim Lenz, by Kai Ruprecht Struck, dated 15th August 20XX.*

And signed with the illegible flourish I recognise only too easily.

"And this was in the system?" I say. "He must have been mad, Mac." I'm finding it a little difficult to breathe.

"I don't think I should tell you how I got hold of it. Let's say I have computer skills I didn't know I'd acquired until I put them to the test."

"I'm wondering how you found the time to produce your programmes."

He ignores this. "Would you think me unduly impetuous," he asks, "if I said Kai Struck is our man, kitted out with a weapon and on the loose in the Tiergarten?"

# Chapter 5

There is the crump of an explosion. The picture window cracks and slowly disintegrates. We have just enough warning to avoid most of the fragments of glass that drop on to our food and drink and cover Maguire's document collection. But I end up with a gashed cheek and Maguire has blood dripping from an ear lobe. The rest of the clientele have moved swiftly to the back wall. Kyriakos struggles to pull the two of us away from our shattered table. Maguire resists, desperately trying to scoop up his sensitive print-outs and stuff them into the pockets of his jacket.

I'm aware of activity outside. Blue lights and sirens.

"Settle up later," Mac bawls at our host.

Kyriakos stares open-mouthed as we rush into the street.

A line of *Bullen* have blocked off Potsdammerstrasse to the south. The tapes are already in place. A uniform spots us and our minor injuries.

"First-aid post," he says. "Just round the corner. Move. Fast. There might be another bomb."

We slip past the tapes. The *Feuerwehr* are hard at it, targeting the ground floor of a building on the other side of the street. I look down and realise I'm walking in something soft and wet.

"Apples and pears," says Maguire. "They've hit my favourite Turkish market, the bastards."

We strain to look closer. We see every kind of fruit and vegetable strewn across Potsdammerstrasse. The road surface is awash with slicks of juice and blood dribbling past body parts and the debris of wooden stalls.

"I said - move." The uniform has caught up with us. He's not pleased to see us again. "Get out of here. Go and get yourselves patched up, you clowns."

We walk on, trying to scrape the pulp from our shoes, and cross the street in the hope of snaffling a cab. There's a stand just outside the Wintergarten theatre. But no taxis. We jog down to Kurfuerstenstrasse U-bahn. The bomb has caused northbound traffic to pile up - three lanes jammed with nowhere to go. Mac steps out into the road, dodging a yellow bus and blue VW Bora whose driver rams his hand on to his horn and curses, unheard, behind his windscreen. I wait for the next convenient gap while Maguire leaps up and down on the pavement doing his impersonation of a flailing windmill. A lone cab emerges from Pohlstrasse and turns south. His light is on. He sees us. We clamber into the back.

"*Brandenburger Tor*," says Maguire, flashing a smile.

"I'll try," says the driver. "But they're closing everything off."

"Try Yorckstrasse," says Maguire. "Turn left on to the Mehringdamm and up Wilhelmstrasse."

Our man does his best without breaking the law, doesn't ask why we look as if we've been in a fight and gets us as far as Leipzigerstrasse. We pay him off handsomely and he smiles as if he's won the lottery.

From here we must walk alongside the plot of land being prepared for the Holocaust Memorial. The crowd thickens.

"Like 1989 all over again," says Maguire. "That was a night. Kids sitting on the Wall. *Vopos* looking up from the other side. *Ossis* waiting to cross over, unsure how the uniforms would react. Then it happened. Reunification in one fell swoop."

"While you're waxing lyrical about the past," I say, "tell me where you think they're going to put the tribune?"

"On the side facing *17 Juni Strasse.* The VIP's will want to walk symbolically through the Gate from Pariserplatz. East to West. The platform will probably be on the spot where Kennedy said '*Ich bin ein Berliner*'."

He's staring hard at the trees on the edge of the Tiergarten. Even with his appalling eyesight, Maguire has the intuition to detect something amiss. And there's nothing wrong with his hearing.

"A sniper in the bushes?" I ask.

"Not such a daft theory after all," he says.

We make our way past groups of demonstrators holding placards and banners. 'We stand for Tolerance and Humanity'. 'No Racism'. 'Commitment instead of Guilt'.

"A curious formula," Maguire observes. "Typically German. Even the younger ones find it hard to bury the past."

"It'll be an hour before the Big Man's here," I say. "We need to trace the route back to its source."

"The synagogue in Oranienburgerstrasse," he replies.

We take a back way, up Luisenstrasse and catch another cab. It takes us as far as the Oranienburgerstrasse S-bahn. We meet more crowds. They're gathering in front of the synagogue, its illuminated gilt and turquoise dome shining like a beacon to defy Berlin and its past. We are jostled and pushed but it's good-humoured stuff. Not a skinhead in sight. The police are moving onlookers back from a space they want to keep free for the motorcade. We can see them. Six black Mercs parked side by side.

They'll head for Unter den Linden by the obvious route, down Friedrichstrasse.

The mood changes. The crowd settles for a passive protest.

"Now they know why they're here," says Maguire.

The street is almost silent. The chief rabbi comes out of the synagogue followed by the Chancellor, the federal president and the speaker of parliament. But they avoid the cars.

"They're going to walk, Mac. All the bloody way."

The four men turn right and slowly make for the Oranienburger Tor U-bahn. The crowd moves in behind, separated from them by a thin line of plain clothes minders and a few uniforms. They turn sharp left into Friedrichstrasse.

"If there's a street encapsulating Berlin's recent history, this is it," says Maguire, longingly. He points to the railway station. "During the Cold War, it must have been the most heavily guarded terminus in the world."

It had been full of *Vopos* checking out western visitors trying to go East and making sure no-one from the East went the other way without good reason. Attached to it a structure called 'The Palace of Tears', where *Ossis* who'd had the luck to be given an exit visa queued for a seat on a west-bound train.

"Totalitarianism at its most depressing," mutters Maguire.

Now we're walking perhaps fifty metres behind the main party. As we move under the railway bridge, the Chancellor stops to acknowledge a memorial recalling the deaths of two *Wehrmacht* privates, murdered by the SS because they refused to go on fighting for Hitler in the last days of the

Battle for Berlin. He bows his head and places a wreath on the pavement below the plaque. There's quiet applause from a section of the crowd. The VIP's are startled. It's only now that they are aware of the massive support behind them.

Someone taps me on the shoulder. I turn to see the radiant faces of Hansi, Udo and David.

"We knew we'd find you here," says Hansi. I don't need to reply. They're in robust health and happy to be part of it all. We form our own line of five as the column presses on towards Unter den Linden.

Hansi sports a pair of binoculars, dangling from a thick polo-neck sweater.

He sees my look of admiration.

"Forester's best friend," he says. "Thought they might come in useful."

The crowd swells to occupy the full width of the street. Looking back, I see it stretching into the dim evening light.

"Heard about the bomb in Potsdammerstrasse?" asks Udo.

We tell them what we saw.

"We carry the scars," says Maguire pointing to his ear and the weal on my face.

"A diversion," says David. "To stretch the police."

"Your mate in Traffic tell you that?" I ask.

He doesn't answer but winks and gives me a quizzical smile.

We move on. The Movement has threatened to make its presence felt and take revenge for the arrest of Lenz. But there's no sign of a counter-demo. The procession turns into Unter den Linden. More protesters join from adjacent streets. To our left strides a group of pious Jews, men in their thirties and forties wearing black suits and stove-pipe hats. One of them breaks into a melancholy chant reminding me of soundtracks from films and documentaries about the Holocaust.

"What is that?" I ask one of his companions.

"It's what you call Psalm 140," he answers. "A prayer for salvation from our enemies."

*"Deliver me, O Lord, from the evil man; preserve me from the violent man;*

*Which imagine mischiefs in their heart; continually are they gathered together for war.*

*They have sharpened their tongues like a serpent; adders poison is under their lips.*

*Keep me, O Lord, from the hands of the wicked; preserve me from the violent man; who have purposed to overthrow my goings.*

*The proud have hid a snare for me, and cords; they have spread a net by the wayside; they have set gins for me.*

*I said unto the Lord, Thou art my God: hear the voice of my supplications, O Lord.*

*O God, the Lord, the strength of my salvation, thou hast covered my head in the day of battle.*

*Grant not, O Lord, the desires of the wicked: further not his wicked device; lest they exalt themselves."*

The crowd lets the echo of his words fly off into the night.

*"As for the head of those that compass me about, let the mischief of their own lips cover them.*

*Let burning coals fall upon them: let them be cast into the fire; into deep pits, that they rise not up again.*

*Let not an evil speaker be established in the earth: evil shall hunt the violent man to overthrow him.*

*I know that the Lord will maintain the cause of the afflicted, and the right of the poor.*

*Surely the righteous shall give thanks: the upright shall dwell in thy presence."*

"Amen," they say in unison.

"Amen," echo the nearest marchers, even though the Hebrew is a mystery to them.

The only sound now is of feet, hundreds of them padding gently down the long thoroughfare, passing the massive Russian embassy and the refurbished Adlon Hotel. All eyes but ours are fixed on the object of the march, the floodlit sandstone of the Brandenburg Gate. We look upwards, scanning roofs, windows and alcoves for any sign of activity.

Maguire moves ahead of us. We must make a detour, skirting the portico on the south side of the Gate. We push through the crowd, until we reach the rim of the *Platz des 18 Maerz*, named after the day in 1990 when what was left of the GDR held its first free elections. I look back at the Gate, then up to the four horses and the goddess of the Quadriga holding her staff topped with an iron cross and a laurel wreath. The murmuring crowd presses against the steel barriers. Maguire and I turn to scour the darkness of the Tiergarten, the branches of its trees almost denuded of leaves but thick enough to hide a million unseemly secrets.

"I know this is stating the obvious but he could be anywhere," he says disconsolately.

We hear music from the other side of the square. A choir is singing, gently but lustily enough for the melody to penetrate the buzz of the crowd. Now there are thousands gathered in front of the tribune. Many light candles, others hold bunches of flowers. They gaze at the podium, positioned so that the VIP's can look down *17 Juni Strasse* towards the infamous Victory Column a mile to the west, an ugly monument to its own dubious symbolism.

There is a subdued gasp as several figures emerge from the central portal of the Gate and make their way to the steps of the tribune. There's my minister, standing behind the Chancellor's left shoulder. Even from here I can see him nervously scanning the area in front of the podium.

A voice resounds through loudspeakers, the voice of the president of the Federal Republic, of a generation that knew and survived Hitler's hell. These are people almost desperate to promote the values of a Germany which once bred the likes of Goethe, Schiller and Beethoven and, despite all the horrors of the 20th century, Guenter Grass, Willi Brandt and Wolf Biermann. A writer, a politician and a troubadour.

"In the last ten years," he declaims, "one hundred people have fallen victim to neo-Nazism. We must not fall backwards into barbarism."

There are stifled cheers and polite applause. No yelling or exultation. At odd moments come cries of support, often to more subdued applause.

Then the Chancellor speaks. He has nothing new to say but says it well. Hc is the consummate politician, dark suit and tie, of an age group that never knew war or Nazism.

"We have walked with you this evening," he says, "from the synagogue, torched and desecrated on this night in 1938, now returned to its full glory as a temple to the God we all worship - Jews, Christians, Muslims and others. We have reminded ourselves that *Kristallnacht* was a day when civilisation and decency gave way to lawlessness and hatred. We have moved together, in reverence and respect, through the heart of this, our restored capital, to the Gate that has witnessed so much of German history - a grandiose militaristic empire, a brutal totalitarian regime, two ghastly wars, the divisiveness of communism, and now a reunified city and a reunified country."

"He knows how to play the part," mumbles Udo. One or two in the crowd throw disapproving glances. Others nod in agreement.

"All this," says the Chancellor, "must mean something to those of us gathered here tonight. We owe it to ourselves, to our children, to our grandchildren, to affirm that what this monument once represented will never again become reality. And that is why we have to be severe with those who make racism, anti-foreigner sentiment and anti-Semitism, the defining characteristics of their convictions."

This time a roar of approval swells from the crowd.

And a shot.

Maguire and I turn and shove our way through the rear lines of demonstrators and head for the bushes and undergrowth of the Tiergarten. The Chancellor is still speaking, the powerful sound system flinging his voice over the heads of the crowd. No-one seems to have heard what we have heard. There's some consternation, cursing and mild protest as we elbow aside those in our way. But the mass stay solid and unmoving, holding their candles and flowers and waving their placards for the benefit of the cameras.

It's Hansi who stops us.

"Up there," he shouts. "On top of the Gate. To the right."

The gunman has dressed himself in a light khaki uniform to blend with the sandstone. Otherwise he makes no effort to hide himself. He pivots on one knee, his left foot planted on the bottom step of six that lead up to the Quadriga. He lifts the gun to his shoulder.

Hansi adjusts the binoculars.

"He's going to shoot," he says. He hands me the field glasses.

"Christ. These are powerful. I can damn near see the whites of his eyes."

A few of the crowd around us are following our gaze.

"How the hell did he get up there?" says Udo. "Somebody must have seen him."

"He's wearing the same as the police sharpshooters. See them? To the left."

"Then how do we know he's not the genuine article?"

"Because that is Kai Struck," I shout. I'm clenching my fists, stifling rage and wondering what to do next.

"But he fired a shot. We heard it," says David.

"No he didn't. Someone fired at him."

It's Maguire. "Someone in those bushes, someone who's got an even better weapon," he says. "Follow me."

We hear another shot and instinctively duck.

The khaki-clad figure wavers and crumples into the prone position. I train the glasses on him. The rifle falls from his grasp and drops like a discarded piece of lead piping, scraping the stonework of the Gate. It disappears into a mass of demonstrators gathered at the base of one of the columns. There's mild panic as protesters try to get out of the way.

The VIP's on the podium are hardly aware of the diversion. The speeches continue. The choir sings another anthem. Kai Struck rolls over and hangs like a rag doll from the edge of the parapet.

A third shot rings out, closer to where we're standing. Maguire plunges into the undergrowth of the Tiergarten.

He trips. I make as if to help him.

"Never mind me. Just keep going. That way." He points to a gap in the bushes. I stumble on, with Udo, Hansi and David in pursuit.

We break into a clearing where the half light from the square exposes a body and a familiar face, crying for air and relief from pain. She lies in a foetal position, clutching her stomach, her uniform neat and trim except for smears of blood and dirt on one of the sleeves. Just of reach, lying useless in a pile of leaves, another rifle with telescopic sights. She calls my name and I kneel, trying to bring her head up and support her shoulders. She stares at me, maddened by her impotence. All her remaining strength goes into pulling me down towards her. I'm vaguely aware of others moving behind me, issuing orders and standing like hunters over their prey.

I can hear the protesters at the Gate and another voice booming from a loudspeaker. There is more distant music, an orchestra playing the slow movement from a symphony. It drifts back and forth, audible at first, then muffled and undecipherable. Some one else kneels at my side. Maguire is trying to mould his jacket into a pillow for Renate's head.

"I watched him take aim," she says. She spits blood and chokes on it. "Then I fired. I got two shots in. I know I did."

"You stopped him, Renate. You stopped him."

She arches her back, coughs blood and gives me a sweet smile. Her eyes close.

"But who shot you?" asks Maguire.

Now I hear nothing, neither crowd, music, sirens nor the crunch of feet.

"I did," says Wels emerging into the clearing. He stands feet apart, with a gun held limply in his right hand. "She was aiming for the podium."

I look up and see the solemn faces of Hansi, Udo and David. Maguire is still cushioning Renate's head. They let me touch her eyelids, lift me to my feet and lead me away.

As I pass Wels, I punch him hard under the ribs. He doubles up, staggers into the undergrowth but stays upright. For all his fulsome airs and graces, he's tough and strong. Two uniforms grab me. Hansi, Udo and David grab the uniforms.

"That's another lie you'll get away with, Wels."

"Let him go," he says quietly. The uniforms back off. "You're still tilting at windmills, Charlie Barrow."

"I'll be the judge of that," I say and walk on.

# PART 6

# Chapter 1

There is work to do. I don't want to linger in Germany but I can't let Maguire down. We have the perfect story and we let it rip. He takes off to places where we need to film, to Dresden and the Ecko Club, to Kittlitz and Zerbst, even Kolonie Paradis and the drab little residence of Friend Fechner. Now that the whole saga is out in the open, no-one stands in our way. The minister has given us permission to interview anybody we want, including himself, which means a re-run of the session I had with him on the morning of the 9th.

We find Marion again, strangely willing to go on camera and tell us everything she knows about the inner workings of The Movement. She names plotters, conspirators and traitors - who's likely to come out on top and who's being paid off by the security services. She seems indifferent to the danger she faces.

"I'm living by my creed," she says. "Risk brings excitement and a zest to life."

I am sure she will die very soon.

We track down Friedrich Kuhls and the Widow Struck. Kuhls is reluctant to have his face on screen but takes Maguire and crew to the school where he taught. We use the opportunity to film the children of the new Germany in a bright new classroom equipped with every conceivable modern gadget.

Their teacher parades them as wholesome adolescents and bridles at my suggestion that they might be susceptible to the blandishments of the far right.

"That is a slur on my professionalism," she says and refuses any further co-operation. But one girl tells us she's thinking of joining the Viking Youth.

Frau Struck relates the story of her husband's death again and finally acknowledges her family links with the Strucks of Hanover.

"I haven't been in touch with them," she says, "but I've been through some family papers. Kai was my nephew. And he corresponded with Otto. I think that's as far as it went."

Behind a façade of dignity, she is still angry. "I hope your film exposes all of them. Kai Struck got what he deserved and so should they."

Maguire and I spend a week with the production team working on a script. We accept an offer from Udo to hide away in his emporium at Pankow, with a profusion of laptops and *Handys*.

David comes clean about his friends in the Traffic Police. "I was at college with them. I used to drink with them occasionally. When this happened, they got very excited. Gave me some useful stuff on the preparations for the Brandenburg Gate protest. All for your benefit, Charlie."

"You do realise I thought you were squealing on us," I tell him.

"But I wasn't, was I?" He gives me that quizzical smile again and I let it rest.

We co-opt his father as an *ex-officio* consultant. He puts numerous calls through to Hansi, on the basis of which we drive up to Grossdoelln and, guided by the forester, film the

*Karinhall* site, the old Soviet airbase and the wreck of the room where I was ditched by my kidnappers.

Who snatched me from the Charite? Renate might have known the answer. Wels insists it was her. He still won't tell me why he rolled up in this big black Merc and took the body away.

We don't hang around waiting for a repeat performance of the neo-Nazis' rally in memory of the *Reichsmarschall*. In any case they stay well out of sight.

"Too much publicity," says Hansi.

We allow our cameraman, Willi, to indulge his passion for lingering shots of lakes and woodland which he assures us will make excellent, even sinister, 'wallpaper' for the final cut. For this he treats us to a slap-up lunch at the Hotel Doellnsee-Schorfheide where we film the rooms once used by party big wigs and visitors from Moscow. We drink several Radebergers and lounge obstinately on the terrace on a freezing but sunny December day.

"Its all part of your rehabilitation," says Maguire. "Designed to make you forget."

"I know that. And I can put on a good act for Willi's sake. But it won't work."

"You want out of Germany ASAP?"

"Sadly, yes, Mac."

"Portugal?"

"I think so. I've always wanted to spend all day looking at the sea with a glass of *tinto* in my right hand."

We worry that there'll be huge gaps in our coverage. Fechner has vanished for a start.

"Probably dead," says Maguire without remorse.

"My sixth sense says 'no'. Abroad maybe. Out of the way until the heat's off."

Later I swallow my pride and ask Wels for help. He surprises me by saying 'yes'. In his office at Jaegerstrasse, he lays on the charm again.

"I don't know where Fechner is, Herr Barrow. Even if I did, I'm not sure I'd tell you."

"Despite orders from the minister?"

He laughs in my face.

"The minister is a politician. There's an election coming up. He won't be there much longer. But I shall - at least until I retire. And that's a long way off. Bureaucrats and officials run this country, not ministers."

"I'm not sorry I hit you."

"I know you're not. I know why you did it. But it was wasted effort."

"You deserved it."

"No I didn't. But I don't take offence. And you know perfectly well why I shot Seelig. Everything I told you about her was true."

It's useless to argue with him again.

"Can we see Lenz?"

"No." It's useless to argue about this too. "Any contact with him will prejudice his case."

"What's he charged with?"

"Murder, illegal possession of drugs and weapons, running a private army, assisting terrorists and stirring up racial hatred. You and I know he's as guilty as hell. But he has a right to a fair trial. The answer's still 'no'."

By all the rules of the game, Wels is right. Maguire and I are arrogant enough to bend the rules. But we still fail to unearth Lenz in any of the prisons and detention centres on the ministry's list.

"He's probably as snug as a bug in a rug on the top floor of Jaegerstrasse," says Maguire. "At least it gives us another angle to play with. Speculation and oblique allegations of cover-ups and conspiracies at the highest level. You can go to town with that."

We notice that after the broadcast, no-one takes us to task for this indulgence.

On the days Maguire doesn't need me, I pursue one of my private passions. I need music. I need to hear the powerful playing of a large orchestra, a hundred musicians in full flow with a complex and inspiring symphony.

I might have found it in Herbert von Karajan's 'Circus Tent' at the Philharmonie, an ugly structure of meaningless curves surrounded by sidewalks where the kids practise their skate-boarding. But I don't like the Philharmonie or the Berlin Philharmonic. I don't like their smugness and their smart and wealthy audiences. They're over fond of Bruckner and Wagner. They even make Beethoven and Mozart sound like flatulent Teutons. In any case, I once committed the ultimate sin of falling asleep at the Philharmonie, right in the middle of a long and dreary second movement. I snored like a pig and let my head droop on to the shoulder of a dear old thing sitting next to me. She was not amused and I fled at the interval.

"Go to the Schauspielhaus in the Gendarmemarkt," advises Maguire. "The orchestra there plays with elegance and wit."

He's right. The music is wafted deliciously round and about the gilded plasterwork and the glittering chandeliers. And I hear Ravel and Debussy, Bartok and Stravinsky as well Mozart, played with a lightness of touch that lifts my spirits. All this from musicians who lived under communism, worked with the aid of subsidies but now have to compete for their cash and beat the Philharmonic at its own game. I feel proprietorial towards them as if I'm supporting a good second division team that merits promotion.

"They also serve a good *Sekt* in the interval," says Maguire.

"And they keep the bars open after the performance," I tell him after my first visit.

There's one more musical thing I have to do. I've ridden in many a taxi from Tegel to Herr Rastrup's hotel, passing the Steinway Shop on Hardenbergstrasse in Charlottenburg. I've always wanted to enter its hallowed portals. Behind crisp white walls and in the golden light from its windows I have seen Aladdin's cave.

It contains row upon row of grand pianos, immaculately polished and very expensive. There is a notice in the window advertising practice rooms for hire.

"We shall go together," says Maguire. "I've often wanted to hear you play."

"You may not like what you hear. I'm rusty - for obvious reasons."

I pluck up courage and walk in with Maguire in tow, looking as if he owns the place. The young assistant is charm itself. I can have an hour for ten euros. And Maguire is allowed to sit and listen.

"In fact, sir, you can have longer, since it's ten minutes to the hour and there are several rooms free right now."

"Is my friend permitted to play jazz on these instruments?" Maguire asks airily.

"That, sir, would be a welcome change." He manages a discreet smile. "One can become bored with endless Bach and Mozart. It's heresy, I know. Keep it to yourselves."

He leads us up a flight of stairs to a large room in which the only pieces of furniture, apart from the biggest concert grand I have ever set eyes on, are a piano stool, an upright chair and two music stands.

"Take your time, gentlemen. Enjoy yourselves."

And for half an hour I set myself free, meandering through pale imitations of Cole Porter and Gershwin. Maguire sits on the chair, closes his eyes and smiles his cherubic smile.

As I play, I think the inevitable - that I might have done this for Renate in some Mediterranean dive on a warm summer's evening. The piano wouldn't have been as good as this, but I might have coaxed the right kind of melodies from it.

The chord floats away and Maguire opens his eyes.

*"Away! the moor is dark beneath the moon,*
*Rapid clouds have drank the last pale beam of even:*
*Away! the gathering winds will call the darkness soon,*
*And profoundest midnight shroud the serene lights of heaven."*

"Shelley is almost as profound as Thelonius Monk," I say.

"Philistine!"

I close the piano. We walk slowly downstairs and pay the young man his ten euros.

"I hope you come again, gentlemen," he says.

"I doubt it," I reply. "But it won't be your fault."

# Chapter 2

I pull out of Berlin the following morning. The cab splashes its way through streets awash with December rain. The shops stay illuminated and the light show from the road surface is as dazzling as ever.

There is another photographer working the Pavilion bar at Tegel. He's younger than Axel and brusque to the point of discourtesy. As I sip my coffee, he approaches.

"Before you ask," I say, "the answer is 'no'."

"Well, you're no beauty, I must say."

The lisp irritates me. I put my cup down and lean towards him. "If you so much as touch the tit on that thing, I'll brain you with it."

He backs off and walks away without another word. Then pulls out a *Handy*. The conversation with his contact last several minutes during which he shoots glances fit to kill.

I hear my flight called. To get out of the bar, I have to pass him.

"Bastard," he hisses as I squeeze between table and chair.

I grab the lapel of his jacket. We're nose to nose. He's terrified. The rest of the clientele are studiously taking no notice.

"The person who did this job before you," I whisper, "was murdered. The people to whom he supplied his pretty pictures killed him in the middle of the night. Take a tip from me. Find another job. You'll live longer."

I release him. He collapses into the chair.

As I walk out of the bar, I see two swarthy heavyweights fall in ten metres behind me.

I check in and pass through the entrance to the departure lounge. They don't follow. Instead they eye me through the glass partition that separates the lounge from the ground crew working at the desk. I stare back. They don't move and I have all the time in the world to memorise their features.

I see the green uniforms of two *Grenzpolizei* strolling along the concourse. Before my watchers realise what's happening, the uniforms have grabbed them. There's a struggle and punches are thrown. More police arrive. The two are subdued, handcuffed and hustled out of the area. Passengers queuing at the desk have pulled back, anxious to get out of the way. The two *Grenzpolizei* restore order and a measure of calm.

They pass through the gate into the departure lounge and approach me.

"Herr Barrow?"

"Are you arresting me as well?"

"For what?" says the one who's clearly the senior partner.

"For molesting a photographer in the Pavilion bar."

"I shouldn't worry about that. He has been asking for trouble for some time. A little too pushy with the customers. Not nice and polite like our old friend, Axel."

The uniform knows he's hit a nerve.

"You've heard all about that then?" I ask. I should have realised a young attentive cop would recognise my face. "So, why are we having this conversation?"

"To warn you. We have examined the passenger list for this flight. It's clean. But if we hadn't intervened just now, you might not have made it to London. We are to tell you that when you alight at Heathrow, British police will be on hand to meet you."

I pull a face and sigh deeply. "It looks as if life's going to be like that from now on."

The uniform hands me a folder. And grins.

"This might help," he says. "You've been upgraded to first class. Have a nice flight."

They turn on their heels. The one who's done the talking looks back.

"And take care, Mr Barrow."

# Chapter 3

I am expecting a visitor. Maguire phoned last week and said he would be on a flight to Porto. I find my battered Seat at the end of the street. It's intact, protected against theft and vandalism by a bunch of lads I pay in new euro notes once a week. Their leader is Mario who makes sure they never let me down.

"Look, Senhor. We washed it."

Mario waves a filthy cloth as evidence of their hard work.

It costs me another ten euros which he duly shells out among his co-operative.

I drive south down what the tourist board calls the Costa Verde, the Green Coast promoted as a rival to the Algarve in the south. It has beaches to die for but gets a lot of cloud and rain. I like it. The tourists stay away and the towns and villages stay Portuguese.

Porto's airport is on the north side of the city. Which means I don't have to cope with too much of the urban sprawl that blights the outskirts of a hundred Iberian towns in the name of development. I negotiate the whirligig of motorways leading to the terminal and park the car.

I enter the arrivals hall and inspect 'Flight Information'. It tells me Maguire's plane will land in ten minutes. That suggests a wait of about half an hour while he passes through immigration and baggage collection. I head for a bar and a shot of caffeine.

Places like this make me think again of Axel Dreissig. He spent half his life in airports, wept away his silent hours in a small apartment and died a painful death in a bleak Berlin street. And he gave us one of the greatest stories of all time. Maguire says he's bringing tapes of our epic and a bunch of cuttings.

I'm not sure I want to wade through it all but the income it provides is definitely doing my bank balance a lot of good.

I stand, like so many hopefuls, at the barrier, waiting for Maguire's cheery face to emerge from the automatic doors. But he doesn't come. I wait a full hour. Then I ask the information desk if they can check the passenger list of the flight from Berlin. There is no Maguire on it. I fish out my mobile and try his Berlin number. No reply. I return to 'Information'. Is there a Maguire on the next flight from Berlin? Again the answer is 'no'.

I go to the bar and down a beer. I'm depressed by all this. It smells. But I'm helpless. I wander out to the car park. I take no notice of my surroundings and fail to see the man who comes up behind me and prods my spine with what I know is a handgun.

"Leave you car where it is, Barrow. Just walk forward. And don't look round."

"Would you like the keys?" I ask.

"Shut up."

I have no intention of playing the hero out here in the open. I know these circumstances only too well. And I know who has the gun in my back. He hasn't disguised his voice.

Hans Best or Heinrich Joachim Lenz, out of jail and free to travel.

I spot the car from fifty metres. Lenz has retained his penchant for silver Audis. As we get nearer, out steps a minder in black shirt and slacks, an odd concession to Portugal's winter sunshine. He too trains a gun on me and opens a rear door. I'm pushed inside. Lenz goes round to the other door. Now we're just a cosy threesome. And I can look the bastard in the eye.

"Well, you got off lightly," I remark as we pull on to the slip road and head north.

"Don't joke, Barrow. Just keep your mouth shut."

He's nervous. This is not his country and not his environment. But he does have the gun.

"I've no intention of keeping my mouth shut. And if you want to shoot me, do it now, because I don't care any more."

It's a lie. It will be a messy death. I'll make sure of that. And he and Black Shirt will have to clear it up. That might present a few problems with the Portuguese.

"What was the deal then? Did you bribe the minister? Or Wels? Never did trust that guy."

"Shut up."

"No, Lenz. It won't work. You've taken the trouble to fly all the way down here to bump me off. God knows what nastiness you've perpetrated on my good friend, Maguire. If I ever find out, I'll kill you."

He opens his mouth to scoff but I keep going.

"We must be very dangerous people, Lenz. A real threat to your political career. I wonder how you propose parading yourself as an acceptable vote-catcher in Germany with such bad publicity, not to mention the blood on your hands?"

He can't work out why I'm so cocksure. He wants to tell me to shut up again. But he's confused. I can see it in his eyes. He's thinking, why haven't I got the upper hand?

What is it about this ageing Englishman with the battered face that bugs me?

I laugh and look out of the window at suburbia turning into a rural slum, the half way house between city and countryside, pitted with little workshops and half-finished apartment blocks. We're not following the coast. We're on the road heading for Braga.

"You defamed me in that film," says Lenz.

"Well, at least you took the trouble to watch it."

I'm in a position to scrutinise the rear-view mirror. I see a four-by-four keeping its distance behind us.

"And those mendacious articles," he goes on.

"Ah, a case of mark, learn and inwardly digest, as the prayer book has it."

He doesn't understand this. He isn't supposed to.

"How did I defame you?" I ask.

He's given up on trying to keep me quiet.

"You accused me of……"

Black Shirt has lowered the window on his side of the car. I sniff the scents of the countryside - rosemary, thyme and myrtle. They reinforce the strange courage I feel.

"I accused you of nothing more and nothing less than what came out of your own mouth during our tete-a-tete in Kittlitz and my interrogation in Zerbst. Actions and beliefs of which you boasted until you were fit to burst. I suspect the cocaine helped."

He pushes the gun barrel into my ribs.

"Fuck off, Lenz. You're a murderer and a fraud. You sanctioned the killing of Horst. You probably did it yourself. Or perhaps you don't have the guts to kill."

The car lurches to overtake a truck. The four-by-four is still with us.

"There's more than enough evidence to connect you to Kai Struck and his assassination attempt. Not to mention your links to Al Qaeda sleepers in Hamburg and the use of *hawala* to finance your revolution. Defamation? You've got to be kidding - yourself more than anybody."

We've turned off the highway. Black Shirt is mumbling curses at the pot holes.

"Shut your mouth," yells Lenz through the blast of air from the open window.

Before they kill me, I want to know how he's managed to stay out of court. I want to entice him into giving me names - officials he's bribed, those sympathetic to The Movement, double agents inside the *BKA* and the *BND*.

"Tell me how Kai Struck wormed his way into a top job at the *Kanal* - why he wasn't spotted - why the reports on political leanings stayed under wraps. Go on. Tell me. You shit."

We turn off the road, through a gateway leading to a derelict farmhouse. The sun still shines but the track is muddy from recent rains. The wheels spin and the Audi bucks and bounces. We never reach the farmhouse. Black Shirt takes a sudden left into a clearing, ringed with timber stacked high for winter fires.

"Out," shouts Lenz.

He's right. This is it. I'll never get answers now. All the intriguing pieces of the jigsaw will remain scattered round the edge of the table.

"Over there," he orders.

I walk towards one of the piles of firewood.

"Turn round."

I think of Stauffenberg in the Bendlerstrasse and wonder whether I should play the fool one last time and shout, "Long live sacred Germany." A chance to be melodramatic with next to no audience. Maguire would have laughed. So would Hansi and Udo.

I hear two shots. Lenz and Black Shirt lurch forward and hit the ground. And don't move.

I take a cautious step towards them and look up. But with the sun in my eyes, I can't see any further. Then I pick out the shape of the four-by-four, parked by the gate to the enclosure.

And a woman, tall, athletic, wearing shades and ridiculously tight clothes. Her fair hair is cropped close to her skull. Next to her, another, shorter woman in a blue skirt and a white blouse, hair done in a German plait. She wears half-moons. Both carry automatic rifles. Behind them stands a man, thin and bespectacled, with a skin that has never been burned by the sun.

They stroll towards me.

"Just in time, Charlie Barrow," says the blonde.

"For people of your undoubted intelligence," I say, "that is about the most unoriginal remark you could make."

I'm grinning at Dagmar, Marion and Fechner. The women hug me and Fechner shakes my hand. A Portuguese squad car arrives. Four uniforms begin the business of tidying up. It's all been well organised.

Maguire flies in the next day explaining how someone had screwed up on his original booking.

"I tried to warn you," he says. "But somebody was jamming your mobile."

The five of us watch the breakers and the sunset and drink cheap wine. Dagmar and Marion become avid beachcombers. I play piano and Fechner inspects my library. Maguire produces a volume of Shelley, retires to a corner and reads.

But it's Fechner who declaims.

*He has out-soared the shadow of our night;*
*Envy and calumny and hate and pain,*
*And that unrest which men miscall delight,*
*Can touch him not and torture not again.*

Maguire looks up, at Fechner, then at me, his eyes glassy with tears.

Three days later, he, Fechner and Marion fly back to Berlin.

But Dagmar stays behind.

THE END.

# About the Author

Jack Thompson was born a long time ago in the North of England. After spells as a bus conductor, teacher, industrial spy and pianist in working men's clubs, he joined the BBC where he eventually landed the job of foreign correspondent for the World Service. He reported from south-east Asia, the Middle East, Eastern Europe and the former Soviet Union. He followed the Vietnamese army into Cambodia as it overthrew the Khmer Rouge and saw the grisly aftermath of Pol Pot's "Killing Fields". He was nearly blown to bits by militiamen in Lebanon and verbally pilloried by Saddam Hussein's information ministry for a report on human rights abuses in Iraq. His superiors at the BBC described him as 'curmudgeonly and subversive', a badge he wears with pride. Which is why he left in 1995 and became a newscaster for Deutsche Welle TV in Berlin. Since 2002, he's devoted himself to writing, playing the piano again and trying to help with the upbringing of his grandchildren. In March 2006, he won the Scottish Association of Writers Pitlochry Award for crime writing.

He lives in London with his wife, Kathryn.

Printed in the United Kingdom
by Lightning Source UK Ltd.
112243UKS00001B/7-48

9 781425 936426